Casco Bay

Willow River Press is an imprint of Between the Lines Publishing. The Willow River Press name and logo are trademarks of Between the Lines Publishing.

Copyright © 2025 by Aja Holland

Cover image by Bliadd Photography

Between the Lines Publishing
1769 Lexington Ave N, Ste 286
Roseville, MN 55113
btwnthelines.com

First Published: January 2025

ISBN: (Paperback) 978-1-965059-24-1

ISBN: (Ebook) 978-1-965059-25-8

Library of Congress Control Number: 2024951714

Casco Bay

Aja Holland

And why are you so quiet now
Standing there in the doorway?
You chose your journey long before
You came upon this highway.
Traveling lady stay awhile…

"Winter Lady"
Leonard Cohen

PART ONE:

The Return

One.

Shiloh was surprised a boat could rock in so many different directions simultaneously, a dynamic distressingly echoed by the turmoil in her stomach. Her queasiness must've been painfully obvious even through all the swaying and dipping and the cold rain blowing into the well of the converted Higgins boat. The man at the helm podium in the stern called out, "Hey, Miss, you gonna need a bucket? I got one you need one."

She was grateful there was no snark or condescension to it, just what passed in typically Maine waterfront gruffness for consideration. She politely waved the question away, afraid to open her mouth for fear her stomach would consider that an invitation to prove she would, indeed, need a bucket. Seated on one of the cargo crates in the well, she tucked herself a little tighter into herself, pulled the collar of her ruined suede jacket a little higher, and tugged her soaked-through felt beret down a bit further around her head. Between bouts of trying to mentally calm her stomach, she scolded herself for making so many bad wardrobe decisions for the trip across Casco Bay.

She should've known better; she kept telling herself. This same Higgins boat - a converted WW II troop landing craft - had been making package deliveries to the islands in the bay when she was a child, and even on a good day, the shallow draft vessel had hardly provided a smooth ride. For a kid, that was fine. She remembered - shaking her head at the memory - even wishing for winds to come whipping up white caps turning a trip across the bay into a giddy roller coaster ride.

Well, you don't like roller coasters anymore either.

The boat shuddered and jumped as a foaming roller exploded against its flat bow and a shower of salty spray mixed with the chill November rain plastering Shiloh's already waterlogged beret closer to her head.

"Whooee!" the helmsman remarked. "That was a rough one. You ok up there, Miss?"

Shiloh managed another unconvincing I'm-ok wave. She stood, trying to steady herself with a hand against the cold hull plate behind her, and went up on tiptoe to peek over the gunwale to see how much further they had to go. This was a mistake; even though it was hardly visible through the sea spray and sheets of rain, the see-sawing horizon only seemed to stir her stomach further. She immediately sat back down.

"Just a few minutes more," the helmsman said, seeming to understand what she'd been looking for.

She envied him. He was draped in what looked to be warmer and certainly more waterproof bright yellow oilskins, and the icy rain pelting his leathery face didn't seem to faze him any more than a cool breeze might. Standing erect, one hand on the spoked wheel, staring unflinchingly into the whipping weather, she thought, *He looks just like the guy on the Gorton's frozen fish boxes*, the idea finally giving her something to smile about.

"Here we go, Miss. St. Aggie's."

The seas had calmed some now that they were on the leeward side of St. Aggie's Island, and still more as the Higgins slowly nosed into the shelter of a small rockbound cove and up to the dock sitting next to the ferry ramp at the head of the inlet. Along the western curve of the cove were anchored a motley collection of small boats bobbing in the waves, modest things, cat boats and bay boats and skiffs. They were tired-looking with long use, the sea-going equivalents of aging family sedans. Some had been tarped over for the coming winter, and still others looked long derelict: rust streaks, frayed lines trailing in the water, windows fogged with layers of salt.

"I don't suppose you'd be any good helpin' me tie up?" the Gorton Fisherman asked, again, no acid to it, just an honest question.

Shiloh shook her head.

Another figure in yellow oilskins, pushing a hand truck, was already jogging down toward the dock from "Granier's Store," a small building of once-white-now-weather-grayed clapboard on the other side of a narrow strip of cracked and potholed blacktop. The Gorton Fisherman deftly sidled the Higgins boat up alongside the dock, cutting the engine and letting the boat glide the last foot or so until it gently kissed the tire bumpers hung on the pilings. He tossed a stern line to the Granier man, then ran forward to toss him the bow line.

"I'm lookin' for four crates, Gabe," the man on the dock called down.

"I got 'em. Gimme some help with the lady first, wouldja? Give ya a hand, Miss?" Gabe the Gorton Fisherman squatted down and made a stirrup of his interlocked hands.

Shiloh smiled a thanks, stepped into Gabe's hands as he gently lifted her up where the man on the dock could take her by her hands and help her step off the boat.

"I don't 'member orderin' *you*," the storekeeper said. He was considerably younger than the Higgins boat helmsman, but just as weather-beaten.

"You can always send me back."

He grinned. "Nah, I'd be a fool to do that!". Then he frowned thoughtfully, studying her. "I know you."

"I don't -"

"Hey, Gabe!" he called to the man in the boat. "I think this is one ah the Vail kids."

"The one who went away?"

She returned the same studying frown, then shook her head in surrender. "I don't remember you."

"You'd 'member my dad. That was his store," and he nodded at the building across the road.

Then it came to her. "Teddy Granier?"

He nodded and smiled; he was missing a canine tooth. "I didn't think you'd 'member. We were a couple years apart in school."

"That's right, but you were always hanging around in the back of the store. *That* I remember."

"Yup, that was me. I 'member you comin' in with your dad, you were always bustin' him to buy you -. What was it? There was a candy you liked." He started poking at the air as if trying to snag a memory. "I wanna say it was somethin' like Almond Joy. Or Mounds."

"It was both, actually."

"Yeah, yeah! That's right!" Then his face went soft and serious. "Sorry 'bout your dad. I guess that's why you're home?"

Before she could get into a conversation she didn't particularly want to have, Gabe called up from the boat: "Eyah, nice you're havin' a reunion, Ted-boy, but I ain't haulin' this stuff up m'self."

Granier gave her drowned-rat appearance a once-over. "You forgot how to dress for here."

"Yes, I did."

"Stop by later, I'll get ya fixed up."

"Headin' t' the ol' homestead, Miss?" Gabe called up from the boat. "'Member the way? Eyah, jus' folla the road, take ya right there."

Shiloh knew the way but waved a thanks anyway and began walking along the deteriorating blacktop road which more or less followed the shoreline. St. Aggie's was small enough, Shiloh recalled, that one could make a circuit of the entire island in thirty-forty minutes, but she was soaked through and cold, and her leather ankle boots were hardly waterproof; she could feel her feet squishing inside wet socks with each step. Even a short walk was going to feel like a Yukon trek.

Shiloh was surprised at how familiar everything seemed after so many years away. It was the same scattering of small homes strewn along the road, she could even remember the names of the families: there was the DeLisles' place, still had the playhouse-and-swing set in the yard. Past that were the Dunellens who had kept adding on to their boxy original house as the family grew, the add-ons looking haphazardly jammed into the main building. And then the Talleys with their one-horse stable in the back, Shiloh remembering how little Lisa Talley would trot around the island bareback on a swaybacked old roan, the deep gulf of the ancient nag's spine keeping the child in place as well as any saddle could.

Familiar...yet bleakly changed. All the houses had the same worn, tired, gray look of Granier's store. Their metal rooves were streaked with rust, a lot of the houses - most of them - were dark, with curtainless windows, some with panes of cracked or broken glass, looking in on barren rooms with walls of peeling paint or shedding wallpaper. The DeLisle yard set looked ready to collapse at a touch, the Talley stable looked in about the same long-untended, rotting shape. Even though the grass had been beaten flat by the rain, it was clear the lawns were overgrown, shrubs around the houses ragged and tangled. Pizza-sized satellite dishes hung from abandoned houses at odd angles by the one or two brackets which hadn't yet rusted through and snapped, propane tanks tucked against the sides of the houses were streaked with green moss.

Just around the western tip of the island on the seaward side, sitting atop a slight rocky rise, was one house with windows glowing with a warm, amber light. It was different from the other houses, brick instead of clapboard, substantially larger, the grounds, though withered with the late fall, neatly manicured.

Shiloh lowered her head against the rain now driving nearly horizontal off the Atlantic, finding her way only by following the puddle-dotted blacktop.

She hesitated at the head of the flagstone front walk. The house was squat and sturdy, built to stand up to the harshness of seaward weather. The deep red brick had always given the house a vibe which didn't fit with the rest of the homes on the island. Back in their day, the white clapboard practically glowing in the sun, those other houses had always seemed more welcoming, friendlier, homier. This one had been built less with a family in mind than as a challenge - a dare - to the elements which could be so punishing. It stood defiantly alone, the only residence on this side of St. Aggie's. *It's not a house*, Shiloh thought, *it's a goddamned fort.*

Cold and miserable as she was, Shiloh found herself having to force her feet to take her up the walk, then the few steps to the portico that ran the breadth of the house.

The wind was strong enough to blow rain in under the portico roof, lashing at her, but still she hesitated at the front door. She turned back toward the sea where the wind stirred the chop into churning froth. There were bright flashes to the left, coming from the Ram Island Ledge Light. She could see waves detonating against the tower's seaward side, completely swamping the light's bed of a low spine of rock. More flashes from her right, from the white tower standing sentinel-like atop the boulder-strewn promontory of Portland Head. The lights, she thought, seemed less like a friendly guide to a safe channel into the Portland waterfront and more like a warning to stay away. Or maybe she was just in a warning-away mood.

It was hard looking out at the roiling gray sea - with the equally dark sky, the horizon line fuzzy through wind-rippled rain - and remembering that as a child, she would sit out on this same portico in the golden warmth of a spring sun, enjoying a soft, salty breeze. Her schoolbooks would be spread out on the deck in front of her, momentarily forgotten as she watched the Down East boats - piled high with filled lobster pots - chugging into Portland, and the rich vacationing men from Boston steering their yachts out of that same harbor, their sleek hulls pulled gracefully out to sea by puffed-out white sails.

It was an image from a million years ago, Shiloh thought, so long ago, so distant, it almost seemed something of a barely remembered movie; something not real, not a part of her.

A fresh gust of wind-driven rain that felt like stones pelting into her face was enough persuasion that she couldn't put it off any longer. She turned, knocked on the door window. No answer. She tried the door, knowing it wouldn't be locked, it never was, never had been, and eased it open.

"Hello?"

If there had been something foreboding about the hard face of the house, inside was a welcoming warmth and the sweet-smelling woody smell of a fire in the front room hearth. The fire was low, she noted, it'd been burning a while. She called out, again, shivering so hard it came out in an almost comic vibrato, but her voice made a hollow sound in the house, unanswered.

She slid her soggy beret off and let it drop on the entry mat by a row of battered footwear: rubber boots, old sneakers crusted in dried mud, a pair of ancient Timberlands their soles so worn on the outside edges the shoes tilted at angles away from each other. *They're leaving it to me, to do the hard thing; throwing his belongings away.*

The furniture had changed since she'd been here last, yet there was still something familiar about the choices: simple, comfy stuff, cushy sofa, cushy chairs. On either side of the picture window facing the Atlantic, the wall was papered with family photos. She looked to see if anything new had been added. There was her sister and brother-in-law with a small boy and girl – *Oh, Christ, what the hell were their names?* - still toddlers so that must've been five years ago or so. Her brother, early twenties she guessed by his patchy beard, making it close to ten years ago. He was standing on one of Portland's working docks in oilskins, wearing the sour face he'd developed in adolescence and had worn without a break since, in front of one of the Down East boats as its crew unloaded its lobster pots.

Most of the photos were even older, images she remembered: the wall was basically unchanged from the day she'd left, frozen. But for the first time, she saw...

It was one of those precepts so obvious you didn't consciously consider it: that when you grow up in a place you simply accept what's around you as a norm. But then you go away for a time, for years, and you come back with fresh eyes and now see what you had never noticed before.

Like that there were very few pictures of the whole family – her mother and father, Shiloh, and her brother and sister – together. There were pictures of her brother and sister together, and of her mom and Shiloh's sibs, her brother and sister sharing their mother's brooding looks: dark hair, dark eyes canting slightly downward at the outsides giving them a look – even when they were smiling – of some inner sadness. There were no pictures of Shiloh alone with her mom.

Most of Shiloh's pictures were either of her alone or with her dad: perched on the rocks along the shore; him holding a toddler Shiloh on the Talley's borrowed horse; her cradled in his lap as he sat cross-legged by the fireplace, a Christmas tree on one side, blazing logs on the other.

There had always been a space between Shiloh and her sibs. She'd chalked it up to the fact that she was older by a couple of years while they were close to each other, just eighteen months apart. Or maybe it had been her bookishness, her nose buried in pages while they gallivanted around the island with the giggling abandon of feral children. They tried to chop down her elder status and super-serious countenance by teasing her about her looks: the dark red hair, brilliant emerald eyes. Even her build was different, willowy where they had their dad's sturdy stoutness. When she'd tried to act the stern Proxy Parent in their teens, the rebellious retorts would come back: "Why don't you go back to your home planet!...Who set fire to your head?" When she'd asked her dad about those differences he told her, "Go look up 'recessive genes'…and then count your blessings."

On the wall on either side of the mantlepiece, as they always had, hung two unimpressive watercolors, cliché stuff: a bowl of fruit, flowers in a vase. Her mother had hated those pictures, so much so Shiloh could remember a bitter fight between her parents over them. She could still hear it, a surly mumble from her father, then her mother's raging shrill, "Because they're ugly! Because they're *stupid!* *Because because because!*"

When Shiloh had gotten old enough to judge the paintings' blandness for herself, she had asked her father what it was he saw in them.

"I like 'em. That alright with you?" He'd said it with such a declarative finality that she knew never to broach the subject again.

That reminded her of something else she'd now realized was equally mystifying. She took a few steps into the living room where she could see deeper into the house to an alcove extending into the side yard. The upright piano no one ever played was still there. She crossed to the piano, lifted the cover, tapped some of the keys. Some were dead, others twanged out of tune. She wasn't surprised; one couldn't expect anything better from an instrument which had stood un-played for as long as she could remember. Like the motel art-caliber paintings, when she'd gotten old enough not to think of the piano as just another piece of furniture and ask about it, her father shrugged, didn't even look up from whatever it was he was half-watching on TV and said something about the previous owners of the house having left it behind when they moved out.

"I thought *you* had the house built."

Then he hushed her and pretended to concentrate on the TV which she took as a sign for her to drop the subject. That had been her dad's way; saying things and saying them firmly...without actually saying them.

Two.

The aroma of hot coffee brought Shiloh into the kitchen. Her dad's ancient Corning Ware pot was sitting on the stove on a low heat. He'd never bought into the Keurig wave, couldn't even abide something like a Mr. Coffee, reacting to such brewing shortcuts as some kind of blasphemy.

She was still a little girl when he'd taken her by the hand into the kitchen to teach her how to make coffee – "This is gonna save your life someday, Sweets!" - showing her how to properly measure out the grounds, sprinkle them lightly and evenly around the percolator basket, then add ground-up eggshells to take out some of the bitterness. "Don't let anybody fool you with all this other fancy crap," he told her as he basked in the vapor over a freshly poured cup, "*this* is how you make *real* coffee!"

When he'd come to visit her at college in Boston, she'd offered to take him to a Starbucks; her first and only attempt. "Look, Sweets, thank you and all that, but I want to go someplace where I sit at a counter, I say, 'Cup ah coffee and a donut,' and I get this big clunky mug I can crack your skull with and a sinker on a plate. I don't want to have a big conversation 'bout la-*tays*, and swirls and all that other stuff 'cause none ah that is *coffee!* I don't want a scone, or a croy-*sant*. 'Cup ah coffee and a donut' and they know exactly what I mean."

She held her hand close by the coffee pot, enjoying the radiating heat, not just because it helped her finally uncurl her frigid fingers. She looked at the percolating brew spurting up into the little glass bubble in the pot lid and felt a warmth inside as well: *Dad.*

There were flashes of light in the kitchen window coming from the backyard. Across the yard, the wind was whipping the open the door of the old storage shed back and forth, thus the flashes from a light inside. Next to the shed was her dad's Chevy pickup, its tires gone, sitting on cinderblocks. He'd had it as far back as she could remember, had refused to give it up even as body rot grew around the wheel wells and a rear-ending had left it as swaybacked as the Talleys' horse. No matter how much he'd tinkered under the hood, it had always sounded like it needed a good throat-clearing. Her sister had emailed her several years ago that they'd only gotten him to stop driving it when his macular degeneration had gotten so bad that even he recognized he wasn't just a danger to himself but to anybody and anything else on the road. Still, he wouldn't let them scrap it.

A strong gust of wind held the shed door open, and Shiloh saw her sister inside. Her back was to the doorway, but Shiloh immediately recognized the wide but slumped shoulders, her thick build looking even stouter in an oversized plaid coat, lumpy jeans, and clunky Timberlands.

Shiloh hadn't yet stopped shivering and the idea of even a short run through the rain was a bit daunting, but she lowered her head, put a hand visor-like over her eyes to keep out the rain and made a quick dash across the yard.

With the clatter of the pelting rain on the shed's metal roof, her sister didn't hear her, didn't turn until Shiloh pulled the door closed behind her.

Startled at the noise, the other woman turned. It took a second for Shiloh's appearance to register, then her face broke into a wide smile as she threw herself at her sister and gathered her up in thick, strong arms. "Jesus! Shy!"

"Zee!"

When it felt like Zoe would never let her go, Shiloh gently pushed herself free, but their hands fell into each other's tight grasp.

"Oh, Shy! I'm… God, I don't know what…Jesus, Jesus, Jesus!" Zoe let one hand slip free to wipe at her eyes. She turned her face away, sniffling. "I'm gonna get all… Oh, damn."

Shiloh put her free hand over the hand she still held. "It's good to see you, too, Zee."

Zoe gave one, final sniff, gathered herself up, and turned back to her sister. "When'd you get in?"

"Just a few minutes ago. I called out, but…" She shrugged.

Zoe waved her free hand at the piles around her, still holding Shiloh's hand with the other, holding it tightly as if afraid her sister would disappear if she let go. The corners of the shed were lost in shadows, beyond the reach of the hurricane lantern Zoe had parked on a tool-strewn workbench, but Shiloh could still make out a jumble of old bicycles, rusting garden tools, dusty car batteries, spare cans of motor oil, water-stained cardboard boxes stuffed with God-knows-what, and tied trash bags bulging with more God-knows-what.

"I was pokin' around," Zoe said with a bit of a sigh, "seein' what was here, you know, goin' through things. We're gonna have to do that, right? Sooner or later? I don't think he ever threw anything away.

Regular pack rat. Look: he still has those bicycles he bought us that Christmas. When was that?"

"I think I was twelve, thirteen, something like that. I remember him spending all night putting them together. I could hear him cursing from all the way up in my room. Goddammit this, Goddammit that. I think that's when I stopped believing in Santa Claus."

They shared a laugh.

"I never understood those bikes," Shiloh said. "There's no place on the island you can't walk to in twenty minutes. Where the hell were we going to ride?"

"Maybe he just liked the idea of it. Maybe 'cause, you know… Well, that was the first Christmas after Mom … I guess he was just tryin' to, um, you know…"

Shiloh nodded. "What do you hear from Jay?"

"He's supposed to come out. Maybe tomorrow. Depends on the weather. It's hard gettin' out here for him when the weather's bad."

"*I* made it and I'm not exactly Captain Nemo."

Zoe shrugged, her way of saying their brother would do what their brother would do. "Jesus, Shy, you're pale as a ghost, your lips're blue, and you're shakin' so hard you look like you're gonna come apart. Let's get you inside; I don't feel like goin' to another family funeral any time soon."

After the hot shower, the chill bathroom set Shiloh shivering again. She wrapped herself in a bath towel and ran on her toes across the cold floor of the hall to her old bedroom. Their house had always been one of the biggest on the island, big enough that each of them had enjoyed having a bedroom to themselves. The master bedroom ran across the front of the second floor. Along the hall were Shiloh's, Zoe's, Jay's rooms, and then across the back of the house, the room that belonged to her father, sort of an office/den/retreat and - at one point - bedroom.

Zoe had gotten the wood pellet stove in her bedroom going for her, and the air now had a comfortable toastiness to it. Her sister had left clothes out on Shiloh's bed, by the looks of them Zoe's spares: flannel shirt, jeans, heavy wool socks. She'd been spending some time at the house during their dad's last weeks, she'd told Shiloh; it'd been easier to have clothes kept at the house rather than truck a bag in with her for each trip. Shiloh smiled at the tent-ish shirt: *When was the last time you wore flannel?*

She started to dress, then stopped, sat at the edge of the bed in front of the pellet stove. The room hadn't changed since she'd left for college, although she felt that had been less out of anybody's sense of nostalgia than there had simply been no need. The same posters were on the walls. On one side of the room: Leonardo DiCaprio from his *Titanic* days, Billy Corgan, David Grohl. On the other: Hemingway in full beard, Steinbeck, a line drawing of a tangle-haired Vonnegut.

Part of her room extended out over the first-floor alcove in something between a bay and a full turret. Her father had turned the space into a "reader's nook," building a platform against the outside window, covering it with a cushion and heavy pillows, an Anglepoise reading lamp extending over the platform. Flanking the platform were roughly made bookshelves (her dad fancied himself something of a carpenter, but he'd had more energy than skill). The books were still there. Along one side were volumes scavenged from library clearances and garage sales, books with cracked and ragged paperback covers: *Slaughterhouse-Five*, *Catcher in the Rye*, *The Grapes of Wrath*. Opposite were books bound in green cloth lettered in gold: Melville, Dickens, Poe, Dumas, Hugo. She'd gotten them through a Classic of the Month subscription her father had given her one

Christmas; her father whom she couldn't recall ever reading anything himself other than the sports section of *The Portland Times*.

She moved to the nook, spread out on the cushioned seat, the rain rattling against the windows surrounding her on three sides. She remembered what it was like to snuggle up on those cushions under a quilt, book in hand. Her dad would crack the bedroom door to call her down to dinner, but then see she was deep in a read, and quietly retreat closing the door softly behind him.

She shook off the memory, finished dressing, and shuffled out into the hallway in the thick socks. She headed for the stairs, but then stopped, turned and headed for her dad's sanctuary at the back of the house.

The door to his room was slightly open and she took that as an invitation. She opened the door gently, the way she would've if she'd been afraid of disturbing him.

It was a sparsely furnished room: a heavily scuffed desk against the windows overlooking the yard, a piece he'd scavenged from his precinct when they had replaced their old office furniture; a second-hand dresser picked up at a thrift store; a single bed.

When her father had started sleeping in that room, he and her mom had explained it to the kids like this: "Your dad snores so loud, I can't sleep"; "Your mom kicks in her sleep, she's gonna break one ah my ribs one day I don't move."

Like everything else now jumping out at her, she'd thought nothing of it as a ten-year-old, the explanations had made sense then, but now she looked back on it in a mix of curiosity and melancholy.

Mounted on a wall was a gun rack, his hunting rifles and shotguns secured behind a lock bar. She could almost feel a throb in her shoulder, remembering him teaching her how to shoot on the shore rocks, him throwing clay pigeons out over the surf: "You don't aim at where it *is*, Sweets, but where it's *gonna* be!"

There was a picture frame on his desk and now she had another of those years-belated epiphanies. It had been taken the day she'd received her undergrad degree at Boston College. She was in her cap and gown, brandishing her diploma, and her father was in his police uniform, pointing to his newly won sergeant's stripes and holding them up against her diploma. Two graduates, smiling with pride at themselves and each other.

The epiphany: except for his one young hitch in the Navy, the man had spent his entire working life with the Portland Police Department. He'd somehow hung on through fallen arches, shortness of breath, and fading eyesight until he couldn't pass his annual physical and was forced out at sixty-three. And yet in the whole house, this was the only photograph of him in his uniform.

She wondered… Was it still there? She slowly pulled open one of the side drawers. In a cracked leather holster, next to his badge and departmental retiree's ID, was his short-barreled off-duty revolver.

"You ok?" Zoe called from downstairs. "You get lost or somethin'?"

"Yeah, I'll be right down."

Shiloh pushed the drawer shut, took another look at the desktop photo, then left, closing her dad's door quietly behind her.

Three.

Zoe set an afghan across Shiloh's lap. She had pulled one of the front room chairs closer to the fire for her sister, thrown a fresh log onto the flames to bring up the heat in the room. The striped pattern in the afghan was unevenly wavy and Shiloh guessed this was probably something Zoe had knitted herself, who - like their dad - had more energy than skill.

"Are the clothes too big?" Zoe asked, pulling another chair up by the fire across from Shiloh.

Shiloh shook her head. "They're fine."

"I got yours in the dryer. That jacket looked nice."

"It was."

"Looked kinda expensive."

Shiloh sighed. "It was."

"Maybe when it dries out…"

Shiloh shook her head.

"Maybe you can take it to the cleaners -"

"It's suede, Zee. It's done. It's my fault. I don't know what I was thinking." *What were you thinking? The beret, the jacket, those cute little boots… Who were you trying to impress? Why?*

"I didn't know what else to do 'bout your clothes," Zoe said. "I didn't see any luggage."

"I'm in a hotel in the city."

"A hotel."

"The Hilton."

"Oh." Shiloh couldn't tell if Zoe was legitimately impressed, or if there was some slight mockery in it. Then, a little wistful: "We always wanted to stay there. You know; maybe just one night." A shrug: it wasn't going to happen.

"My firm has an account with them, Zee, it's not a big deal."

"Still, the Hilton."

"Did you think I was going to stay here? The man died in this house, Zee. I wasn't going to, well, you get it, don't you?"

"You could stay with us. Anthony wouldn't mind."

"That's polite bullshit, my dear."

Zoe sighed knowing it was true. "Doesn't matter. For now, we're both stuck here. At least for tonight." She nodded at the rain still splattering violently against the front window. "They're not gonna run the ferry in this. Storm's worse than it was -"

Shiloh turned to look out the window. There were explosions of spume against the shore rocks, shooting sprays of water nearly as tall as the house. "Good Christ! It *is* worse!"

Zoe laughed. "Boy, you have been away a long time! You forgot how it can get. This is kinda bad, but you shoulda been here for Irene, then there was Sandy. We had some pretty ugly Nor'easters last year, too. You think the bay is rough now? I 'member one storm, nobody could get a boat out from the city, the cell tower got knocked down, the land line to the mainland was out. If it wasn't for the radio at the police substation down in West Village, it was like we were stuck on the moon or somethin'."

"I saw a lot of empty houses when I was walking in. Is that why?"

Zoe looked into the flames starting to wrap themselves around the fresh log and let out a long breath. "Oh, I s'pose that was part of it. Thing is, St. Aggie's is dyin' out; I guess that's how you'd put it. Young people, some of 'em, went off to school and didn't come back -"

"Like I did."

Zoe made an apologetic face; she was sorry it had been taken as a dig, and Shiloh nodded her own apology for taking it as such.

"Some just wanted a life on the mainland -"

"Like you."

Zoe smiled at the reversal. "Like me. Place like this might be fun when you're a kid, but it gets to be tough when you get older. When the kids leave, it gets harder for the adults to keep things goin' 'cause they're gettin' up there in the years. Some move back to the mainland. Sometimes, like old Mr. Talley, when he died in his house, his wife said, 'That's it, I'm outta here'."

"Jeez, who's left?"

"On this part of the island? Nobody, really, but there's still families down in West Village."

"And Teddy Granier. I saw him when I came in."

Zoe laughed. "I think Teddy stayed 'cause he don't know what else to do with himself! You warmin' up any? How 'bout a cup ah coffee?"

"I could do with that."

Zoe went out into the kitchen and Shiloh heard the clatter of her rifling around in a cabinet for mugs. "You want somethin' in it?" she called out.

"Black is fine."

"I mean like a little sumpin'-sumpin'."

"What've you got?"

"What're you drinkin' these days? When all the big lawyers get together in those D.C. cocktail lounges, what're they puttin' down? Cosmos? Martinis? Somethin' with an umbrella in it?"

It was a gentle poke and Shiloh laughed. "We just call them bars, and no umbrellas. What's on the wine list?"

Through the archway between the front room and the dining room, Shiloh saw Zoe carry two steaming mugs in from the kitchen, set them down on a sideboard and look into one of the sideboard cabinets. "Dad wasn't exactly what you'd call a conna-swar of the fine la-koors. I just see that battery acid he liked for God knows what reason." She came out of the cabinet brandishing a whisky bottle. She unscrewed the cap, took a whiff and pretended to stagger. At least Shiloh thought she was pretending.

"Not too smooth but I guarantee it'll warm you up."

"Maybe a light dose."

Zoe poured a short shot into each coffee mug, came back into the front room, handed Shiloh one mug and went back to her seat. She held up her mug in salute, Shiloh returned the gesture, and they each took a sip.

Shiloh wasn't sure what hit her hardest: the heat from the coffee or the napalm explosion in her stomach from their dad's bottle. Zoe managed to down hers without so much as a flinch. *Practice,* Shiloh thought.

Zoe laughed. "I can't figure out if this helped kill the ol' bastid or it's what kept him goin'."

Shiloh laughed, too.

Then it grew quiet. The two cupped their coffee mugs and listened to the rain for a while.

Zoe looked into her cup. "Um, you gonna see Mom?"

Shiloh lay her head back on the chair. She got the very faintest whiff of cigarette smoke from the upholstery, her dad's unfiltered Camels. "I don't know, Zee. And say what? Thanks for the birthday cards I haven't gotten since you left? You guys were in touch with her, not me."

"You were away."

"Not when she left. I suppose she knows about Dad."

"We told her."

"*You* told her. Jay doesn't give a shit about any of us. Including Mom."

"Don't say that," but it came out weakly; she knew it was true.

"Ok, I won't say it. Not out loud." Shiloh let her head loll from one side to the other, looking around the house: the pictures on the front wall, her dad's footwear by the front door… "We're going to have to go through everything, go through the house, the shed…everything."

"Oh, that reminds me! You got a letter!" Zoe sprung out of her chair, went back into the dining room to a stack of mail on the sideboard.

"I got a letter *here?*"

Zoe nodded. "I guess he didn't know your address in D.C."

"He *who?*"

Zoe quickly rifled through the stack and pulled out a business envelope. "Here," and she brought the letter to Shiloh.

"H. McNair, Esquire," Shiloh read from the pre-printed return address.

"That's Dad's lawyer. Was Dad's lawyer. I guess he's still Dad's lawyer."

Shiloh took the letter, opened it. The single sheet of heavy bond paper inside was letterheaded with Harold J. McNair's name and an office address in Portland. The message was just a few lines. Shiloh looked over the top of the page and saw Zoe suddenly – and badly - pretending to be uninterested.

"Go ahead and ask, Nosy," Shiloh teased.

"I wasn't, I mean -"

"I'm playing with you, Zee."

"You're evil."

"You learn that in Big Law."

"I'm guessin' it's 'bout Dad."

"Apparently, Dad appointed me executor in his will. This McNair wants me to come in and talk about it." She handed the letter to Zoe to show she wasn't holding anything back.

Zoe plopped back in her chair and gave the letter a quick scan. "Shouldn't we all go in? For, like, what do they call it? The reading?"

Shiloh smiled. "That's in the movies, Zee. He's just going to give it to me, tell me what's in it, then I'll bring it home and go over it with you and Jay."

"And Anthony, right?"

Shiloh took another sip of the coffee, winced against the new explosion in her stomach. "Maybe you should wait and see what's in it, first. I'm not crazy about having Anthony and Jay in the same room if something in the will is going to provoke a – um - *spirited* discussion."

Zoe processed that for a second, Shiloh could see her looking for some flaw in the proposal, then coming to the truth of it, making a reluctant accepting grimace. "Um, yeaaaah,,,"

Zoe handed the letter back to Shiloh, there was another silence broken only by the sound of the rain now hitting the front window so hard it sounded like pelting gravel.

"You know who you should see?" Was Zoe smirking a bit?

"Who?"

"He's been comin' 'round a lot since Dad started gettin' really sick, seein' if he could help out 'round the house. He always used to stop by, I guess you could say him 'n' Dad got to be, like, friends, but 'specially after Dad got worse -"

Yes, she *was* smirking and Shiloh thought she knew why. "Don't tell me."

Zoe's smirk turned into a smile as she nodded.

"Ben Cole."

An emphatic nod.

"Zoe, I really don't…" *Don't what?* The only response Shiloh could come up with for Zoe and for herself was to flap her hand and wave the subject away.

"Dad really liked him. Well, he always liked him -"

"Good for Dad. They should've run off together."

"I thought you liked him. Seemed like you liked him."

"Zoe!" And Shiloh slashed a finger across her own mouth signaling her sister to *Zip it!*

Zoe made some sort of vague shrug and hand flutter which was her own signal that, fine, she'd drop the subject…but then…

"I'm just sayin'…" The smirk was still there.

"Sayin' what?"

The smirk changed to something else, something softer. "I mean, well, yeah, at first, he was comin' 'round 'cause ah you mostly, askin' how you were doin' down in Washington there, if you were comin' up for a visit or somethin'; you know. But after a time, well, I don't know how to put it; him 'n' Dad hit it off honest. I don't want to get all Dr. Phil 'n' everything, but what with Jay bein' - well, Jay bein' Jay - Ben was, um…"

"A nice change."

"Maybe more."

"You going to tell me Ben was The Son He Wished He Had?"

"I know that sounds kinda goopy, but I do think it was somethin' like that."

"That must've really pissed Jay off."

"What doesn't? Ben even tried helpin' Dad with Jay, got him his first job on the boats. Took him on himself for a while when word started goin' 'round Jay was a pain in the ass when he crewed."

"But even Ben canned him I'm guessing."

"Put up with him longer 'n he should've, I think 'cause a Dad. Toward the end…"

"What?"

Zoe sank deeper into her chair. She took a deep draw on her spiked coffee. Her face, even her voice, grew mellow. "You 'member Ben played the guitar? Had that band in high school?"

"Yeah."

"When the pain started gettin' bad, Ben would come out 'n' play for Dad, take his mind off stuff. There was this one song Dad got really likin' which was strange 'cause what I got was it was 'bout dyin' 'n' stuff. A Foo Fighters song. Some reason, it worked for Dad."

There was a long silence broken, again, only by the sound of the wind and rain outside, and the crackling of the fire in the hearth. Zoe pulled herself out of her chair, grabbed a poker from the fireside and stabbed at the logs though the fire didn't need any stoking.

"You weren't here, Shy. I'm not gettin' on you; I'm just sayin' you didn't see. Dad wasn't afraid. He was like, 'Hey, it's ok; when I go, I go'. Maybe it was all those years bein' a cop 'n' all, seein' what he saw, he was ok." She set the poker down, went back to her chair, her eyes aimed past Shiloh at the gray ocean, then shifted back to her sister. The fire cast a flickering, melancholy glow on Zoe's face. "What I'm sayin' is Ben was a big help. Sittin' with Dad 'cause I couldn't always be here, the kids 'n' stuff, 'n' Jay…"

"Useless?"

"Pretty much." A smile – a sad smile – came to Shiloh's sister. "But it was nice seein' Ben there with Dad, strummin' his guitar, singin' to him, 'n' Dad would lay back 'n' it didn't seem to bother him so much, the pain, havin' trouble breathin'.   I guess what I'm tryin' to say, Shy, 'n' I know it might be, ya know, awkward 'n' stuff, but you should say somethin' to Ben when you see him."

"If I see him."

Zoe grinned. "Shy, I'll put money on the table right now he's gonna make a point you bump into him."

"Shit."

Puzzled now, Zoe asked, "Whatever happened to you two?"

Now it was Shiloh's turn to sigh. "Jesus, Zee, it was high school for Chrissakes. We were kids. What happened? We grew up is what happened." It all came back to her with a dull ache. "*I* grew up."

The quiet, again. After a bit, "You eat today? There's not much in the house. Dad wasn't eating much the last few weeks, but I could scramble us up some eggs. I know it's not the same service you'd get at the Hilton…"

"Maybe, but I like the staff here better…even if it sometimes has a big mouth."

Zoe hadn't exaggerated: there hadn't been much in the kitchen refrigerator. Two eggs apiece, a slice of toast apiece. They ate quietly at the small Formica-topped kitchen table. In the harsh, flat light of the kitchen overhead, Shiloh noticed things about her younger sister she hadn't picked up on earlier; the flecks of grey in her tangled hair, the lines in her forehead and at the corners of her mouth and down-canted eyes, the rough skin of her hands; working hands. Shiloh thought of her own nighttime rituals - the hand cream, the face moisturizer - and found herself burying her manicured hands in her lap.

Zoe gathered up the plates, set them in the sink, poured them each another cup of coffee, and offered another shot of their dad's fire-in-a-bottle. Shiloh smiled the offer away, but Zoe poured some into her own cup. They sat and listened to the rain for a while. Outside, the dim gray light was fading, and the world was going dark.

"Hadn't occurred to me," Shiloh said, "but I missed that."

"What?"

Shiloh nodded at the rain. "Rain on a metal roof. When I went to school in Boston, first time it rained, I couldn't get to sleep. Couldn't figure out why, and then it hit me."

Zoe smiled. "Too quiet."

Shiloh nodded. "No metal roofs. I'm in an apartment; I don't even have a roof. It's funny what you get used to." And that reminded her of the two paintings in the front room, the silent piano, the family photos that never showed a whole family. "Funny what you get used to," she softly repeated more to herself than aloud.

They were quiet again.

Zoe began fidgeting with her cup. Shiloh had sat in on enough witness prep sessions to recognize the signs. "What is it?"

"Hm?"

"You look like you want to say something."

Zoe frowned. "Uh, well, I guess you should know…"

"What?"

"I mean, if Jay makes it out here tomorrow."

"Ok."

"See, Jay was kinda pissed you didn't come up for Dad's service."

"I told you, Zee."

"And I told him, you know, 'bout your job 'n' stuff. I'm just, like, I guess I'm warnin' you he's probably gonna be, well, you know…"

"I get he was pissed off I didn't come. And if I had come, he'd've found a reason to be pissed off about that. Jay would've been pissed no matter what I did because Jay is *always* pissed off."

Zoe nodded in glum acknowledgment. "He's probably gonna be a little worse 'n usual. See, I don't know if Dad told you, but Jay was livin' with this girl."

"I didn't know."

"Couple years, two years, like. Some girl. I don't know how he met her; she was kind of a…" Zoe made a face like whatever description she could come up with wasn't going to be very flattering. "Well, look, I don't want to go into the whole story, but anyways she gets pregnant, there's a kid, they break up. So now he's pretty much broke, livin' in some Bayside dump down by the cove. He's on the hook for child support but the boats don't go out so much this time ah year, this 'n' that…"

"I'm getting a picture."

"Like I said, just so's you know, he's gonna be, well…"

"I get it, thanks."

Quiet, again.

"How long you stayin'?" Zoe asked.

"I don't know. I want to help you guys get things settled. See what's in the will, talk about that, start going through Dad's things, then I'll go home and come back after the will is probated and help with the dispositions. Why?"

"Thanksgiving's next week. Be nice, you know, if you stayed."

"Zee –"

"You haven't seen the kids, not face-to-face. We all haven't been together in I don't know how long."

"Your husband thinks I'm a snot and Jay's a dick on a good day. I'm not sure I'd be missing a Hallmark moment. Besides, by the time I get back to D.C., so much crap will have piled up on my desk…"

Zoe stared down into her lap, nodding but not really agreeing.

Shiloh felt another of those pangs.

Again, the quiet, the rain. Shiloh yawned. "I don't know what time it is, but I feel beat." She finished the last of her coffee and stood. "I'll help you with the dishes."

Zoe nodded the offer away. "It's not much. I'll do it."

Shiloh turned to leave.

"Hey, Shy?"

Zoe was staring into her cup. She didn't say anything for a while.

"Go ahead, Zee. What is it?"

"I know what you said 'bout the job, you couldn't get away. You know; for Dad's thing."

"You didn't believe me?"

"No, no, it's not that. I just thought, well, you not comin'… I mean, you know…"

"Know what, Zee?"

"You bein' his favorite 'n' stuff…"

Shiloh dropped back into her chair. "Christ, are we going to go down that road?   You don't think Dad loved you guys?"

"It's not that, I'm not sayin' that it's… Look, I got kids, I know you love 'em all, but I know you love 'em each different. Dad was different with you is all I'm sayin'. C'mon, Shy, you know it. The books 'n' stuff, all those times -"

"And Mom treated me like shit so maybe it evened out."

Zoe seemed to shrink a bit inside her flannels. "I'm sorry, Shy. I didn't mean to, you know… It just seemed funny to me, you not bein' there."

Shiloh pulled her chair around to Zoe's side of the table, took one of her sister's rough hands between hers. "I'm here now, Zee, and I'm glad I'm here. Screw Jay, I'm glad I'm here for you. And right now, that's all that matters, right?"

Zoe put her other hand over her sister's and nodded.

Shiloh kissed her sister on the forehead and stood. "Sure you don't want help with the dishes?"

A small but sincere smile. "Shoo."

Shiloh headed for the stairs and her bedroom. As she climbed the stairs, she felt a heaviness, almost a pain in her chest. *You're right, Zee, he did treat me differently, I know that. And that included him not wanting me here to watch him die.*

Four.

"Shy! *Shy!* C'mon, wake up!"

The shaking only half-roused Shiloh, just enough for her to blindly bat the hand on her shoulder away.

"Shy, for Chrissakes!"

But the hand came back, the shaking grew more violent. Shiloh finally forced herself awake but not so much that she remembered she wasn't in her bed but curled up in her reading nook. The reminder came in the form of her head thunking rather solidly into one of the bookcases built into the side of the nook.

She finally squinted up at the figure looming over her. The rain which had lulled her to sleep drumming on the nook's metal roof had stopped and there was now a clear sky. A bright moon caught her sister's face, streaked by the bleaching pale light and strands of uncombed dark hair falling across her face.

The sharp pain from colliding with her bookcase had done a lot to clear Shiloh's mind. She sat up, rubbing the swelling bump under her tousled hair. "What the hell do you want?"

"There's someone in the shed."

31

"What?"

"Someone broke into the shed! C'mon, I'll show you."

Before Shiloh could move on her own, Zoe grabbed her hand and practically dragged her across the room and out into the cold hall and then to her father's room at the back of the house.

Shiloh was only wearing the flannel top Zoe had given her and her panties, not enough to fend off the chill in the room or the way the bare wood floor stung her feet with cold. Zoe pulled Shiloh to her father's desk under the bank of rear windows and pointed down at the backyard shed. The yard was washed with a bright, decolorizing moonlight.

"What am I looking at?"

"See the door?"

There was a steady wind, strong enough that gusts sent the windows rattling. The shed door blew back and forth as the wind picked up and eased then picked up again.

"So, you didn't lock it right. Maybe the lock broke. That old wood is pretty rotten and the wind -"

"Shuddup and watch. See it?"

A small, narrow beam of light occasionally swept around the dark interior of the shed; it was a flashlight.

Shiloh no longer felt the cold in the room or under her bare feet. An odd, unpleasant warmth crept up her neck and into her face. "We should call the police."

"It'll take 'em an hour to get out here."

"I thought you said they had some kind of station down in the West Village."

"They shut the substation down last year."

"They shut — "

"It's a story for later, ok?"

Shiloh watched the sweeping flashlight beam for a few seconds. *It's not random.* "Is there anything worth stealing in there?"

Zoe shook her head. "Unless he wants a twenty-year-old bike. Maybe somebody just wants to get in outta the rain."

"There's a whole row of empty houses; why break into a crappy old shed?"

Her father's voice in her ear: *God forbid it happens, Sweets, but you need to know what to do if something comes up and I'm not here...*

Shiloh opened the top side drawer of the desk, reached into the dark and came out with her father's off-duty pistol.

"What're you gonna do?" Zoe, her voice tight.

Your heart's gonna go like a jackhammer, but you still need to have a steady hand...

And he was right; she could feel her heart pounding against her chest, but to her surprise she found she could force a sense of...if not calm but a certain *stillness* about herself.

She pushed the latch on the side of the pistol and the pistol's cylinder dropped to the side. The moonlight glinted off the brass base of the six shells in their chambers. She snapped the cylinder shut. "You stay here." Shiloh turned for the door, felt as much as heard Zoe right behind her, almost close enough to touch chest to back. "Zee, I told you to -"

"I'm not lettin' you go down there by yourself." Zoe said it with such an unwavering firmness that Shiloh was suddenly overwhelmed with a flash of guilt about how she'd always underestimated her sister. If there'd been time, she would've hugged Zoe so hard she would've cracked her ribs. Instead, she smiled a quick smile, nodded an acquiescence and the two headed for the door.

They made their way down the hall then down the stairs to where Shiloh slipped her small, pale feet easily into her father's sneakers still sitting by the front door, then quietly shuffled through the house, through the kitchen to the door to the yard. She set her free hand on the doorknob, paused and looked to Zoe, an unspoken, *Are you ready?* Zoe nodded back, and Shiloh opened the door, swinging it slowly open.

It was clumsy walking in her dad's sneakers, like trying to walk in swimming flippers. Some part of her that could stand off and take in the scene saw the comic absurdity of her standing out there in a billowing flannel shirt, bare-legged, shuffling along in her dad's clunky footwear, and carrying a pistol. The gun was going to have to carry the day; she sure as hell didn't cut all that intimidating a figure. She only took a few steps into the yard, putting herself about fifteen yards from the swinging shed door.

You set the hand with the pistol in the palm of your other hand, like a coffee cup in a saucer…

She raised the pistol, setting her gun hand in her other hand. She felt Zoe's hand on her back. Support? Fear? Didn't matter; it felt good there.

"You in the shed!" she called out. The flashlight went out.

You aim from your eye to the rear sight to the blade at the front…

"I know you're in there, asshole! I'm counting three for you to come out and take off! I have a gun, I know how to use it, and if you're not out of here on 'three,' I'll show you how well! One…Two…"

Take a breath, let half of it out, don't jerk the trigger, you just squeeeze it…

The .38 jumped in Shiloh's hands as the yard lit up with the muzzle flash, the report muffled by the wind. The round thudded with a splintering impact into the aged wood over the shed doorway.

"The next one is going lower. *Three!*"

The wind had blown the door shut at just that point, then it exploded outward as a figure, shadowy even under the moon's illumination, flew out of the door and ran off into the night. Shiloh fired a second round into the ground, a confirmation to the running man that he should keep running. She kept the pistol up and at the ready, aiming off toward where the man had disappeared into the shadows of the empty houses along that side of the island.

Shiloh let a minute or so go by, looking for any movement off in the dark, before she lowered the pistol, surprised at how heavy it suddenly seemed, and just as surprised to find herself pulling in deep breaths, as if at the end of a long, flat-out run.

"God*damn*, Shy! God*damn!*" Zoe's face was all wide o's – wide-open eyes, a gaping mouth.

Shiloh tried to get control of her breathing. "Go get that lamp you had this afternoon."

When Zoe returned with the lit hurricane lamp, they headed for the shed, Shiloh keeping an eye on the dark space where the intruder had disappeared in case he tried for a return appearance. She let Zoe go into the shed while she stayed in the doorway where she could watch her sister while also continuing to keep watch outside. "Did he take anything?"

"Hard to tell."

Shiloh took a quick look inside the shed. She could see that boxes and bags had been opened, their contents scattered on the floor. "I don't think he did. It feels more like…he was looking for something."

"Like what?"

"You tell me."

To which Zoe could only shrug.

As they left the shed, Shiloh checked the padlock on the shed door. "This was cut with a bolt cutter. He came prepared. This wasn't just somebody looking to get dry." They propped the door closed to keep the weather out with a cinderblock from some spares her father had piled up by the pick-up and went back into the house.

They were sitting in the kitchen sipping re-heated coffee and this time Shiloh welcomed the added shot of her dad's cheap whisky. Zoe had gotten the afghan from the front room and thrown it over her shoulders.

The cold Shiloh felt wasn't completely from being half-naked outside. Her eyes were glued to the pistol sitting on the kitchen table in front of her. *If I had to, could I...?* She pushed the question off with a deep pull on her spiked coffee. "Are you supposed to go into the city and meet Anthony tomorrow or is he coming out?"

"I was supposed to go in."

"I hate to ask this. I don't want to leave the house empty. I want to get my stuff from the hotel tomorrow and come back to the island. I'll be staying here. I just need somebody to keep an eye on the place until -"

"You're going to stay here alone?"

"Zee, you've got the kids -"

"My sister-in-law Marie, you 'member her; she's good. She's been watchin' 'em for me, she'll do it as long as I need her to. 'Sides, she's their favorite aunt."

"Zee, I appreciate -"

"I don't want you out here alone, Shy." A slight smile: "Deadly as you are."

Shiloh got the same feeling she'd had when she'd felt Zoe's hand on her back out in the yard. "You should talk it over with Anthony first."

Zoe took another hefty draw of her coffee; the whisky flushed her face with a red glow. She started grinning, shaking her head, even giggling a bit. "I can't wait to tell Jay 'bout this. He's always goin' on 'bout how you're like some princess, Miss Hoity-Toity he likes to call you. But you're a goddamn Dirty Harriet!"

"He'll be more impressed if you don't tell him about the part where I kind of peed in my pants a little. You got some underwear I can borrow?"

PART TWO:

Legacies

Five.

Shiloh wearily sat up in her bed. She had thought she'd slept lightly, tuned to any strange noise signaling their visitor had returned, but Zoe had managed to lay out her dried clothes in her reading nook, her now-dry boots nearby, and she hadn't heard her come and go. She pulled herself out of bed, still groggy; she and Zoe had only slept in alternating two-hour shifts through the rest of the night in case their intruder came back.

What had stirred her that morning was raised voices from downstairs. No – a single raised voice.

Dressed, she went out into the hall, looked toward the master bedroom sitting behind a closed door at the front of the house. The voice below was clearer now, but she'd known when it was just an undecipherable murmur leaking up through the floorboards who it was. Her brother could wait.

She opened the door to the master bedroom and was immediately hit with the smell: gauze, antiseptic, disinfectant, urine…and something else. She couldn't define it, couldn't describe it, but there was a sense to it: decay, death.

The bed was unmade, the sheets and blankets pulled down and piled at the foot of the bed. There was a hamper overflowing with towels, hospital scrubs, pee-smelling linens; a medical waste container; a waste basket stuffed with rubber gloves and disposable adult diapers. An IV stand with two empty solution bags stood on one side of the bed. She stepped closer for a look. One bag was Ringer's lactate: that would be for dehydration. And the other: oxycodone for pain. On the other side of the bed: an oxygen tank with the mask and feedline coiled around the regulator. *God, how he must've hated looking around and seeing this was how he was going out. This is why he didn't want me here.*

Zoe had emailed her two months ago telling her they had moved their father back to the master bedroom needing the larger room for their dad's medical needs. Besides, it would be more comfortable for him. He'd argued against it, saying it wasn't his room, hadn't been his room for years, but Zoe had made the case that they couldn't take proper care of him in the room at the back of the house. They never really persuaded him, Zoe had said: "I think he just got tired of arguing."

She looked down at the rumpled bed. There was still an impression on the sweat-stained pillow. Her hand began to move toward the pillow, toward where her dad's head had lain.

"This is total bullshit, Zee! How the hell could there be no food in the house? Were you starvin' the ol' man?" It came up the stairwell, filled the upstairs hall. "I didn't eat breakfast 'cause I figured I'd get somethin' here, now you're tellin' me you gave the last eggs to the princess?"

Shiloh's fingers retreated from the pillow, slowly balled into a fist as she wondered if her brother ever spoke in anything less than a shout.

"Maybe if you'd come out more than once a week, you'd ah seen he wasn't eatin'." Zoe, her voice not loud but hard.

"I was out here."

"Yeah, Jay, you were a huge fuckin' help, did I ever thank you? Huge."

"Gimme a fuckin' break, Zee. I'm so fuckin' hungry I got a headache now. I come out here thinkin' -"

"Go get somethin' at Teddy's, bring it back, I'll cook it up for -"

"Yeah, I come out here to go fuckin' shoppin' at ree-tard Teddy's place. I had to get up 'fore the sun to help Donnie load up traps so he'd drop me off -"

"Glad to see you've mellowed, Jay," Shiloh said from the kitchen doorway.

Jay turned to her, went silent, but it was only the pause of someone taking time to switch weapons and adjust his aim.

He was bulkier than she remembered, and it wasn't just because of his oilskins and boots. His face, shadowed by a faded Boston Red Sox cap, was bloated and blotchy, a bad combination of windburn and liquor. What had, in his wall photo, been a patchy beard was now full but - like the long, scraggly hair creeping out from under his cap – unkempt. And even though he was almost two years younger than Shiloh, she saw it was peppered with gray.

"Ah, I see her majesty has decided to grace us with her presence!" A mocking smile of tobacco-stained teeth, a voice gravelly from too many cigarettes and too much booze. *You're going out like Dad only no one will be mourning you.* "Didn't mean to disturb your majesty."

"I've been up."

"Were you waitin' 'till I leave, Shy? You were gonna have a long-ass wait, sister."

"Coffee, Shy?" Zoe offered, looking more bored than annoyed by her brother.

"Of course!" Jay said with a deep bow and a sweep of his arm. "Don't forget, Zee; pour with your pinky out! Pinky out!

"Christ, Jay," Zoe sighed, "you couldn't wait to start in, could you?"

Jay's tone switched from acidic mockery to angry declaration: "I want to be there when you see this lawyer guy what's-his-face; McNair? Yeah, I know 'bout that letter."

Shiloh hadn't flinched through any of it but had ambled across the kitchen to sit at the table as Zoe poured her a cup of coffee. "I don't remember that it was addressed to you, Jay," she said evenly. "So..." She savored her first sip of the warming nectar. "No."

He hung over her shoulder. He smelled of the ocean, of fish...of beer. "Just 'cause you're some half-assed seckatary for your big deal law firm, don't think I'm gonna let you pull some bullshit over the will! I been talkin' to people who know how this stuff works. I'm sure Dad prolly left you every-fuckin'-thing 's not nailed down, but I'll take that shit to court, Big Sister. 'N' I'm tellin' you right now; I'm gettin' his guns."

Shiloh calmly beckoned to Zoe. "Do we have milk?"

Zoe grinned, shook her head.

"What were you saying about his guns?" Shiloh asked.

That he hadn't been able to rile her only steamed Jay more as Shiloh knew it would. He began angrily pacing around the kitchen, spastically jabbing an accusing finger at her. "You had plenty ah time with Dad with 'em, so I figure I earned 'em."

Shiloh sat back in her chair to face him. "You done? Everybody will get whatever the will says they get, and nobody – including me – is getting a goddamned thing until the will clears probate. So go sit on an ice cube and cool your ass because you've got a bit of a wait on your hands."

"I'm not blinkin' on this, Shy! Yeah, I heard 'bout last night, but fuck you, big deal, I'm not impressed. If I'da been here, whoever it was wouldna run off; they'd be leavin' in a rubber bag!"

Shiloh shrugged and turned back to her coffee. "I didn't feel like killing anybody last night. Maybe it's a woman thing because I don't have to worry about what people think about the size of my dick."

Jay let out a half angry/half exasperated blast of air and turned to Zoe. "Didn't I tell you? She was a snotty bitch when she left, and she's a bigger, snottier bitch now!" He turned to Shiloh, back to Zoe, back to Shiloh, saw there was no satisfaction to be had from either direction, and stormed out of the kitchen bleating, "I'm gettin' some air and fuck ya both!"

Shiloh answered Zoe's apologetic look with an it's-ok smile. "You did warn me."

Zoe poured herself a cup and sat at the table next to her sister. "Yeah, but it was worse than even I thought it was gonna be. I'm sorry, Shy. Dad's gone, you come all this way, and this is what you get."

"Forget it. I've gotten worse at the firm. One client even called me an instrument of Satan."

"Really?"

"No lie. Bring your coffee; come upstairs with me."

Shiloh sat at her father's desk in the upstairs back room, started going through one drawer after another, Zoe standing nearby. "Is there any other place Dad kept his papers?"

"Papers?"

"It's going to come up when we go over the will: where he kept his money, anything else having to do with holdings. Here's his bankbook. Almost $6,000. Cut up three ways, it's not much."

"You think that's not much?"

"In D.C., my share wouldn't cover one month's worth of bills and not because I'm living the lush life. That's just what living in D.C. costs."

"Ouch."

"Well put. But I don't see anything about the house: mortgage contract, deed, anything about his property taxes. I'm guessing the house is going to be the big-ticket item, but I don't see anything. I've got some bank statements here, but I'm not seeing any checks or automatic withdrawals indicating a monthly mortgage payment."

"I think he kept all his tax stuff up in the attic."

Judging by the clutter in the shed, Shiloh assumed the attic would, if anything, be a worse mess. She picked her coffee up from the desk, sat back in the chair. Her eyes went out the window. The last shreds of yesterday's storm clouds were gone, the sky was the deep, rich blue she remembered went with a Maine autumn. She could see past the shed, across the island to where an amber sun lit up the now calm bay with a thousand sparkles.

Her eyes dropped back to the shed. *What the hell could he have been looking for?*

"Zoe, I don't want to leave you alone here too long but when I go to pick up my stuff, I want to see if I can see this McNair guy, see what he has to say about the will, and then I'll hustle back here as fast as I can. I don't think our visitor'll be back during daylight, but I still -"

Zoe laid a light hand on Shiloh's shoulder. "You weren't the only one he taught how to use his gun."

It wasn't meant to be a dig, but it was coming to Shiloh how lopsided her father's attentions had been when it came to his kids, and maybe, for the first time, seeing how unfair it had been.

"I'll be ok, Shy. Like you said, he probably won't be back any time soon. But if he does..." She made a pistol of her fingers, a cartoon tongue-out expression of concentration as she sighted down her index finger barrel, and then in a badly imitated Clint Eastwood rasp: "Ask yourself: Do I feel lucky? Well do ya...*punk?*"

It was impossible for Shiloh not to laugh, and just as impossible for her not to lean her head and rest her cheek on the hand on her shoulder. "Ok, Deadeye."

There was a rapping on the glass of the front door, a muffled voice from outside: "Hello?"

"That can't be Jay," Shiloh said. "He wouldn't knock."

"He wouldn't even say hello," Zoe said. "Be more like, 'Guess who, motherfuckers!'"

He was already standing just inside the open door on the entry mat. He offered what Shiloh thought was intended as a disarming smile. "Apologies, but the door was unlocked..."

"So, sure, come right in." Shiloh said.

A slight bow of his head. "Apologies, again."

He was somewhere around Shiloh's age, she guessed, and the kind of handsome even men admired, a face of strong angles but not pretty, sharp dark eyes under a strong brow. His face had seen enough wind and sun to have a good amount of color and lines in the right places without looking weathered and worn. That bright, apologetic smile was filled with teeth just imperfect enough to telegraph they were natural. Despite the oilskin hoodie, faded jeans with their ragged hems, and the battered New England Patriots cap, he was no denizen of the Portland docks. No tobacco stains on the teeth, and when he doffed his cap in deference to the presence of ladies, Shiloh saw the kind of $100 + haircut she was used to seeing on the partners at her law firm. Even under the baggy hoodie Shiloh could see he was free of the tired slump of the men on the docks, but had the broad, square shoulders and tapered torso of someone who took care of himself, had the time for it, but didn't overdo it.

But what grated on her from the moment he'd stepped inside was the vibe that he was a good looker who knew he was a good looker, who had the gliding ease of someone whose accomplishments, whatever they might be, probably owed more to that smile and charm than any ability.

"Hello, Zoe," he said with a nod to her sister, then to Shiloh: "Notice I used the preferred pronunciation: "'Zoh,' and not 'Zoey'," for which he seemed to feel deserving of some kind of credit. He flashed those pearly charmers and pointed a manicured finger at Shiloh. "And that would make you Shiloh Vail. And, unless I miss my guess, that's your brother Jericho out by the water throwing rocks at the seagulls. He have something against seagulls? Defecate on his car, did they?"

Shiloh looked to Zoe, saw the look on her face. "You know this guy?"

"He was at Dad's service."

"And I apologize, again, for my father's absence that day," the man said. "He wanted to be there, but, well, business. You know. I'm afraid business has always come first for Dad. And, he hasn't been well."

The question on Shiloh's face must've been clear: "He's one of the Cleary boys," Zoe explained.

"Sean," the man said. Then, with a look of false embarrassment: "Sean, Junior, actually."

Shiloh again turned to Zoe looking for clarification.

"At the service, he said Dad and his dad did some kind of business together."

"Dad was a cop." To Sean Cleary: "My dad was a cop."

"And a very good one, too," Sean Cleary said. "Patrolman to lieutenant; you should be proud. Actually, my father and yours go back a long way. They were in school together, went in the Navy together. The Three Musketeers my father calls them."

"Three?"

"There was a third friend. I never met him, but I believe he was your dad's partner on the force when he was still on patrol."

Shiloh took a few seconds to take it in wondering why she'd never heard any of this from her father. Then another thought: "Cleary," she mused. There was something familiar about the name that had nothing to do with her father. "Your family still has that big house on the point?"

"Ahh, you remember! Yeah, the family manse, as it were."

"I like that: 'manse'."

"My brother likes it, but it's a little ostentatious for me. I have an apartment in the city."

"Wasn't there a thing…" Shiloh probed back into her memory. Again, back to Zoe: "Zee, wasn't there some big thing about something the Clearys were trying to pull out there at the point? Back around the time we were in high school?"

Zoe grinned. "Oh, yeah! You guys were trying to get the name changed from Cypress Point to Cleary Point. I remember everybody at school making fun ah you guys for that."

"As well they should've," Cleary said with a surrendering nod. "I'm afraid that was dear old Granddad. He's no longer with us, but in his time, he could be a little ostentatious, too."

"You weren't in school with us," Shiloh said.

A bowed head in what seemed to Shiloh a well-practiced gesture of humility. "Waynflete, I'm afraid," he said, naming one of Portland's private schools.

"So, you're a preppie."

He held up a finger. "Not by choice. Look, I understand I have intruded, and this may be a difficult time for you, what with your father's recent passing. But there's something I'd like to discuss with you ladies. I told Zoe at the service we should talk; there must be a more comfortable way of doing that."

Shiloh looked at Zoe, and Zoe gave a why-not shrug and started down the stairs. "I'll warm up the coffee."

They sat around the kitchen table, Sean Cleary making some pointless remarks about what good coffee Zoe made which, considering it had been sitting on the stove all morning, Shiloh dismissed as a painfully transparent attempt at ingratiation.

"So," Shiloh said, trying to push the conversation to something purposeful.

"Ah, so!" Sean Cleary said, nodding his head. "As it happens, I consider myself lucky that you're here," meaning Shiloh.

"How is that lucky for you?"

"Well, this is something for the whole family, but I think you might be of particular value here. You went into law, didn't you?"

"Your research is a little off. Paralegal."

"But for a boutique firm in D.C."

"You've been doing a lot of homework."

"Habit. Always know the ground. I handle a lot of my father's legal affairs."

"You're a lawyer?"

This time it was an honestly embarrassed smile. "Not quite. I started law school, got through the first year at the University of Connecticut."

"U-Conn," Shiloh said, nodding, "Pretty decent."

"But Dad needed me around, so... Why didn't you go?"

"I was thinking about it, but then I started working with lawyers."

"Turned you off the profession?"

"Understatement. So, what is it you think two not-quite-lawyers need to discuss?"

"When did you get in?"

"Yesterday."

"Good God, you weren't out on the bay yesterday, were you?"

"I made it in before it got really bad. Still, I was proud of myself. I managed the trip without puking once. Close, though."

"Ah, some of Maine is still with you."

"Nice chat. Now back to business."

Cleary chuckled. It had a mellow, warm sound. "Oh, you would've been a hell of a lawyer."

"Thank you. Business."

"Your father and my father had some dealings."

"So, you said. But my dad was a cop, so I don't see what kind of business anybody would have with him."

"I don't know how much you know about my family – "

"I know they tend toward ostentation."

Cleary laughed. "Good shot! Well, my father has his fingers in a lot of pies. Some are business pies; some are political pies."

"I've been hearing about the Clearys since I was a kid," Zoe said. "Big wheels."

"Bluntly put, yes, at least the old man likes to think so."

"Still trying to see a connection," Shiloh said, and she exchanged a look with Zoe who was having the same problem.

Cleary took a moment, sipped his coffee, Shiloh could see he was trying to figure out a clear, simple explanation. "Because your father was a policeman, sometimes he was in a position to hear things that were advantageous to my father. Oh, nothing illegal, nothing like insider info, nothing like that. More like a heads-up; 'Hey, the talk in the locker room is the union wants a seven percent pay hike in the next contract,' or – and this is pertinent to you – 'The city's doing an audit and they found out St. Aggie's isn't really within municipal boundaries so they're closing down the substation'."

"Is that true?" Shiloh asked.

Cleary nodded.

She looked to Zoe.

"I thought they just didn't want to keep paying for it," Zoe said. "I didn't know about this stuff, about us not being part of Portland."

Shiloh turned back to Cleary. "Ok, I see what you're saying, but I still don't get what that's got to do with – "

Cleary held up a hand; a silent way of saying, "Stop, allow me to explain." Shiloh nodded for him to go ahead.

"There was some material pertinent to a project your father was helping my father with. It was quite some time ago, years, actually. Dad wanted to see if it was possible to locate those materials, that maybe as you were figuring out the estate, you might come across them."

"In order to…?"

"He'd like them returned."

"Returned. They were his?"

"Well, as I said, it was something the two of them were working on – "

"Some time ago."

"Yes."

"So why now?"

"Oh, you would've been hell on wheels in a courtroom."

"Flattered. Again. And you haven't answered the question. Again. You do that a lot, you know; find a way to not answer my questions. You would've been hell on wheels in a deposition."

Cleary grinned at that, then frowned and this seemed a true expression of puzzlement. "In all honesty, I don't know what my father's interest is. Dad wasn't clear about that. If I had to guess, I think he might be interested in resurrecting the project, whatever it was."

"In all honesty."

"Is that what working with lawyers does? Makes you naturally skeptical?"

"No, that's what working with lawyers' evasive clients does."

Cleary threw his head back and laughed, slapping the table. "By damn, you're something! Even while you're looking at me like you think I'm picking your pocket, I like you, Shiloh."

"Ms. Vail."

He nodded. "Per your wishes, but only -" and he held up a warning finger "- until we become friends."

"And you're confident we'll become friends?"

He scrunched up his face in a way that was almost little-boyish. "Not confident. Hopeful."

"Well, tell you what, Mr. Cleary -"

"Sean, please!"

"- Mr. Cleary, we haven't even begun to go through my father's things. I don't know that he even had files. So far, all I know is my dad kept my bicycle from when I was a kid. That you can have if you'd like. I haven't even seen the will yet. And there's still probate -"

"I know, I know, but my father was kind of anxious -"

"Since, according to you, this has been sitting around for years, it doesn't seem so time-sensitive to me, so…"

"So tough shit?"

"Kind of, yeah. Not trying to be a pain."

"No, no, I understand. I'll tell my dad to be patient."

"Real patient. It's a big house, lots of stuff to go through."

"If it would help, I could come out and -"

"Mmmmm," delivered with an icy smile that said, No way that's going to happen. Cleary smiled in response, partly in resignation, but also partly amused. He was enjoying the verbal fencing...and Shiloh reluctantly admitted to herself that she did, too.

"If we find something I think you and your father should know about, I'll let you know."

Cleary pulled a small notebook out of his hoodie pocket and a nub of a pencil, scribbled something on a page, tore it out and handed it to Shiloh. "That's my personal number. If you -"

"Like I said, if and when, and it's something – in my judgment – you should know about..."

He gave her a you-*are*-something shake of his head and stood. "Zoe, thank you for the coffee, I can let myself out."

As he started for the door, "Hey!" Shiloh called.

Sean Cleary stopped and turned. "Found something already?"

"A question."

He nodded for her to go ahead.

"Whatever it is your father's interested in, is there anybody else with the same interest?"

"Why? Has someone been by asking?"

Shiloh shook her head. "In case someone does..."

"As I said, this was something between my father and yours. I think you should consider those materials proprietary. But, no, I don't know of anyone else who would be interested. I don't know if anybody else even knows about it."

Shiloh nodded and Cleary took that as a dismissal and left. She waited until she heard the front door close behind him and turned to Zoe. "Do you have any idea what the hell he's talking about?"

"I didn't even know Dad knew ol' man Cleary until this dude showed up at the service. You think this has anything to do with what happened last night?"

"It's a hell of a coinky-dence if it doesn't."

Six.

As Shiloh stepped out onto the portico, it was hard for her to believe she was looking out on the same bay – the same icy rain-whipped world – she'd experienced the day before. The sky was cloudless, a rich sapphire blue that went up forever, the sun a warm yellow, giving everything an autumnal glow. There was still the occasional whitecap out on the Atlantic, but the ocean rolled calmly, quietly, barely making a burble as it swept onto the rocky shore by the house. There was a November edge to the breeze coming off the ocean, tangy in her nose and on her lips with the taste of the sea, but it was more bracing than biting. From where she stood, she could see the jumble of coal-black boulders at the base of Cape Elizabeth, and beyond, on the grassy flat atop the bluffs, lit up to a brilliant, shining white by the sun, the spire of Portland Head light and the cozy little lighthouse keeper's cottage at its base.

Yesterday, listening to the sound of rain on the Vail house's metal roof, she had told her sister she hadn't realized it was a sound she missed. Her father had once told her the same thing before she left for college in Boston: "You'll be glad you left," he'd said, "but you'll be surprised what you miss. You may not even realize you miss it until you come back."

She'd gone to school in Boston, worked and lived in D.C., her job had taken her to New York City and Philadelphia, and measured against them, Portland was easily in the junior league of cities. But, it was still a city, and like all cities, it was busy, it had its share of urban noise. Only the people who lived on the islands of Casco Bay were treated to what Shiloh was letting wash over her now: an empty, endless sea and sky, the faint calls of gulls and terns, and a quiet – almost solemn – natural majesty.

You may not even realize you miss it until you come back.

It was only the muted nagging that there were things needing doing that day which finally pulled her off the portico. On the road along the shore, she weaved this way and that around the potholes and dips still filled with water from the previous day's storm. As she made the turn around the west end of the island, she heard a low thrum she recognized as boat engines, diesels; she'd heard the sound often enough growing up to know it.

She looked up and saw a cabin cruiser – forty-footer, she guessed, maybe fifty – slowly easing its way across the inlet. It wasn't like the other boats in the inlet, rust-streaked and tired-looking. It's gleaming white hull and brass fittings popped against the blue water. Clear of the inlet, the engines changed pitch, the boat picked up speed curling up a foamy wake as it headed out into the bay.

She couldn't make out the figure at the helm but didn't need to; she knew it was Cleary, heading back to Cypress Point lying obscured behind the other islands of the bay; Junior no doubt heading home to report to Daddy.

"Ewww," Teddy Granier said as his eyes did a quick up-and-down of Shiloh's used-to-be-suede jacket. "Casco Bay was not kind to you."

"Merciless," Shiloh agreed. She'd felt pretty much the same way when Zoe had handed it to her, mottled with water marks and looking as if it was suffering a case of mange.

"Anything you can do for that?"

"Give it to Goodwill. But I'm not sure they'd take it." She slid a piece of paper across the counter to Teddy. "Those are my sizes. Throw together a couple of flannel shirts, jeans or twills, wool socks and Timberlands if you have them, Carharrts if you don't. Leave it all at the house. I have to go over to Portland for a while, but I'll settle up when I get back."

"I trust you," Teddy said without looking up from the paper with her sizes.

I trust you. When had she ever heard anything like that expressed over a counter since she'd left? She felt an odd... She didn't know what to call it...a pang? A twinge? It was like someone telling you a relative you'd once been close with but hadn't seen in years, had passed.

"I'm going to need something to wear now, too, because this -" and she plucked dismally at her ruined jacket "– isn't going to cut it."

Teddy brightened. "Got something," and he beckoned Shiloh to follow him along the cramped, narrow aisles.

The store had a musty smell, not off-putting but comforting; a sense of the place having always been there...and always would be.

Her father had liked taking them on long weekend drives away from the coast – "Expeditions," he liked to call them, blowing past lumber trucks on the two-lane rural highways as he bellowed out the window, "Outta me way; I'm an expedition!" "The whole world isn't Portland," was his explanation for these excursions, and she remembered burgs that were sometimes no more than a convenience store with gas pumps and a church, color explosions of fall foliage, derelict mills crumbling alongside the rivers that had once powered them. Oddly, that was the same rationale he used to push her off to school in Boston: "The whole world isn't Portland."

These little towns often had general stores which reminded her of Teddy Granier's; truly general because these isolated pockets relied on them for almost everything. St. Aggie's may not have been off in the Maine hinterlands but was just as isolated and Granier's served the same function since the locals couldn't just hop on a ferry every time they needed toilet paper or a quart of milk. Teddy's store stocked some of everything: food, liquor, household products, some clothing, a bit of hardware, even a few kitchen appliances. He took her to a back corner of the store where there were some clothing racks and plucked out a fleece-lined denim jacket with a hood attached.

"How's that?" He looked pretty proud of his choice.

It was hardly a one-for-one replacement for a $400 Ralph Lauren number, and Teddy's eye was a little off on the size as the jacket was a bit baggy, but it was comfy and warm. As she snuggled into it, something about it felt like Shiloh'd pulled an old favorite from a long untouched trunk. "Perfect, Teddy, thanks."

"You'll probably need one a these, too, you don't mind it messin' with your hair." He reached into a bin of knit wool watch caps and handed her a fire engine red one. "Next time you're crossin' the bay in a storm, we'll see ya comin' a mile off!" He thought this was funny for some reason, laughed, flashing that missing canine space. Shiloh couldn't help it; she laughed, too.

She followed Teddy around the clothing corner of the store as he started putting together her order, throwing one article after another over his shoulder, sometimes holding up a flannel shirt for her approval – "Don't like the gray? How's the blue?"

Then he was back at the counter, toting things up.

"Teddy…"

"Mmm."

"You hear anything funny last night?"

"Whaddaya mean funny? There was a helluva wind after the storm cleared. Makes funny noises. You mean like that?"

"More like maybe a gunshot. Or two."

Which froze him. "Shots? Like bang-bang?"

"Somebody was rooting around in our backyard shed. I popped off a couple to scare him off."

"Wow."

"What's wow?"

"Just…wow."

"You didn't hear it?"

"Like I said, it was pretty windy last night. I was in my storeroom out back puttin' away all what come in with you yesterday. I like to crank up the radio when I'm alone like that. Maybe if I'd ah been outside…"

"So, you didn't hear anything."

Teddy shook his head. "Coulda been some ah those West Village kids. Sometimes they go horsin' 'round those empty houses. You know; kids."

"Maybe," but Shiloh didn't believe that. Bolt cutter? No, that wasn't "just kids." "What about the ferry, Teddy? When's the next one?"

"He's going to tell you you've got a loooong wait, right, Teddy?"

"'Fraid so. They still haven't bounced back from the storm. It happens."

But Shiloh wasn't listening to Teddy. Among the many functions Teddy's store fulfilled on the island was as a morning coffee stop, and to that end he'd set up a small counter against a far wall with coffee urns and the usual coffee stand accoutrements, sugar and Splenda packets, stirrers, take-out cups and so on. And loitering on a single chair by the counter, tipped back against the wall, was a vaguely, not-completely-welcome-or-unwelcome familiar figure.

"Ben?"

"That's it?" and he leaned forward, the front legs of the chair hitting the store's warped floorboards with a deep thump. "'Ben'? No running into my arms in slow motion? Sweeping me off my feet?" Ben Cole took a deep sip of his coffee as if to fortify himself, then slowly unfolded from the chair.

Cole was like the authentic model Sean Cleary had been imitating: the same good looks but with the lines and creases from someone who didn't just cruise the sea but worked it. The same kind of clothing – flannels and twills – but faded and frayed, topped with a duckbill cap carrying the emblem of the U. Maine Black Bears, and anchored at the bottom with work boots worn down at the heels. He carried the same sense of physical strength as Cleary, but it wasn't the product of regular gym workouts; rather someone whose job demanded it.

And yet…

All that seemed to look better on Cole than Cleary's carefully composed faux dock worker air. Or maybe, Shiloh warned herself, it was just bound up in her with echoes of long-ago days.

She tried not to smile, managed to keep it to a wry twist of her lips. "Not to be sexist, but I think *you're* supposed to do the sweeping. And that's not an invitation."

"In lieu of a romantic sweeping, can I offer you an alternative to the ferry? I've got my boat."

"And you just happened to be sailing by?"

Cole shrugged. "Finished up laying my traps this morning, just hangin', you know; shake off the chill. Gets cold out there on the bay early in the morning."

"Laying traps. Don't you usually circle around and start pulling them in after, what? An hour or something like that?"

But Cole was unflustered. He smiled an exaggerated smile. "How sweet you remembered!"

"That's what we in the legal profession call an evasive answer."

"Ah, he's been comin' in here most every day last coupla days," Teddy put in.

Shiloh did a quick calculation: "Since my dad passed."

"Well, yeah, I guess."

She turned back to Cole.

He nodded. "I guess."

"Figuring sooner or later I'd be here."

"Sue me, I was hoping to see you."

She was already shaking her head. "Ben -"

Cole waved his free hand to slow her down. "No big thing; just to see you, ok? Shy, the ferry's gonna be a while. Last harbor bulletin I got said another hour meaning probably two. I promise, no *Love Boat* maneuvers, just a friendly lift across the bay."

She turned to Teddy. "Why do I feel like I'm getting suckered?"

"'Cause that's how it sounds?"

She laughed.

After Cole settled Shiloh in the pilothouse of his boat with two cups of Teddy's hot coffee – "Trust me, you're gonna need it out there" – he climbed back out onto the dock, slipped off the bow and stern lines and hopped lightly back into the open after deck. He came into the pilothouse, took his coffee from Shiloh, turned over the engine and then one-handedly steered the Down Easter away from the dock as easily as anyone else might pull a car away from the curb. This wasn't the awkward rookie lobsterman Shiloh remembered; every move had the smoothness of a practiced veteran and reluctant as she was, it was hard not to admire the skill and how at home Ben Cole looked at the helm. She could see in him that in twenty years, maybe even ten, he'd look as married to the helm – and as weather-beaten – as the Gorton Fisherman type who'd taken her across the bay the day before.

And that, she remembered, had always been the issue.

As the boat moved out of the shelter of the inlet, there was more of a swell, but a casual, even comforting motion. Still, as Ben had warned, once on the open water there was a wind with a bit of a bite to it rattling the pilothouse windows, and she was glad for the hot coffee.

"You want, I can take a lap around the bay," Ben offered with a hopeful smile, "see the old sights."

She looked out at the slow rolling waters of the bay. "Maybe another time."

"As in never."

"Ben…"

He shrugged it off. "'S'ok, Shy," taking one of the coffees from her, "I get it."

She didn't think he did. For a few minutes, there was only the sound of the boat's growling diesel. She watched him squint against the morning sun's glare on the water, though he seemed to be trying too hard not to look her way.

"I want to thank you," she said.

"No need. I had to head in anyway."

"Not this. Well, yeah, thanks for the ride, but Zoe told me how nice you were to Dad."

"It wasn't all about you, ya know."

"I didn't think it -"

"I mean," and his head dropped sheepishly, "it *was*, in the beginning; you know, after you first went down to Boston for school, yeah, I guess it was. About you. Around the holidays, I'd hang around the house, hoping, well, you know…"

"I remember."

"But…"

"But?"

A sad frown. "Well, you know what my dad's like. Sometimes I thought the only reason he had so many of us, he figured we'd be a crew he wouldn't have to pay. Your dad, it was different with him. I could talk to him about stuff I couldn't talk to my dad about. Some ways – I know this is gonna sound corny, like a what is it? A cliché?"

"You mean he was more of a dad to you than your own father?"

"Yup, that's the cliche. What I'm sayin' is I was glad to be there for him when he got sick. No offense, but it had nothing to do with you."

"None taken."

"But he did talk a lot about you those days. So how is life down in the snake pit of Washington, D.C.?"

"I'm not involved in government, Ben, no political stuff."

"Ok, then, so how's the boutique law firm business?"

"A snake pit."

They both laughed and that seemed to put them in a place where they were both comfortable.

"It must pay well," Ben said. "That jacket you ruined looked like it'd been a nice piece of goods."

"It was."

"Expensive, too."

"It was."

"You were supposed to go to law school. What happened?"

"I started working for lawyers is what happened. Some of the stuff I see, if I did it, I'd have to go home and scrub myself with a Brillo pad every night. If you can do that stuff without feeling like you need a

Brillo scrub, it can pay for a summer house in the Hamptons, a boat you keep here to use one week out of the year, and vacays in Cabo. But I couldn't get my head to that place."

"I don't see that as a bad thing." He mulled a thought for a moment. "Even doing what you do, that's not the direction I figured you for."

"Oh? What'd you figure me for?"

"I know it was a long time ago…"

"C'mon; what?"

"I remember when your big interest was *li-tra-chur!*"

Shiloh groaned.

"C'mon, Shy, you were gonna be the next what? I remember you read a lot of Hemingway and some other guys."

She laughed at that: *Some other guys.* And then she thought… *Some other guys.* The phrasing seemed to define the space between them.

"You got that prize," Ben went on, "big deal with the school literary magazine -"

She looked out through the rear windows of the pilothouse, past the stern of the boat and widening V of their wake, out to where she could see the crown of Portland Head light still floating above St. Aggie's Island. She could just make out the stout figure of her family's house on the southern shore of the island. It was a view which had been cloaked by yesterday's storm, but now it was clear, familiar, and brought with it a lot of things she'd forgotten, and still more she'd pushed away. "Christ, Ben, it was kid stuff. I did take a few classes at Boston which was enough to see I wasn't ever going to be better than a high school hot shot, and that killed that."

Ben's face clouded, a combination of sadness…and puzzlement. "So, from aspiring Hemingway to aspiring Perry Mason to… So, what's this?"

Her coffee had grown cold. She stepped out onto the after deck, poured the cold liquid into the bay. "It pays for my life, Ben."

He killed the engine, but she didn't mind. He came out on the after deck, sat on the gunwale across from her. As the boat lost its forward momentum, it fell into a soothing, easy swaying, the water lapping against the fiberglass hull in quiet licks.

"It's worth it? It's that nice a life?"

"It's different for you, Ben." She waved at the expanse of the bay, its islands and lights, the bells of channel buoys gonging quietly in the distance. She could see the allure of it even if it didn't hold for her. "This was always what you wanted to do. Wasn't it? That's what I've always thought."

He shrugged. "I dunno. It was in the family. Seemed natural. Tell you the truth, I don't think I ever thought about whether it was something I *wanted* to do. This is just what we did."

"But you're ok with it. You stay."

He looked out over the same bayscape, flashed a puzzled smile at some inner thought, then the smile evaporated as he turned to her. "I won't lie, Shy, it killed me when I saw you weren't coming back, but I get it. If you're lucky, you find something that feels like you found your place. This," and he nodded out at the waters of Casco Bay, "even on the worst days, cold enough I can't feel my fingers and toes, every part of me aches at the end of the day and the catch sucks... This feels like my place." He turned back to her. "It's not yours. Have you found your place, Shy?"

In that moment, she envied him. *You're home, you've always known this was your home...and always would be.* "Sometimes I wonder if I even have a place. Maybe some people don't. But I still have bills to pay."

He pondered that for a bit, looked out at the bay as if some clarifying answer was out there, then nodded, went back into the pilothouse and re-started the engine.

They passed through the channel between House Island and Peaks Island, then far off in the distance they could see the white dart of the Cleary cruiser cutting a frothy wake across the bay toward Cypress Point.

"That's him," Ben said. "I saw him heading toward your house this morning. Mind my asking; what'd he want?"

She shrugged. "I'm not sure I know."

She stood next to him, and they both watched the Cleary boat grow smaller in the distance.

"Nice boat." Ben shook his head in a begrudging admiration. "Must be nice to be the king."

"He's really only a prince," Shiloh said.

"Still. Easier than working for a living."

Ben sailed them past the cruise ship and harbor ferry docks, the marina where the Boston rich kept their yachts, then to the commercial wharves where other Down East boats were already unloading their first catch of the day. After Ben docked and tied up, he helped Shiloh up onto the wharf.

"Consider yourself delivered," he pronounced. "Now what?"

"My hotel."

"Where you staying?"

"The Hilton, and don't give me that faw-faw-faw look; I got enough razzing about that from Zoe. I want to pick up my things then go on back to the house. But before that, I need to go by my dad's lawyer's and talk about his will."

"I have my truck -"

"And I have my car."

"Oh. Well…Would you think I'm being too stalkery if I walk you to your car?"

"As long as you don't ogle or drool. I'm parked at the Casco Bay Garage. When did that go up?"

"It's been up for a while, Shy. It's not like you haven't been back."

"It's been a while. And even then, I'd go straight out to the island. It's years since I've been down here. I um…" The thought faded as she looked from the brickwork of the Old Port on the landward side of Commercial Street, to the new, sleek buildings along the waterfront, and felt…something. Like a shadow passing over her heart.

They followed Commercial Street toward the garage. Shiloh had been born after the Old Port's resurrection in the 1970s and 1980s which had turned a neighborhood of derelict and decaying old buildings dating back to the Victorian age into a tourist draw of quaint shops and equally quaint eateries, cafes, and bars set along narrow cobblestone streets. When she and her friends had been old enough to cross the bay on their own, they had roamed those streets, hung out in the ice cream shops and coffee bars and then, when they'd gotten a little older, had had their first giddy taste of legal, bar-served alcohol. Sometimes – and later often times – sitting across from her in those days had been Ben Cole.

What Shiloh didn't recognize was the ultra-modernness on the waterside, like some bit of Manhattan cool had been forcibly jammed into the Old Port waterfront. What had once been open to the water was now home to fancier stops; upscale club-like restaurant/bars aimed at a younger partying crowd. Some of the working wharves had been converted into foundations for condo complexes giving the inhabitants of its high-priced residences a panoramic view of Casco Bay, and another wharf was now home to a still shiny terminal for the cruise lines.

Cole must've caught the look on her face – not so much put off by what she saw as somewhat disappointed. "You ok, Shy?"

She nodded.

"I heard what you were saying to Teddy about last night. What happened out at your house?"

She told him.

"And then today that Cleary guy went out to see you."

"You think they're connected?"

Ben shrugged. "But I know I'm not happy about you staying out at the house."

"Maybe Teddy's right, just some West Village kids."

"Not making me happier. Tell you what; remember Micucci's? What if I bring out a pizza tonight, a couple of 'em, for you, Zoe, her family. I'll get a cooler of Allagash brews… Think of it as a welcome home thing for you, kind of a salute to your dad. I'll bring my guitar, and you can throw your empties at me."

"What if Jay is there?"

"Do me a favor and throw a few at him. You know how many boats tossed him?"

"Jay thinks he should be a captain."

"Jay thinks he should be the fucking fleet commodore."

They were at the garage, Shiloh ran her Visa through the pay terminal, and then they climbed the stairs to the third deck. Before she went for her car, Shiloh walked to the end of the deck and leaned on the low wall where she could see the night-and-day contrast of the old Old Port and the new Old Port waterfront.

"Hey, Shy?"

She'd been lost in thoughts of what used to be and no longer was, so she hadn't heard him come to stand beside her. "That Cleary guy, you got the slick one. I saw him walking back from your house."

"You know him?

"A lot of Portland knows him. I mean, they know the family. They buy this, own that, control the other. They wanted my dad's boats for a while until they got tired of hearing no. Got a little ugly for a bit."

"Cleary said his dad and my dad had some kind of business together. Dad ever say anything to you about anything like that?"

"With the Clearys?" Cole shook his head dismissively. "I don't recall him saying anything. He just used to tell me stories from when he was a cop...and stuff about you. A *lot* about you," this last was said with a smile knowing it would make her fidget uncomfortably.

And it did.

"Look, last night, I'm not saying the Clearys had anything to do with it, maybe Teddy's right, just some kids, hope he's right, but you be careful around those people. When it comes to the way they do business, they have a reputation for using a mallet when a gentle tap would do the same job. I got to see that close up when they came after my dad's boats. The nice one, the one with the smiles, Junior, he shows up and makes an offer, Dad says no. The next day, one of the boats wouldn't start because somebody put sugar in the fuel tank. Somebody said they thought they saw the other brother poking around the night before; Aidan."

"Did you tell the police?"

"Told your dad but he said, 'Somebody thought they saw' isn't evidence. Told me I had to let it go. I'm just saying, you see somebody who isn't slick Mr. Smiles poking around, you give me a holler...and be careful. This Aidan guy, he's got a rep makes your brother look like a Boy Scout."

"I'll be careful. See you tonight, Ben." But she stopped for a last look at the two faces of the Old Port.

He grinned. "You don't like it, do you? I mean the new stuff."

"'Let us hush this cry of 'Forward', till ten thousand years have gone'. Tennyson. Another one of 'those' guys."

He laughed. "Yeah, you get something, you lose something. I'm thinking, give it a few years and none of my boats is gonna be allowed to dock here anymore. Few years after that, nobody'll remember they ever did."

Seven.

Even with her GPS homing in on the address for Henry McNair, Esquire's office, Shiloh missed it because it was easy to miss. The address was on the quietest stretch of a quiet side street off – far off – Congress Street, downtown Portland's main artery, well into the West Bayside neighborhood, almost halfway to Back Cove. The address was nothing more than a doorway squeezed between a walk-up and a sleepy coffee shop. The doorway opened to a narrow set of stairs leading to a floor over the coffee shop shared by a one-man travel agency, a one-man insurance agency, and Henry McNair's one-man law firm.

Even during her intern days, Shiloh had managed not to work for one of these little outfits, but her firm had, occasionally, bumped into them. Some were bottom-crawlers, taking on the kind of bad-smelling cases and clients no reputable firm would touch, but her father never would've had much to do with that kind of operation. McNair, she suspected, was the other kind; nice guy who'd been practicing law so long he'd probably forgotten why he'd gotten into it in the first place, and now it was all he knew how to do, making a modest living handling

71

the small things: wills, house closings, penny-ante slip-and-fall cases and the like. That seemed more like her dad.

There was a small outer office with a lumpy sofa and an equally lumpy, sweet-faced middle-aged woman behind a reception desk who asked her to have a seat on the lumpy sofa; Mr. McNair would be with her in a minute and would she like something from the little coffeemaker sitting on one of the two file cabinets along one wall? Shiloh gave her a polite shake of the head, let her eyes wander across the dusty landscape prints on the walls, the dusty plastic plants standing sentry on either side of the sofa, and the so-old-they-were-brittle issues of *Portland* and *Down East* on the dusty cracked-finished coffee table in front of her.

The door to the inner office opened, a man's voice called out – "Katie, ask Ms. Vail to give me a few minutes" – as a woman in a Dunkin Donuts employee hoodie wrestled her way through the door dragging a sour-faced boy of maybe ten behind her while carrying a squirming, younger girl in her other arm. Shiloh nodded at Katie that she'd heard her boss's request and was fine with it.

The woman with the two kids plopped them both on the sofa next to Shiloh and did more wrestling trying to get their uncooperative selves into the coats she'd evidently left behind on the floor.

At first, Shiloh thought the woman was older than herself, but seeing her close-up realized she was probably near Shiloh's age but with the same kind of wear-and-tear on her face she'd seen taking a toll on her sister.

"I once saw a guy wrestle an alligator on TV," Shiloh said. "It looked a lot like this. Can I help?"

The woman grinned. "Yeah, it is a lot like this. If you could just hold him in your lap. Cal, for Chrissakes, sit still! Carrie, don't you go wanderin' off!" which the little girl did.

"It's ok," Katie called scooting out from behind her desk. "I've got her!"

"She'll get into stuff 'n' next thing I'm payin' for stuff gettin' broke," the woman said.

Her face was closer to Shiloh now as she managed to get the boy's coat on him. Shadows under the eyes, a bad blonde dye job growing out. But there was also something…vaguely…

The woman finished with the boy – "Just hold 'im so *he* don't get into anything" – stood up to catch her breath, finally got a good look at Shiloh. "Hey…"

"I'm not sure, but I think we know -"

"Shy Vail!"

"I can't quite -"

"Well, yeah, it's been, like, a million years! Tracey! Tracey Killian! Well, it *was* Tracey Killian. Then it was Tracey Newberry and now it's still Tracey Newberry but there's no more Mr. Newberry. That's why I'm here with Mr. McNair, tryin' a get my ex to cough up the six months child support he owes. I gave up on alimony a long time ago."

Shiloh gave a profession-polished smile and nod of understanding. She had a vague high school memory of Tracey - too much make-up and pinching boys on the ass in the halls between classes.

"Hold on to this one while I get the other one," Tracey said as she went to relieve Katie of her squirming daughter and tried to get a coat on her. "I thought you – would you hold still, Jesus, Carrie, ya wanna get sick out there? – thought you moved away or somethin'."

Young Cal tried to buck free, but Shiloh managed to keep her arms locked around his middle. "I went to college out of state. Then I got a job and, well, you know, one thing leads to another…"

"Don't I know it!" Tracey grunted as she finally got little Carrie properly enwrapped. She pulled her daughter to her while she collapsed on the sofa, winded. "I tried college. I did a semester – well, most ah semester – at Southern Maine, but then I met this guy… Well, school wasn't really my thing anyways. Then that didn't work out, 'n' like you says, one thing leads to another, this is one thing - " and she gave a nod at Master Cal " - so then Hal – Mr. Newberry – steps up which was nice ah him, but then I guess he got tired a steppin' up when another thing come along - " another nod, this time toward the girl in her lap.

It was pouring out of Tracey Newberry nee Killian the way Shiloh had seen it pour out of people in front of a lawyer, a police officer, a social worker, not because it was necessary or even wise but because for the first time somebody had in front of them a set of ears willing to listen to frustrations and disappointments which had been percolating a long time.

Something seemed to suddenly come to Tracey: "Oh, crap! Do you have the time?"

Keeping one arm wrapped around young Cal, Shiloh fumbled her phone out of her jacket pocket: "Almost noon."

"Oh, *crap!* I'm late! 'N' I gotta hand these two off to my mother 'fore I go in! You got a gift, you two, gettin' off school today, now Gramma's gonna stuff you full ah junk! Shy, you gonna be in town long? I'm at the DD over at City Center. Come by, I'll slip you a freebie, maybe we can hang after work 'n' catch up."

"We'll see, I've got a lot of running around to do. I'm not in town very long."

Which she could see Tracey took as a no, but still, the woman smiled, grabbed her kids, mumbled something along the lines of hope you can make it, and wrangled her brood out the door.

A sad little something tugged at Shiloh. She'd known a dozen Tracey Killians in high school, some getting pregnant instead of a diploma, some walking from the graduation ceremony into a marriage and kids and a two-out-of-ten chance of winding up like Tracey.

There was a time when she was home on vacation from Boston, her dad had taken her out to eat somewhere – she didn't remember, some diner-type place, a cop hangout her dad had said, probably long gone since Portland had begun fancying itself up – and the waitress was somebody Shiloh had graduated high school with. In the little bit of catch-up chatting they'd done, it was clear this wasn't something the waitress was doing to pay for college or as some kind of interim thing while waiting for something better. She was already married, a baby at home being watched by her mother, her husband worked the docks, and this was the second income they needed. Period.

After the waitress had turned away to put their order in, her dad had turned to her: "*That's* why I shoved you out."

Henry McNair was about what Shiloh had expected; a short, pudgy, pleasant-faced old gent, bald except for a feathery white fringe, lost in a baggy off-the-rack suit. He sat behind a large, heavy desk in about the same battered shape as the coffee table in his reception room. There were the usual family pictures on the desk as well as an edge-to-edge clutter of manila folders, sticky notes on everything from his phone to his goose-neck desk lamp. There wasn't much in the way of décor. On the plaster walls: McNair's law degree, a photo of a Little League team (Shiloh didn't think McNair earned enough to sponsor the team so assumed a grandchild was tucked in the player ranks somewhere). On the windowsill, a bowling trophy.

And that was it.

Based on some of the other small firms Shiloh had dealt with combined with the weary condition of McNair's office suite, her guess was the lawyer probably spent as much time chasing down clients to get his unpaid fees as he did representing them.

McNair had handed her an envelope of heavy bond. Printed on the front, in gothic letters: Last Will and Testament. Filled in with a ballpoint pen on a line underneath: Edward Everett Vail.

Up until then, her father's passing had been an abstract, if a sad one. Even standing over his deathbed hadn't brought it home in a way looking at the neatly blocked letters of his name under those oppressive gothic ones did. She ran her index finger slowly along his name. *You're really gone, Dad. Damn...*

"Are you alright, Ms. Vail?"

Shiloh flashed him a smile of thanks for the consideration, pulled on her law office composure as she slid the blue-bound document out of the envelope and began to scan its contents.

McNair pointed to his own copy of the will on the desk in front of him. "I'm sure you've dealt with enough of this kind of thing at your firm that you can see this is pretty routine, I mean you being a paralegal. Yes, I know about your work down in Washington; I knew your father a long time. Not that we were close in any way, more friendly than friends because I had been his attorney for so many -"

"I understand."

"What I mean to say is he always bragged about you. He was very proud."

"That's nice to hear, Mr. McNair. Actually, I'm a paralegal manager, and my firm doesn't do family law. Corporate, criminal... Things along those lines."

"Impressive."

"Doesn't feel that way when you're reaching for the Maalox."

"Funny you should say that." McNair reached into a lower desk drawer to show his own bottle of Maalox and they both laughed.

He turned back to his copy of the will. "As I was saying, it's pretty standard. My letter mentioned that the will designates you as executor of the estate. As far as the estate goes, equal division among the three siblings. I don't know what your father had in terms of savings, you'll have to go through his personal papers and see what accounts he had. I don't believe he had anything in the way of stocks and such."

"Dad wasn't a stock market kind of guy."

McNair smiled in agreement. "You should check with the Portland Police Association to see if there are any survivors' provisions under your father's pension plan; I'll give you a number and a contact name over there. He may also have had some kind of life insurance through them. Of course, as you know, his Social Security benefits ceased with his passing.

"The main asset, at least as far as I know, is the house on the island, and the will bequeaths joint ownership to the siblings. You and your brother and sister will undoubtedly have a conversation about what to do about the house. Be forewarned: the market for houses on St. Aggie's is, well…" He sighed.

"I've been out there, Mr. McNair. I know; people are moving out, not moving in."

"The three of you should discuss it. If it comes to it, I can give you the names of several reputable realtors, but I think you'll find it hard to get someone to handle a sale. Selling the house at any price is going to be, um…" That sigh again.

"Difficult, I get it. Easiest thing to do would be to light a match."

McNair looked up at that, his face somewhere between alarm and disappointment.

"It was a joke, Mr. McNair."

At which the lawyer's face slackened.

"Mr. McNair, I'm not seeing any provision here for my mother."

He frowned. "Mmm, no. Well, understand, they'd been divorced for what? Almost twenty years?"

"Give or take. Still, I thought, well, you know; *something*. I didn't know he was still that bitter."

McNair took a moment. Shiloh could see he was having some sort of debate with himself, then he seemed to reach a decision with a shrug and a nod. "Um, well, Ms. Vail, as I told you, I wasn't, you know…close to your father. But he always struck me as a decent man. There being nothing in the will for your mother… So, you know, that wasn't his choice."

It took Shiloh a second or two to work out the meaning of what the lawyer was telling her. "Hers?"

"Your father hadn't updated his will since you were children. When his health started to fail, that's when he came in to redraft it. The only major change was removing anything having to do with your mother. I asked him if he was sure that's what he wanted to do. You know what happens; someone gets cut out of a will, the deceased, well, they decease, the omitted party thinks they were somehow treated unfairly and sues…"

"I know how it goes."

"I wanted to prevent that possibility, so I asked him: are you sure about this? And he told me he'd reached out to Delia to see if there was something specific she might want, and he told me she'd said no. I know sometimes clients, well, they, um, are not always accurate in what they tell their attorney, they might, you know…"

"Lie."

"Say things they think will make matters go smoothly. But he told me if I had any doubts about what he was saying, I should give her a call myself. So…I did."

"And?"

McNair winced at the memory. "She told me in no uncertain terms that she wanted nothing from your father. And she was pretty…um, *forceful* in how she phrased it."

Shiloh had enough memory of her mother to know "forceful" probably meant a heavily obscenity-laced tirade.

"I handled the divorce, you know. For him, I mean. I don't usually handle domestic matters. With a five percent divorce rate, a lawyer in Portland could build a comfortable practice on nothing but divorce, alimony claims, and child custody cases, but…"

"But?"

"There's a particular ugliness to those kinds of cases. Especially when children are involved. I don't have the stomach for that, even with…" and he nodded at the desk drawer with his Maalox stash.

"But you're handling Tracey Newberry's case. We passed each other in your reception office. Seems we knew each other in high school."

"Small world. I'm not really handling her. I referred her to a firm that does that kind of work. She came to me because I'm the only lawyer she knows. I helped her and her husband with some paperwork when they bought a place, well, not so much a place…A mobile home up in Gorham, some place called Friendly Village. I think the bank has it now." A certain sense of resignation passed over McNair's face and Shiloh's impression was that a painful number of the lawyer's clients got themselves into these kinds of fixes.

"Anyway, as far as your mother is concerned, Delia was clear she wanted nothing: no alimony, no settlement." He slid a manila envelope out from under his copy of the will and handed it to her. "I took the liberty of notifying probate that you're the executor and gave them your contact information. I hope you don't mind."

"Thank you."

"Things in our neck of the woods move slower than you might be used to; it could be well into next year before the will clears probate."

"How well into next year?"

"In time for your summer vacation."

"Ouch."

"With luck."

"Oof."

"I know, sorry." McNair shifted around in his seat as if he couldn't find a comfortable position.

"Something else, Mr. McNair?"

"In that envelope you'll find another copy of the will, three copies of the death certificate..." He paused, leaving some unsaid thing hanging in the air.

"Something else?".

He nodded. "Something else." He took a moment, looked to be gathering his thoughts and gave up on the attempt. He pointed to the envelope he'd handed Shiloh. "It's that I don't know what to make of it. There's a letter in there. It's why I addressed my letter specifically to you, because your father's instructions to me were to see that I put that letter -" nodding at the envelope " – directly into your hands. I don't know what's in it, so I thought perhaps it'd be better if you came in alone."

She looked in the large envelope and sitting among the other folded documents was a sealed business-size envelope. She pulled it out. Across the face of the envelope, written in her father's scrawling script, was her name.

"So, you haven't seen what's in this?" she asked.

McNair shook his head. "He never discussed it with me. When he came in for the will signing, he gave that letter to me, sealed, told me when the time came to hand-deliver it to you."

"I don't see any reason you shouldn't know what's in it now," Shiloh said. She tore open one end and pulled out a single piece of lined loose-leaf paper written on both sides. The family used to joke that her father's handwriting looked more like an EKG printout than cursive handwriting, but Shiloh had long ago gotten the hang for deciphering his scribbles. But here, it was clear to her, her father had made the effort to be particularly legible.

She read it aloud:

"Hey, Shy –

"If you have this letter it's because I'm gone. You and Jay and Zee will be going through my stuff at the house and figuring out what to do with it all. I named you executor so you can referee those fights and I wish you luck with that. Be patient with them. Keep in mind I probably never did as right by them as I should've.

"If while you're going through everything you come across some special documents, it's up to you, Shy, and only you to decide what to do with them. I trust your judgment but any decisions you make should be because it's good for the family and by that I mean all three of you.

"I feel like I should say a lot more, but I wasn't a reader like you, so I don't have a lot of words. I'm not doing this to be a pain in the ass even though I figure that's what it'll be. I'm not sure what the right thing to do will be when the time comes or even if there is a right thing, but if there is, I'm talking to you because I know you'll be the one to figure it out.

"For all the things I should've talked to you about but never did, I'm sorry. If you ever find them out, remember that.

"One last thing from the old man - make yourself happy. Life gets in the way of that a lot, trust me I know, but try not to let it.

"Love you, Shy,

"Dad."

After a long silence, "Like I said," McNair said quietly, "a nice man."

Shiloh found her voice didn't want to work just then but managed a nod. After another pause, "Mr. McNair: 'special documents'?"

The lawyer shrugged helplessly. "Maybe something in his personal papers? I don't know. As I told you, he never discussed this letter with me other than to say, 'Make sure my daughter gets this'."

She also wanted to ask about *all the things I should've talked to you about but never did*, but assumed she'd get the same answer. She frowned at the letter as she tucked it back into its envelope. "Do I even show this to my brother and sister?"

McNair swiveled in his chair to look out his rain-spotted window, his head bowed in thought, then he turned back to her. "This is something personal between your father and you, so I don't feel it proper for me to offer an opinion. I can only repeat what he says in there: that he trusts your judgment."

She stood, thanking McNair, then had a thought. "They're going to ask about the house."

"No doubt."

"If we decide to sell, at some point I'm going to need paper on the property, and so far, I haven't found anything at the house."

"I would suggest the Tax Assessor's office and the Register of Deeds. I'll write down directions."

The Register of Deeds was one of those blocky but dignified edifices of granite in the Federal style government buildings favored before local governments started opting for structures lean and shiny. Shiloh found the service desk and its squad of clerks and wound up in front of a pimply young guy who, she guessed from his ill-fitting white shirt and badly knotted polyester tie, had yet to learn how to dress for his first real adult job.

She told him what she was after, he turned to the computer terminal at his station, spent a little time *tick-tick-tick*ing his fingers across the keyboard, frowned slightly before his face slid into disinterest.

"I'm not seein' it, ma'am."

"It's on the south shore -"

"No, I'm not seein' the island."

"What do you mean you're not seeing -"

He huffed slightly at her not understanding what seemed so clear to him. "There's no St. Aggie's Island."

"Trust me; it's there."

He pointed to his computer. "Ma'am, I'm puttin' in St. Aggie's Island 'n' I get 'No Records Found'. Ok?"

One of the many life skills Shiloh had learned from her years in law offices was even in the face of frustrating obstinance, to keep her cool, because once you blew up at someone, they'd throw themselves into a wood chipper before they'd cooperate. So, very cooly, she said, "I just came from there this morning."

Another huff, and irritated now: "Lady, I tried St. Aggie, St. Agnes, there's no Saint Anything anywhere in Casco Bay. There's nothing there, ok? I can't make it show up if there's nothing there."

Shiloh took a breath and smiled. "You want me to take you out there and show it to you?"

"Problem, miss?" The man had come out of a small office behind the service area, one of those little cubes where civil service managers get tucked. At the sight of him, Shiloh's smile turned sincere; it was impossible for it not to be.

If they were ever casting another remake of *Miracle on 34ᵗʰ Street*, Shiloh thought, I found their Kris Kringle! He was a large, round man, Santa Claus-ish in almost every way, from his snowy full beard to the gold wire-rimmed glasses parked far down on his cherry of a nose. Not that he needed the extra touch, but his bright red cardigan added to his Santa-between-Christmases look. His only break in the image – and it was barely that – was his long, white hair tied back in a neat little ponytail.

He delicately touched a pudgy finger to one ear. "Pardon, dear, but I couldn't help but overhear." The "dear" may have been inappropriate for 21ˢᵗ century sensibilities, but there was such an old-fashioned courtliness to him that Shiloh saw no need for a corrective updating.

"My father passed away recently -"

"My sympathies."

She nodded a thank you. "- and I'm trying to find paperwork on his house. Which is on St. Aggie's Island. Which this young gentleman tells me doesn't exist."

The old gent's beard rippled with a slight smile. "Technically, it doesn't."

"Well, technically, I grew up on that rock, so I know it's there."

"Well, it is…and it isn't."

She wanted to be angry with him, and maybe it was because of the Santa Claus vibe, but she couldn't be. "Whatever's going on, you seem to be enjoying it."

He laughed.

Jesus, he even laughs like Santa!

"Apologies, dear," and he made a sweeping gesture of his arm at the offices around them, "but the Register of Deeds provides so little amusement, I find it where I can. But you're right, that was rude of me," and he bowed his head in apology.

"I don't mind some fun at my expense as long as at some point you untie the knot."

"If you were to trek on up to Augusta and dig into the state records, you'd find that the, um, what I suppose you would call the formal name, the historic name is West Bay Island."

"St. Aggie's is really West Bay Island?"

"St. Aggie's is sort of a nick name. It's just that everyone's been calling it that for so long, I'm not sure many people not as ancient as I even remember it had another name. I think even some of the newer maps call it St. Aggie's. But on the books, it's still West Bay Island."

"So how does it go from West Bay to St. Aggie's?"

"That takes a bit of unraveling so why don't you come with me, and we'll make ourselves comfortable while young Louis here -" a pointed look toward the young clerk meant as a command "- looks up the properties on West Bay Island and locates your father's house."

Santa showed her past the service desk toward his little office cube where the name plate beside the door told Shiloh his name was Sinclair. He gestured her to a seat in front of his government issue gray metal desk. "Coffee? I've got this nice little Keurig here," pointing to the machine on the credenza behind his chair. "I can make you coffee, espresso, seems like a hot cocoa day."

"No thanks. The knot."

"Ah, yes." He fed a cartridge into the Keurig which, Shiloh guessed from the brown-stained mug Sinclair set under the spout, was likely hot cocoa. "Well," and he took his seat, "as I said, it's a bit of a story so bear with me. It starts in World War II."

"So, not a story but a saga."

He chuckled. "I suppose. You're from Portland?"

"Originally, yes."

"Then perhaps you know that during the war, Portland was a very important Navy base."

"My father was in the Navy; I seem to remember him saying something about that."

"I don't think locals under a certain age are aware of how close the war came to Maine. Providing you young folk remember the war at all. If you're ever of a mind, one of the boat tours can show you some of the vestiges: the submarine spotting towers, you can see where there were coastal artillery placements where Fort Williams Park is out on Cape Elizabeth. You can even see the little buildings where they had the winches which opened and closed anti-submarine nets across the mouth of the bay. The bay was home to a flotilla of destroyers. They would pick up convoys coming up the east coast and escort them across the North Atlantic."

"I didn't know it had been that big a deal around here."

"No reason you should, I suppose," though he said it with a touch of sadness. "It's long-ago history. It's even before my time if you can believe it, but I heard the stories from my father when I was growing up."

"Mr. Sinclair, much as I'm a big fan of The History Channel, I'm still eagerly – *eagerly* - waiting to see what this has to do with -"

He daintily held up a finger calling for patience. "I cautioned you it was a bit of a story. So. You have all these young sailors, you have all these young men on these convoys heading off to war, a lot of them had never been away from home before, they're wondering if they'll ever see home again, you had a lot of men who'd come to Portland to work in the shipyards which were running twenty-four hours per day. That's a lot of young men…with money in their pocket." He paused and Shiloh got the impression he was waiting for her to make a deduction which didn't come.

"Ok," and she nodded for him to go ahead.

"*Lonely* young men."

"Oh."

He nodded to confirm she'd understood the unspoken part correctly. "A woman named Agnes – no one remembers her last name – showed up in Portland and saw this as a business opportunity. You know; providing a, um, a certain kind of, uh, service, mmm, the kind of entertainment which would most likely be of interest to, ahem, lonely young men."

She grinned. "Agnes. So, Aggie, I get it. Mr. Sinclair, is this your tactful way of telling me this Agnes/Aggie woman was a prostitute?"

Shiloh wasn't sure but she could swear Sinclair blushed under all that facial hair.

"To be accurate, my understanding from the stories I was told was her role was primarily managerial."

"So, she was a madam."

"I believe that's the proper term. Evidently, Miss Agnes felt it would be to her advantage to operate in a location which would not antagonize the propriety of the good citizens of Portland."

"The island."

"Away from possibly offended eyes, yes." Sinclair turned to the Keurig for his fresh cup of cocoa. "Are you sure?" and he pointed to the cup.

Shiloh waved a no-thank-you.

Sinclair cupped the mug in his fleshy hands, seemed to enjoy the warmth of it. "She had a house built on West Bay Island where ships returning to Portland would be able to see the red light on her porch from miles off. And for years…*years*…her house was the only, um, residence of any sort on West Bay. Eventually, Miss Aggie died or left town or something, I don't think anyone knows for sure, but there was always someone willing to take over running the house after she disappeared from the scene. And it seems that even after the war, there was always some, uh, demand for such services. Until, at some point, the city finally got around to closing it down. But the house – the actual building – remained."

And then Shiloh saw the cosmic joke of it all, the kind of cosmic joke which leaves someone drifting between laughing and crying. "Jesus..."

"Excuse me?"

She shook her head, still digesting it and not smoothly. "Mr. Sinclair..."

"Yes?"

"Mr. Sinclair."

"Yes, dear?"

"Mr. Sinclair, are you telling me I grew up in a whore house?"

Sinclair winced. "Well, to be clear, a former whore house. And that term is a bit on the coarse side. Brothel is a tad softer; bordello has a musical feel to it..."

"A whore house by any other name. But that's my father's house."

"Possibly. Where's it located on the island?"

"Sounds like where this Aggie lady put it; on the south shore and it's the only house there."

"And how long had he owned it?"

"I grew up there, so at least thirty-plus years."

Sinclair closed his eyes and did some mental calculations. "When your father acquired the house, it would've still been the only building on the island, or right around the time the island was acquired for development. I'm old enough to remember when all the construction was going on. What I'd heard was the developer at the time was hoping to make it another Peaks Island, a regular offshore community."

Shiloh was still shaking her head over the nature of her childhood home. "Ok, I get the Aggie part. But *Saint* Aggie?"

Sinclair laughed his Santa Claus laugh. "It was sort of a joke, I imagine. You see, there really was a St. Agnes. I looked her up. She was the patron saint of chastity and died a virgin martyr. So, St. Agnes; chastity. St. Aggie…"

"Not so much."

"I guess that after a long, dangerous sea voyage, some of her young clientele might've viewed her as a blessing."

She had to laugh. "I guess."

He took a sip of his hot cocoa, stood, and beckoned her toward his cube door. "Now that we know your father's house is on West Bay Island, let's see what we can find out."

Shiloh stood, but the idea came back to her strong enough to stop her in her tracks. "My home…a whore house."

Sinclair offered her a comforting smile. "Look at it this way, my dear. You grew up in a place that I'm sure saw much joy."

"Hm," pimpled Louis said, again *tick-tick-tick*ing at his keyboard as one page after another flashed across his terminal screen.

"Still a problem?" Sinclair was standing with Shiloh behind the clerk.

"I don't see any property records in the Vail name or for that location."

"Let me in there, Louis." Sinclair stood at the keyboard, and after examining several unsatisfactory pages, put up a diagram Shiloh recognized as the shape of St. Aggie's/West Bay Island. "This is a digital version of the plat book of the island. All the individual properties are outlined here and marked with references to pull up ownership. Show me where your father's house is."

Shiloh pointed to a large square area on the south side of the island. It was the only plot with no markings.

"This is very, very odd," Sinclair said. "As far as our records go, that's just open land."

"I understand Portland recently found the island wasn't part of the city. Would that have anything -"

Sinclair was already shaking his head. "We would still have a record of any transactions prior to the audit. As far as our registry is concerned, there is no house there, never was a house there, and no one owns or has ever owned that lot."

"How is that possible? "

Sinclair turned to her with a look that said, It's not.

Shiloh stared at the image on the screen again comparing the empty space on the south shore to the other marked properties. There was where the DeLisles' house was, and all the other houses of her childhood neighbors, there was Teddy Granier's store... All lots like every other lot with some sort of reference designation. But not the place where her father had lived with his wife and raised three children.

A void.

"Who was the developer?" Shiloh asked. "They might know something."

"That's a thought. It was actually the same company that's been buying up properties since people started abandoning the island. The formal name is the West Bay Development Corporation; that's what goes on the paperwork, but nobody calls it that. It's a private company, a family operation, everybody knows who it is."

"What family?" although for no good reason, Shiloh felt she already knew.

"The Clearys. They live out on Cypress Point. Maybe you've heard of them?"

Eight.

Shiloh had barely gotten the last words of her father's will out of her mouth before Jay stopped his pacing and planted himself in front of her. "I want his guns."

"I know," Shiloh said. "So, you said."

"You can't use 'em -"

Shiloh and Zoe exchanged sympathetic here-we-go-again looks.

"We've been over this, Jay. Shake your head; maybe it'll come back to you. Nothing happens until the will clears -"

He turned his back on her and went back to his pacing. "Blah blah blah, which is when?"

"McNair says maybe middle of next year. With luck."

Which stopped her brother in his tracks again. "You fuckin' kiddin' me?"

"Yes, Jay, isn't it a great joke? Trust me, anything that'd shut you up about this that I could do sooner, I would."

Jay looked over at Zoe's husband as if they shared confidences even though they rarely talked to each other. "See? What I'm always sayin': attitude."

They had been waiting for Shiloh when she got back to the house. She considered herself lucky Jay had let her shrug off her jacket before badgering her about the will. He'd already been halfway into his second bottle of the Allagash Ben Cole had brought out to the house with a couple of pizzas as promised and was pacing around the living room like a caged puma waiting to take a bite out of his keeper.

Zoe's husband was there, standing behind the chair where his wife was sitting across from Shiloh, patting her shoulder in an awkward and insincere display of comfort and care. But that was typical of Anthony Kling; trying to make a certain positive impression without quite knowing how to do it. He was a tall, lean but shapeless sort, nondescript in every way. Shiloh would sometimes joke to herself that he was the kind of guy who could get lost in a crowd even when there wasn't a crowd. After he'd been out to the house a few times when he was first dating Zoe, Shiloh had once asked her father what he thought of Anthony - never "Tony," Anthony would correct, always "Anthony".

Her father had seemed surprised at his own answer: "Ya know, I don't think of him at all unless he's right in front of me!"

Anthony was an assistant manager of a NAPA store in South Portland and favored a wardrobe suggesting he thought this a braggable accomplishment: NAPA cap, NAPA jacket over his NAPA store twills. Ever since he'd been made assistant manager, he'd been under the grossly mistaken impression his promotion testified to some expertise in big business and high finance.

Anthony had brought their kids with him (Zoe saved Shiloh the embarrassment of fumbling for their names by working "Benji" and "Josie" into the introductions). They didn't seem particularly impressed or even interested in the Aunt Shy they only recalled meeting a few times on Face Time calls. Their sole reaction of note had been from Benji: "How come your head looks bigger on the phone?"

Ben Cole had gotten a quick read on the room when Shiloh had come through the door and whisked the kids off to the kitchen with him – "This looks like it's for family and grown-ups" – to re-heat the pizzas after their trip across the bay.

"And as executor," Shiloh went on, putting a sharp edge to it, "Jay, you're not getting a damned thing I don't say you're getting, so you might consider kissing my ass maybe just a little bit."

Jay turned his back to her, stuck out his buttocks: "After you kiss mine, sweetheart."

Anthony cleared his throat, trying to change the course of the discussion. "It, uh, seems to me, I mean, the way I see it, it looks like the big item – asset, I mean - is the house."

Shiloh nodded. "Yeah. I haven't checked into his pension or any insurance through his -"

"But the house, um, the house, right? That's probably the big thing."

"Probably," Shiloh said.

His shoulder patting of his wife had gotten so rapid, now, that Shiloh could see it had less to do with comforting her sister than his own nervousness. It had gotten to the point of being annoying enough where Zoe shrugged his hand off.

"Fuck it," Jay said wandering into the dining room and back. "Fuck this place, let's dump it."

"McNair says the market is in the toilet," Shiloh said. "It'd be hard to —"

"'N' I'll bet that fucker's got a good buddy who's a realtor just standin' by to do us a favor -"

"Christ, Jay," and Zoe gave an exasperated sigh. "Use your goddamned eyes! This whole end ah the island's a ghost town 'n' you can bet money the rest ah the island'll follow."

Anthony cleared his throat again. "Well, see, I was thinking, you know, the house being in the family all this time, it'd be a shame to give it up."

Jay took a deep swig of his beer, shaking his head not so much in rebuttal as an attitude of are-you-just-stupid-or-what? "'N' do what with it? Decorate it for Christmas? I sure as hell ain't livin' here! 'N' Princess Hoity-Toity here's got her fancy-ass penthouse in Washington Big Fuckin' Deal D.C."

"You're a walking headache, Jay," Shiloh said, "you know that?"

Anthony cleared his throat again.

"Get a cough drop or a drink ah water or somethin'," Jay snapped. "You got somethin' to say, for Chrissakes just say it."

"What I was thinking, well, just so it doesn't stand empty until we make a decision, maybe we could move in. You know, Zoe and me. Especially if we have another kid, our place is a little on the small side -"

"Whoa, whoa, whoa!" Zoe said, waving a halting hand for emphasis. "When were you thinking this? *Any* ah this? When did we talk about havin' another baby?"

Anthony took a step back from Zoe's chair. "It's just something I've been thinking -"

"'N' you want to stick me out here with the kids, gettin' 'em cross the bay for school? 'N' you ferryin' in 'n' out every day, missin' work every time a strong wind comes up 'cause the ferry isn't runnin'? They may like you at that store, sweetie, but you start missin' days like that 'n' I don't think they're gonna like you as much. 'N' another baby? When were you gonna talk about -"

Anthony started patting her shoulder again, apparently hoping this would get her to put off an argument for another time. Zoe whipped her shoulder out from under her husband's hand, shot out of her chair to go stand by the living room picture window facing the sea. It was only three or so, but the sky was already going purple. It was November in Maine and Shiloh remembered that by four, four-thirty it would be dark.

Jay faced off with Anthony, gave him a poke in the shoulder. "I got another point I'd like to make, like who the fuck're *you?* Just 'cause you knocked up my sister -"

"Fuck you, Jay," Zoe muttered.

"- 'n' married her don't make you no blood kin! Will says's between the siblings 'n' I don't need no DNA test to know you ain't one of 'em."

Anthony tried to ignore the painful poking of his shoulder and not doing a very good job of it. "I'm just saying, Jay, it'd be a shame -"

"Yeah, a fuckin' shame you don't get to live in a place with no rent 'n' no mortgage, right?"

Shiloh let out an ear-splitting whistle like a referee calling a time out. "Before you two bring out the knives, you should know that when it comes to the house, there's a wrinkle."

Which pulled all eyes to Shiloh.

"What kinda wrinkle?" her brother asked.

"More like a crevasse."

"Listen to her," Jay said, nodding at Anthony like they were once again on the same side. "Miss Word-a-Day: *crevasse.*"

Shiloh began with the lack of documentation on the house, took a moment, steeled herself for some tacky, tasteless reaction from her brother, and went into an abbreviated history of the house.

Jay performed as expected, cackling, "This was Aggie's whore house?"

"Jay," Zoe said, "the kids can hear."

Jay ignored her, just kept gasping out "Aggie's whore house!" between what had now grown to guffaws.

"You knew about Aggie?" Shiloh asked.

Jay's laughter had stirred up a phlegmy cough he soothed with another pull on his beer. "I heard stories growin' up. Alla guys used to talk 'bout it. Didn't know it was *here*. Hey, how you think the ol' man got the house?" He seemed struck with a thought. "Heeeeey…"

"What?"

His face twisted into something between an ugly grin and an outright sneer. "What if it was him took over the house. I mean, you know, when it was still a, you know…*house*."

"Are you out ah your mind?" Zoe said.

Jay was laughing again, stomping from living room to dining room as he did so. "Ol' Eddie the pimp! 'N' him always lecturin' me 'bout all kindsa shit!"

"Dad was a cop!" Zoe said. Her hands balled into fists, and she looked ready to cross the room and lay one on Jay. Anthony – for once making a smart decision – started moving to where he could block her if she made that move.

"So what? You never heard of a dirty cop?"

"You're insane, you know that?" And now Anthony was there, hands on Zoe's shoulders, holding her back, her shrugging them off, him putting them back. "You'd just love that, have something to take Dad down a notch, wouldn't you? Think that'd make up for you being such a fuck-up?"

"Fuck you, sweets, he didn't ride your ass like he rode mine."

"Maybe he didn't have to."

"Did I say fuck you? In case I forgot; fuck you!"

"Jay," and Anthony started making calm down motions with one hand while he kept the other one holding his wife in place, "let's not get personal -"

"Fuck you, too! This is family shit, 'n' brother-in-law or not, that don't make you family to me so butt the fuck out! Tell your husband to watch his ass, Zee! Fucker's circlin' this house like a goddamn vulture -"

"I give up," and Zoe turned back to the seaward window. Outside, the sky was already going from purple to black. "No talkin' to you," she muttered, shaking her head, "No talkin' to you."

Jay looked ready to toss another barb at her sister and Shiloh jumped in with a loud, *"Everybody shut the fuck up!"*

Jay waved a teasing tsk-tsking finger at her: "Language!" and he pointed to the kitchen. "The children, remember?"

Still, it was enough of a whipcrack to bring everyone to heel. Anthony gently led Zoe back to her chair, Jay propped himself against a far wall, a distance between him and everyone else.

"Let's get a couple of things straight," Shiloh said. *"I'm* executor and anything *I* decide within the terms of the will goes. Anybody has a problem with that, they can get their own attorney and take it to court. Number two: nothing – and I repeat for the millionth time - *nothing* can happen until the will gets through probate. And here's the biggie: as far as the house goes, probate or not, it's frozen until we can find out what's what. You want to sell the house, Jay? We can't prove we own a house that, on the books, doesn't exist on land the books say we don't own. So, learn how to meditate or something, because you've got a loooong goddamned wait before anything happens."

She turned to Anthony. "For the same reason, it might not be a good move for you to move your family in. I didn't go to the Tax Assessor's office because after I was done at Deeds, I didn't figure it was a good move to flag the city that Dad's been living here for over thirty years without paying a penny in property taxes. But the Clearys have been buying up the abandoned properties on the island -"

The three of them perked up at that. "The Clearys?" Jay said.

"Yeah, and if they get interested in this house and start poking around to see what the provenance on the house is, we could have a hell of a mess on our hands. So, everybody just chill while I see what I can find out. Ok?"

A nod from Anthony, a sullen shrug from Jay.

"Ok." She turned to Jay: "You spending the night? No? Good. Then why don't you get your ass across the bay. Do your usual drink-yourself-into-a-stupor because I've reached my capacity for you for today."

"Back atcha, Princess. But 'fore I go…" He swung back into the kitchen, came back out with a full bottle of beer, drained what was left of his other one and left the bottle on the stairs to the second floor on his way out.

"I suppose we should go, too," Anthony said to Zoe after a few moments of welcome quiet. He nodded at the picture window where the Atlantic had disappeared into the night, his way of saying it was getting late.

Zoe shook her head. "I'm stayin' here with Shy tonight. I don't want to leave her here alone."

"Well, Zoe, I mean, what happened last night, I'm not sure I'm too comfortable about you -"

"I'm not leaving her here alone, Anthony," she said more firmly.

He did his annoying throat clearing, then, "I think your sister can take care of herself, right, Shiloh?"

"It's alright, Zee," Shiloh said. *You've already got enough for you two to fight about.*

Zoe shook her head adamantly. "Anthony, do you mind if I spend some time with my sister I hardly ever get to see? Besides…" She didn't seem to need to fill in the blank; she needed some space between herself and her husband.

Anthony shrunk a little bit as the message sank in. He made one more try: "The kids," he said weakly, "they have school -"

"Yes, they have school. God forbid *you* take 'em." With a resigned sigh, "Take 'em back to Marie's, they'll be fine with her. I'll call her 'n' let her know you're coming. Take one of the pizzas."

"What about, you know…" and he nodded toward the kitchen, presumably to indicate Ben Cole.

"You're right, Anthony, that's my secret plan; get you outta here so we can have a mad threesome. Just go, alright? We'll be fine."

Anthony shuffled off to the kitchen, came back with his children and a pizza box. "You'll call me if -"

"Yes, Anthony. And Anthony?"

He winced, sensing what was coming.

"When I *do* get home? You 'n' me're gonna have a loooong talk 'bout all this stuff you been 'thinkin' about'. Another baby, Anthony?" Her voice started to rise. "Another baby?"

"Um," and he nodded at their kids.

"We gonna have another baby?" her daughter asked.

With a sharp look at Anthony, Zoe said, "Doubtful, baby. Doubtful."

"Good," Josie said with an emphasizing nod. "No room at our house anyway."

The children gave their mom a hug and goodbye kiss, and on their way out the door, Shiloh heard Benji ask his dad, "What's a threesome?"

Shiloh managed not to laugh until the door closed behind them. To Zoe, she said, "Now that's a conversation I'd like to hear!"

"You're welcome to it."

Ben came in from the kitchen, set plates of warmed pizza down in front of the women - to which they nodded their thanks - then stood back, putting on the dopiest of grins. "Somebody say something about a threesome?"

"In your dreams," Shiloh said.

Ben had brought his guitar with him. "I figured, you know, just to distract the kids," which Shiloh didn't buy.

"Were they distracted?" Zoe asked skeptically.

"I shoulda brought my amps," he said. "But even cranked up, I don't think your kids woulda heard this ol' Gibson over the brawlin' goin' on in here."

Zoe sighed. "'Fraid they're used to it." She seemed to feel Shiloh's questioning look and returned it with a resigned shrug.

Zoe had gotten a fire going in the hearth, the three of them had worked through one of the pizzas and a few beers apiece, and then Zoe started to cap things off for herself with shots from their father's belly-burning whisky.

The heat from the burning logs, a full belly, a couple of beers and Shiloh found herself slipping into a warm, golden glow. The years behind her collapsed, and the house, the island, and the dull, distant rumble of the surf were no longer revived long-ago memories but things no older than yesterday.

Ben sat across from the two of them, his Gibson across his lap. He started strumming, falling into the songs they'd grown up with, deftly translating them from barroom rock into lulling acoustics: Kenny Wayne Shepherd's "Blue on Black," the Black Crows "She Talks to Angels," Springsteen's "Human Touch."

This wasn't the gawky, young Ben she used to watch play at birthdays, high school events, and his first "professional" gigs at dive bars, fumbling with his sound equipment as it shrieked feedback; his voice thin, trying too hard to sound like his rock idols - trying too hard to impress rather than connect. No, now the guitar looked as at home in his hands as the helm of his boat, and he'd learned when to hit the strings hard and when to barely caress them. His voice had gained something with the years as well. There was a deepness and a bit of a rasp, giving songs an earnest feeling he hadn't had a dozen years ago; he wasn't singing *at* them the way he used to - but *to* them.

Maybe this is how you sound after you've been living for a while.

He didn't sing the songs all the way through; sometimes just a verse and a chorus, then some random, gentle strumming before he eased into the next one. "Hey, didn't you have a thing for that bald bastard Corgan?"

Shiloh blushed.

"Sometimes you couldn't shut up 'bout that guy," and he fell into the chords for "Cherub Rock." Toward the end, his voice went soft, he flicked her a bit of smiling eye as he sang,

Tell me all your secrets…

He took a pause to take a pull on his beer. They sat quietly for a bit, listening to the crackle of the burning logs in the fireplace. Shiloh had a feeling Ben had brought them back – or was it just her? - to an earlier time, a time when each of them hadn't been laden with so much dragging weight.

He took another sip and shook off the somber mood. "Hey," he said with a forced brightness, "My band is playing tomorrow night. You should come. Both of you. Zoe, bring Anthony. But you guys can leave Jay home you don't mind."

"I've heard them," Zoe said to Shiloh. "They're pretty good." But her lopsided grin told Shiloh she was pushing more than Ben's music.

Shiloh gave her what she thought was a reprimanding frown, but that only pushed Zoe's grin into a chuckle.

"Yeah, both of you come! It's a long ride, Farmington, college town out in the boonies, but it'll be fun."

"We'll see," Shiloh said. The names were foggy, but the mood of the night brought back high school faces with their pimples, greasy hair falling over the eyes, pseudo-serious sullenness. "I can't believe you still have the band."

Ben laughed. "Well, it's not the same band." His guitar provided a witty accompaniment to his tales of the fates of The Maine-iacs. Ben hung his head in shame at his own mention of their oh-so-lame name. There was Ben's drummer, Tats — so named because both his bony arms had been sleeved with tattoos — who'd committed himself to archetypal rock-drummer-self-destructiveness. Only a year out of high school, "He got himself so wasted after a gig, wrapped his truck 'round a utility pole. Shame is, it didn't kill him. Banged up his brain so much, his mom's got to take care a him. Don't know what's gonna happen to him when she goes."

And there was bass player Barney – they called him Barney Rubble because he had a laugh like the cartoon character –who'd gotten tired after a few years of playing for nothing more than beer money, took off for New Hampshire or Vermont "or some damned place" looking for steady work and nobody'd heard from him since.

Ah, then there was busty Sandy Torrance who favored low-cut crop tops — which should've been worn by a slimmer girl – and who used to switch off vocals with Ben.

"I heard she slept with everybody in the band," Zoe teased.

"I heard she slept with every boy in school," Shiloh said.

"I admit she tried," Ben said, and batted his eyes theatrically at Shiloh, "but I resisted her fleshy charms. I only had eyes for the one gal who'd captured my heart."

Zoe, flushed with their dad's liquor, made a moony face toward Shiloh while pounding her chest in a passionate heartbeat.

"Screw both of you," Shiloh said.

"Ah, so we're talking threesome again!" Ben said, and to that both ladies raised middle fingers in his direction.

"So, what happened to Sandy?" Shiloh asked.

"Oh, she met this guy, nice guy but a bit of a doof, got herself knocked up 'n' left town. He got himself a job as a grinder down in Groton, workin' at Electric Boat on submarines. Like I said, nice guy, but if you met him, you wouldn't want to be on any sub you knew he worked on. Glug, glug. Know what I mean?"

"I'm surprised you kept it up all this time," Shiloh said, "I mean the band."

"It's somethin'," he said as if that was some kind of answer. "After a while you know it's not goin' anywhere, you put the guitar away, but then you get to missin' it. I can always find some kids who want to play. I guess I just like ..." He couldn't seem to find the words. Then he started in on the chorus of Nickelback's nostalgic "Photograph." He looked at her, eyes fixed on eyes, as he sang the third verse, then stopped, knowing she understood he really meant the part about it being hard to stay and too hard to leave.

They fell quiet again. Zoe got up, grabbed the fireplace poker and stirred up the flames. "What was that song Dad liked you to sing when he was sick? Some Foo Fighters thing, wasn't it? Something about the heart's final beat?"

"I was surprised he knew it."

"Jeez, Ben," Shiloh said, "he didn't grow up with the dinosaurs. What; you thought he listened to Harry James and Artie Shaw?"

"Who?"

"Never mind."

Ben's fingers flowed slowly, lightly across the nylon strings for "These Days."

He let the last notes hang in the air, then seemed struck with a puzzling thought: "There was another one, another song, I had to look it up, but he really wanted to hear it. He only had me play it once. Only time I ever saw that man cry." It was Tom Paxton's "The Last Thing On My Mind."

Shiloh had never heard the song, never heard her father play it on a CD or tape, never heard mention of it in the house.

Ben let the words about leaving with no goodbyes hang in the air.

There was silence, again, after the last note faded away. Zoe looked to Shiloh, asking without asking if she knew what their father wanted from the song, but Shiloh could only shrug helplessly.

"Well, guys," Zoe said through a yawn as she stood. She finished off the last of her most recently poured drink. "I'm tired and a little drunk. I'm goin' to bed. You two try to behave, 'n' if you don't, keep it quiet. I've had enough ruckus for one day."

Ben kept strumming his guitar as Zoe trudged upstairs, saying nothing until they heard her bedroom door shut.

"Well."

"Brought your guitar to distract the kids."

Ben grinned. "I could stay, ya know. I mean, well, I don't mean anything. I'm thinkin' 'bout that guy pokin' 'round your shed last night."

"I'll bet. Go home, Ben."

He gave a conceding nod, carefully set his guitar back in its case, and pulled on his coat. "Will you come see the band tomorrow?"

"I said we'll see."

"This was nice, Shy."

"It was. Let's keep it that way."

"Walk me out?"

For a moment, she thought she shouldn't...but then she was stepping out on the portico with him. It was cold, but not bitter, the wind off the ocean had no edge to it and tasted pleasantly of salt. The sky was brilliantly clear, filled with a million stars, and the moon – glowing so greatly it looked carved from crystal - cast a glade across the waters so bright, it looked solid enough to walk on, clear across the ocean to far places.

It might've been the music taking her back, or maybe too many beers, but Shiloh found her side against Ben's side, the back of her hand touching his. His fingers reached out and intertwined with hers and she didn't pull away.

Then she was against him, chest to chest, looking up into his face shining with moonlight. He bent down, she felt his lips against hers, chapped and dry from his days on the bay, but still, the old days came back, and she felt her lips pushing back against his, but then – as if a fresh gust of sea breeze cleared her head – she pushed herself gently away.

"Please, Ben."

He stepped back, nodded. "Can I ask you something? Do you want me to stop because you don't like it? Or because you do?"

She looked out at the ocean, wave tips twinkling as they caught the moonlight for a brief second. "Be nice, Ben."

He let out a long sighing breath, hefted his guitar case in his hand and started down the walk, silhouetted against the moonglade. He stopped when he got to the road, turned back to her, raised his free hand not in a wave, but something more like a surrender.

Then she watched him walk down the road until he disappeared into the night.

...because you didn't like it? Or because you did?

She sat down on the portico stairs watching the ocean roll in the night like a black velvet blanket decorated with glitter. She sat there a long time before she went up to bed, still unable to answer the question.

PART THREE:

Blood Ties

Nine.

After some long, meditative chewing – which Zoe deliberately made long and meditative just to tease Shiloh – Zoe did some thoughtful frowning before she finally smiled. "It's good."

"Jesus, they decide Supreme Court cases faster."

"Well, I was a little confused about what it was. Are these just badly scrambled eggs?"

Shiloh looked down at the tasty mess on her own plate; she could see the problem. "It was supposed to be a Western omelet, but I've never mastered the flip."

Shiloh had set the alarm on her phone to get up early so she could get in some quick grocery shopping at Teddy Granier's store. When Zoe finally woke up, she'd find a breakfast of sort-of omelet, toast, hot coffee, and two aspirin waiting on the kitchen table for her. Zoe had dropped into her chair, looked down at the spread in front of her and knew why it was there. A look between the sisters said it all:

After what you went through last night…

I know, Shy, thank you…

Zoe made some kind of appreciative yet surprised *humph* between bites.

"What? You didn't think I could cook?" Shiloh said.

"I dunno, I just don't see you bent over a stove."

"I have to admit, I don't always have time at home, but, c'mon, Zee, I used to cook for you guys a lot after Mom left. Somebody had to. If it was up to Dad, we'd've been living on nothing but Kraft mac and cheese and Hamburger Helper for breakfast, lunch, and dinner."

Zoe laughed, nodding at the memory. "I 'member him tellin' you not to drain off the grease on the hamburger. Said that way it'd make more."

They laughed, again, and Shiloh liked how it felt, remembering the things that made them laugh together.

But then they were into that quiet time when the food was done, each nursing their second mugs of coffee. Shiloh saw Zoe's face cloud and she had a feeling about what was coming.

"Ya know, Shy," and Zoe looked down into her coffee mug, "what Jay said last night -"

"Doesn't matter, Zee. That was just Jay being an asshole like Jay is always an asshole. Always was, always is, always will be, amen."

Zoe nodded but Shiloh could see she still felt the need to say it: "It's not true. You know; 'bout me bein' pregnant when me 'n' Anthony -"

"I know."

"Josie was a bit of a preemie, a couple weeks early, 'n' Jay -"

"And Jay won't let it go, I know."

"It's not true."

"It's not true."

They were quiet for a bit, and this time it was Zoe seeing something in Shiloh's face.

"You don't believe me?" Zoe asked.

"It's not that. It's... Well, last night, the way you and Anthony were going at it -"

Zoe let out the long, sighing breath of someone who'd had to explain this too many times before. "We're ok, Shy. Really."

"You said the kids were used to it."

"When you get married, and you're married as long as we are, you'll see. You're gonna have good days 'n' some not-so-good days. 'Member Mom 'n' Dad?"

"I don't remember many good days."

"Ok, bad example. But it's up 'n' down. That's life, right? He takes good care of us, Shy. Yeah, I wish he helped out more with the kids but he's good with 'em, 'n' some stuff 'round the house.... We're fine. Really."

I'm not hearing anything about love, Zee.

They were both relieved when the awkward silence which followed was broken by a knock at the front door. Before Shiloh could say anything, Zoe was out of her chair – awfully fast, Shiloh noted – and heading out of the kitchen.

"You sit," Zoe called back, "I'll get it. 'N' don't touch those dishes! You cooked; I clean."

But Shiloh was already clearing the table. "If it's Jay," she yelled after her sister, "tell him he starts in this early, I'm going to gut him with a butter knife."

But then there was nothing; no blustering Jericho, no give-it-a-rest type rebuttals from Zoe. Curious, Shiloh turned from the sink and saw Zoe in the kitchen doorway, her face stuck somewhere between puzzlement and concern.

And from that, Shiloh could tell: "It's not Jay."

Zoe nodded. "It's two cops."

"Oh, Christ, what'd he do?"

"It must be really bad 'cause one's a detective. They won't tell me anything, Shy. They say they need to talk to you."

She could see their silhouettes through the frosted glass of the front door: one short and sturdy, the other tall and lean. She took a moment to take a deep breath, get into her law office mental armor, then opened the door.

The short, thick one was in plainclothes. Thirties, a chest and biceps which even through his overcoat Shiloh could see loved the gym, and a thick middle that said he loved his steak and beer just as much. His shaved head, ruler-straight posture, and just the tip of a tattoo leaking above his dress shirt collar had her thinking former military.

The tall one was about the same age but in a Portland Police Department uniform.

"Shiloh Vail?" The plainclothes officer produced his badge cover, showed his shield and ID. "I'm Detective Sergeant Karras, this is Officer Whelan."

"I thought you gentlemen didn't have jurisdiction on the island." *Never let the other side get momentum.*

For a moment, Karras lost his practiced cop-in-your-door composure. "Uh, yeah, yes, that's true, but I'm only here to ask a few questions. You are not, as they say, a person of interest."

"Person of interest in what?"

"You know an attorney named Henry McNair?"

Which threw Shiloh as she fully expected police on her porch to be something involving her brother. She re-focused: "You know I do or you wouldn't be here. What happened to him?"

"What makes you think something's happened to him?"

"Again; you're here."

"I'm afraid Mr. McNair was found dead in his office last night."

"And if it was a heart attack you wouldn't be here."

"It does look like a homicide."

Murders and lethal accidents were not uncommon cases at Shiloh's law office. And somebody – a friend, a relative, a spouse – always said the same thing about those jarring here-yesterday-gone-today deaths, that was now going through Shiloh's head: *I can't believe he's dead.*

But she shook off the surprise and got down to business: "What time last night?"

"A little after seven."

"I was here, my sister can corroborate that. You can also check with my brother-in-law and my brother even though since it's before noon you'll have to wake him up. There was also a man named Ben Cole -"

Karras beckoned her to slow down. "Ms. Vail, as I said; you are not a person of interest. Do you mind if we talk inside? It's kind of chilly out here."

"You should wear a hat."

"My wife tells me that every day."

"And like a typical husband, you never listen."

He smiled. "I guess." He had a broad, not unpleasant face, almost boyish when he got the sheepish look he was now wearing. And then he asked with all the obvious discomfort of someone who rarely had to ask such a question: "Ms. Vail, I'm here because I really need your help."

"I don't know that I can tell you anything useful, but…" As she let them in and pointed them toward the living room, she whispered to Zoe who'd been standing behind her: "Don't say anything about the break-in."

They sat in the living room cand Zoe brought them all coffee. Karras had a padfolio open across his lap, flipped back and forth through his pages of notes.

"Mrs. Rutherford – that was Mr. McNair's assistant - said you had an appointment to see him yesterday morning?"

Shiloh'd been through enough Q&A sessions to know to be meticulous and thorough. It would save a lot of time: "I arrived in Portland three nights ago, stayed at the Hilton. Came out here the next day."

"You came out in that storm? Ms. Vail, you've got more guts than me."

"I won't say it was the smartest thing I ever did. There was a letter from Mr. McNair waiting for me here, telling me I was the executor of my father's will. My dad passed away last week."

"I know. You weren't at his service?"

"I, uh, couldn't get away."

"From your office in Washington."

"Yes." *He's good; he's done his homework. And he says "assistant," not "secretary," He works hard at this.*

"So, you know, the department sent a delegation in recognition of his years of service. If there'd been a burial instead of a cremation, we would've had a color guard at the cemetery."

"I appreciate that, thank you."

"I'm sorry; you were saying?"

"I spent that night on the island, went back into the city yesterday to check out of my hotel so I could stay here. I called Mr. McNair from the hotel before I checked out, asked him if he could see me, and he was kind enough to have me come in."

"That would've been at eleven yesterday morning."

Shiloh nodded.

"And this was to talk about your father's will?"

She nodded again. "He provided me with a copy of the will, death certificates… It was all very routine."

Karras looked down at his notes, seemed to be mentally ticking off one item after another. "Did Mr. McNair seem worried or concerned about anything when you saw him?"

"About the will?"

"About anything. Did he seem like anything was bothering him? Edgy, nervous in any way…"

Shiloh shook her head. "No. Like I said, all very routine."

"And you had no further contact with him after your meeting?"

"That was the first and only time I spoke with Mr. McNair."

Karras closed his padfolio, sat back in his chair with an unhappy look. "This all matches what Mrs. Rutherford told us."

"Sorry, Sergeant. I told you I didn't think there was anything helpful I had to say."

"That's not the main reason I came out here, Ms. Vail. I mean, yeah, that part was routine, had to be done, but you said everything I expected you to say."

"So…"

An odd look went between Karras and Whelan, as if they were silently debating whether or not – and how – to proceed. Karras frowned, the debate turning in on himself, and there it was, again: somebody who never needed someone else to carry the other end of the log asking for a helping hand. He sank a little, Shiloh seeing himself resign to a necessity. "Ms. Vail, do you know how many homicides we had in this state last year? I mean excluding that nutcase who went on a shooting spree up in Lewiston."

"No idea."

"Less than two dozen. That's in all of Maine, the whole year. We had four in Portland. Four. That's less than the weekly average for D.C. I know; I looked it up."

"Ok, I live in a war zone and it's all peace and love up here."

A wry smile. "Not quite. Point is, Ms. Vail, there's hardly anybody in the department who has much experience with homicide investigation. Our forensics 'division' consists of a whopping four techs. I drew the call on this one and it's my first homicide."

"Congratulations."

"I'm not looking at it as a gift. I just got my detective's badge six months ago. I'd like to prove I deserve it. Ms. Vail, I don't want to go back to chasing the homeless out from under the Casco Bay Bridge."

"That's a thing?"

"It's a thing."

"It is definitely a thing," seconded Whelan.

Shiloh looked over to Zoe to see if she had any idea where this was all going, but she seemed as lost as Shiloh. Back to Karras: "I still don't know what any of this has to do with me."

Karras flipped open his padfolio, leafed through his pad to a page marked with a sticky note. "You work for what I believe is described as a 'boutique' law firm. Meaning small but high priced because your outfit deals with a lot of heavyweight cases."

"I guess that's a way to put it."

"That includes murder cases, wrongful deaths, stuff like that."

"At times."

"My point is…" He paused, took a deep breath before deciding to push ahead: "My point is you've seen a lot more of this kind of thing than I have."

It took Shiloh a moment to understand and process what she was being asked. She almost laughed. "Let me get this straight; are you asking me to -"

"I'm asking you for help, Ms. Vail."

"Sergeant, I'm just a paralegal -"

Karras referred to his notes again. "Actually, you're the boss paralegal which I figure means your firm thinks you've got an edge on all the other paras."

"You've been doing a lot of Googling," she said, earnestly impressed. "But I think you're grossly overstating what I can do. I'm not an investigator."

"I know. But you've sat in on depositions, read case files and interrogatories, autopsy reports, seen the crime scene photos, you've worked with the lawyers who worked those cases... I'll bet you've even been in the room when a police officer has had to explain himself."

"Sergeant -"

"And you're the daughter of a police officer. From what I'm told, a pretty good police officer."

"So? You think investigative technique is hereditary?"

"I think maybe he taught you a few things he thought you could use on your job."

Which, Shiloh had to admit to herself, he had.

"All I'm asking is for you to come out to the crime scene with me," Karras said. "You might know to look for things that wouldn't occur to me. Just look it over, that's all. I've got a Marine Patrol boat to take us across the bay and a car waiting for us at the docks. I'll have you home by lunchtime. Please, Ms. Vail. So far, the only person I've talked to is this Mrs. Rutherford and the cleaning lady who found him. And what I got from them is this McNair, seems like he was a nice guy."

"Seemed so to me."

"So, ok. I'd really like to nail the sonofabitch who got behind this nice guy and caved in the back of his skull."

When you put it that way... "Do me a favor, Zee, and get me my coat."

The three of them – Shiloh, Karras and Whelan – had just made the turn in the road away from her father's house to where she could see down the shoreline; she froze at the sight of the dock.

"I know it's a small boat," Karras said, thinking it was the Marine Patrol workboat which had stopped her, "but if you came across during that storm -"

"It's not that. I know *that* boat," and she pointed to the Down Easter moored ahead of the Marine Patrol vessel. They began walking, again, Shiloh picking up her pace as she kept her eyes on the lobster boat, looking for any sign of Ben Cole.

As they drew close to the dock, Teddy Granier stepped out of his store, walking toward her. He had undoubtedly seen the Marine Patrol boat pull in, seen the uniformed officer, now saw Shiloh being escorted toward the dock. "Shiloh!" he called out. "Is everything ok? Are you awright?"

"It's ok, Teddy, thanks," she called back. "Is Ben in the store?"

Now it was Granier who stopped in his tracks. "No. I thought he spent the night at your place. I saw his boat pull in yesterday, but I never saw it go out."

Shiloh, like Teddy Granier, had grown up in a place where she'd heard the stories of men working the docks who'd lost a finger in an accident, a foot, maybe even a limb. Maybe even died. And, like Granier, she'd also heard the stories of the Down Easters and fishing boats which went out and never came back, and of the lobster boats found adrift, no sign of their one-man crews. For all of Portland's changes over the years, there were still people who made their living from the sea, and these stories were a part of that life. Which meant that for people who knew the men who worked the docks and sailed the boats, there was - on the back burner - a constant low-simmering paranoia, and it didn't take much to bring it to a boil.

And that's why, at the same time, Shiloh and Granier both started walking faster toward Ben Cole's boat, almost breaking into a jog as they got to the dock. Then Shiloh was close enough to see through the pilot house windows – "Jesus!" - Ben Cole sprawled face down on the pilot house deck.

Shiloh jumped down into the open after deck, Teddy and the policemen close behind. They crowded into the pilot house as she knelt down beside Cole, felt for his jugular. "He's alive. Teddy, he's ice cold. Go down into the cabin, see if you can find a blanket or something."

She rolled Ben over onto his back and as soon as the back of his head touched the metal deck, he groaned, shooting up into a sitting position, protectively cupping the back of his head.

Shiloh, pushing his hand away, gently felt around. "You've got a nice little lump back there. Didn't break the skin, though."

Another groan and he opened his eyes, seemed to have trouble focusing.

"How many fingers?" and Shiloh held two up in front of him.

"You know I'm bad at math."

She turned to Karras and Whelan. "He's fine."

Granier was back, draped a ragged blanket around Ben's shoulders. "You're lucky you didn't freeze to death overnight."

"I had the heater on for a bit," Ben said, still groggy. "Guess I'm lucky it held the heat in here."

"What happened?" Karras asked.

"Not sure. Something…*somebody* come up, hit me from behind."

"You didn't hear anybody climb on your boat?"

"Had my EarPods in. Hey, where's my EarPods?" Ben started feeling around the deck around him. "You know what those things cost?"

"Yeah, that should be your big worry," Shiloh said, emphasizing the misplaced priorities with an eyeroll.

"What were you doing out here last night?" Karras asked.

"Hm?"

This was not Ben still being fuzzy, Shiloh saw. This was Ben trying to think of a good answer. She flashed him a look hoping he could pick up the cue: *Be careful.* She wanted no mention of the shed break-in.

"I asked you what you were doing out here last night?"

Shiloh jumped in: "We had a family get-together last night, Sergeant. You know, sort of a memorial thing because of my father. Ben is an old friend of the family, so…"

"Ok, I get that, but what was he doing *here*," and he pointed to the deck. "And I'd like *him* to answer, if you don't mind."

"Oh, yeah, well." Ben was still stalling, trying to put a good story together.

Shiloh, trying to keep her back to Karras so he couldn't see her smile, "Well, Ben, you did have a bit to drink last night."

"Yeah, yeah, that's right! So, I figured maybe I should wait for my head to clear before I tried to take my boat out. Safety first, right?"

It was clear from the way Karras' face wrinkled all the way up into his bald pate that he wasn't buying. "I want to make sure I understand this: you've got a buzz on, you decide to sit out here stargazing, and you're so looped you don't hear anybody climb on your boat?"

"I did have my EarPods in. I'll bet the sonofabitch who clonked me took 'em. You know what those things cost?"

Shiloh rose from the deck, took Karras by the arm and led him out onto the after deck. "I don't want to embarrass the guy, Sergeant, but here's the thing: Ben and I had a thing years ago. I don't think he ever got over it, know what I mean? So last night, he comes over, has a bit too much to drink, I tell him it's time for him to go home... Getting a picture?"

"So, he's like some high school kid outside his crush's house at night?"

"Something like that."

"You were right to dump him."

The two of them looked back into the pilot house where Granier was helping Ben to his feet. Ben gave them a wary look, and Shiloh gave him a theatrically disarming smile and a wave.

Shiloh and Karras went back into the pilot house.

"Ok," Ben said, "I've got a question: what're you cops doin' here?"

Karras explained and that seemed to be all it took for Ben to shake off the last of any fogginess. He started to say something to the detective, Shiloh had a feeling she knew what it'd be and gave a slight shake of the head to cut him off.

"You might have a concussion," Karras told Ben. "You should have yourself looked at. Why don't you follow us in, and I'll have Patrolman Whelan ride with you in case you start getting woozy. If you want, we can take you to the Mercy E.R."

"I have a better idea," Shiloh said. "Why don't I ride with this guy." She gave a wink to Karras. "I think he and I need to have a talk."

"I've got two small daughters. Is this what I've got to look forward to?"

"Probably."

Karras gave Ben a scrutinizing look. "How harmless is he?"

"Tell you what, Sergeant. He gets out of line, he'll be swimming home. I can handle the boat; I steered it more than once back in the day. And I can handle him."

Karras nodded – reluctantly - waved Whelan to follow him up on the dock. Before the two policemen headed toward the Marine Patrol boat, Karras – his paternal side evidently coming out – gave Ben a stare, pointed to his own eyes before pointing a targeting finger at Ben.

"What was that about?" Ben asked as he began to untie his mooring lines.

"All I've got to say is you better behave," and Shiloh laughed.

The waters of the bay were quiet, but Shiloh was still glad she'd opted for Ben's Down Easter instead of the small workboat which seemed barely more than a step or two up from a skiff, bouncing on the smallest of waves.

Ben was at the helm, and he'd been frowning ever since they'd left the dock. "Just what did you tell that cop?"

"Well, he was having trouble with that story you were spinning – and spinning pretty badly, I might add - so…"

"So…"

"So, I told him you still had a high school boy crush on me, that you were out here last night mooning over me, and that's why after I sent you home telling you nothing was going to happen you were still hanging around. Which is kind of true, right?"

An unhappy grunt from Ben. "High school boy crush?"

"His words. But it catches the spirit of the thing, doesn't it?"

"Boy, when you set your mind to it, you can be kind of a - …"

"Bitch?"

He held up a warning finger. "Didn't say it!"

She laughed. "Now why don't you tell me the truth about why you were out here last night?"

"Besides mooning over you? Ok, ya got me; that was part of it."

"Just a part?"

"I was worried 'bout you, Shy. 'Cause a whoever broke into your shed the other night."

"So, you don't think it was like Teddy said? Just some of the village kids being jerks?"

"Even if it was the village kids being jerks, that doesn't make me feel any better 'bout it. Why didn't you want me to tell the cops 'bout that?"

"They have no jurisdiction on the island."

"They don't?"

Shiloh shook her head, disbelieving. "Jesus, Ben, I've only been in town three days, and I know that much. Don't you ever pay attention to the news?"

"Sure, tide and weather. Anything else: irrelevant. Still, maybe the cops -"

"It's like I said last night. Any government agency starts putting their nose into anything involving that property, and sooner or later they're going to find out about the house. Best case: the house gets taken away."

"Wow, that's the best case?"

"Worst case: Portland – or the state - throws a lien against the estate and they sell off everything of my dad's to pay for back taxes. I'll be ok, I just go back to D.C. the same way I came, and I could give less of a damn about Jay. But I would like to see Zoe come out with something."

"I see what you're sayin', Shy, but I still wish you'd said something. If I was worried before, I'm gettin' downright scared. Now you got this thing with your dad's lawyer? I'm startin' to think all this stuff is connected."

"Don't forget you getting clocked last night."

Ben shook his head, surprised at himself for the omission. "Oh, Christ, yeah! God knows what woulda happened if I hadn't been there. I'm gettin' a really bad feelin'. I want to come with you to the lawyer's office."

"Ben, I appreciate you wanting to play Sir Galahad -"

"It's not just about you. I mean us. I mean -. My feelings aside, thing is you're your father's daughter."

"Meaning?"

"I loved that old man. He was my second father, Shy, my better father. I think you might be in trouble 'n' I want to have your back not just 'cause, you know… But for him."

There was, Shiloh saw, no arguing with that.

"I see he didn't have to swim home," Karras said, "so I take it he was on his good behavior."

Shiloh was standing with Karras on the Portland dock while Ben tied up his boat. "We'll follow you to McNair's office; he has his truck."

"He's coming?"

"I'm trying to let him down easy. You know; the ol' let's-just-be-friends thing."

"Do me a favor if you're back in town in a few years; teach my daughters how to do this. As a dad, I might be more blunt," and he flipped open his coat and suit jacket to flash the holster on his belt.

"You and my dad would've gotten along great."

There was a uniformed officer posted at the door to Henry McNair's office. The doorway was crisscrossed with police crime scene tape.

"The door was closed when your officers got here?" Shiloh asked.

"No." Karras was flipping around the pages in his padfolio. "The body was found by a cleaning lady. Nine-one-one logged her call at 7:04 last night. The door was closed when she got here, but not locked. When she saw the body, she ran out -"

"Understandable."

"– and left the door open."

"But it was closed when she got here. And not locked."

"Mrs. Rutherford always left the door unlocked for the cleaning lady, and then she was supposed to set the lock when she left."

"Before we go in; have your people moved anything around?"

Karras shook his head and tapped a manila folder sticking out from his padfolio. "I've got crime scene photos; you can compare to make sure. The techs have already been through for fingerprinting, so you won't need gloves and don't have to worry about touching anything."

At a head nod from Karras, Whelan peeled back the police tape. Shiloh turned the doorknob, gave the door a push, but stayed in the doorway as it swung open.

You take a scene in, Sweets, her dad had told her. *Big picture first, then you look at everything. You look hard. At every. Little. Thing.*

She gave the outer office a slow sweep of her eyes before slowly stepping inside, her eyes still taking time with every angle, every object. The office looked as she'd remembered it from the day before.

She stopped at the filing cabinets, ran a finger along their top. "This cleaning lady…"

"She always made the rounds of the offices after business hours. This was usually her first stop."

"I think you should bring her in."

Karras was surprised. "You think she had something to do with this?"

"No. Bring her in for fraud." She held out her fingertip grey with dust from the top of the cabinets. "What the hell does this cleaning lady clean?"

"She says it wasn't unusual she'd find McNair working late. Mrs. Rutherford said the same thing. Sometimes he had a late client, people who couldn't make it in during working hours. The cleaning lady said he was always nice, would chat, make her coffee."

"Anybody in the other offices last night?"

"Everybody else on the floor had gone home around five."

Shiloh pointed to the open door to McNair's inner office. "His door was open?"

Karras nodded. "Mrs. Rutherford says unless he had a client or he was on a call where he needed privacy, the door was always open. They could b.s. back and forth, and it made it easier for him to go back and forth to his files.

"Ok, his door is open, the outer door is closed but unlocked. He would've heard someone come in."

"Could they, ya know, maybe sneak in?" Ben said. "Like, been really careful?"

"Unless he was staring out the window or tucked in a far corner of his office, he'd still have to see anybody who came in," Karras said. "His desk and half his office has a direct line of sight to the outer door."

Shiloh stepped into the doorway to McNair's office and, again, held for a moment. And, again, everything looked as it had when she'd been there…except…

On the right side of McNair's desk, about a third of the way down, there was a blood smear about a hand's width, that ran for a foot or so, then the smear changed to a flow running down to the floor. The blood had pooled on the thread-worn carpet in a rough "C" with the back of the C against the foot of the desk. The bloodstain was narrow there but then had spread into two widening wings.

"It's a lot of blood," she said.

"I know. That much blood, I'm thinking the hit didn't kill him. Maybe incapacitated him, maybe even knocked him unconscious, and then he bled out."

"You sayin' this poor bastid bled to death?" Ben said. "Damn..."

"What's your M.E. say?" Shiloh asked. "They finish the autopsy yet?"

The look on Karras' face told Shiloh bad news was coming.

"All autopsies in the state are done by the Chief Medical Examiner's office in Augusta." He checked his watch. "They should just be getting the body now. I told you; this isn't D.C."

She pointed to the blood. "Photo?"

"You sure you want to see it?"

"Not my first rodeo, Sergeant."

Karras still didn't look happy about this but fished an 8 x 10 out of his manila folder.

McNair had evidently fallen against the desk, the back of his head sliding down until his body had come to rest in a half-seated/half-prone position. The blood had continued to run down the desk behind him then pooled around his body.

Shiloh felt an unexpected heaviness pass through her. She'd seen crime and accident scene photos before, more than she could count, and sights much more devastated than poor luckless McNair. But they'd been abstracts, no more real to her than a scene from a movie or TV show. This...

She'd sat with Henry McNair, knew how he sounded, seen how his face furrowed with puzzlement, wrinkled with concern. She knew what he was like alive and that made a difference...

Focus, girl, the job is still the same job...

She let the feeling go like a passing chill and handed the photo back to Karras. He'd seen that moment in her, she could see the concern in his eyes, was about to say something but also saw she was putting it behind her and gave a subtle nod of agreement to do the same.

"Is there anything missing?" she asked, and she heard a slight strain in her voice she hoped only she could hear.

"Later today I'm going to have Mrs. Rutherford come in and we'll inventory the office, but it doesn't look like it. She says he didn't keep cash in the office, his wallet was still in his pocket: forty-two dollars, all his credit cards seem to be there. Assorted change. Still has his wedding ring."

Wedding ring.

Shiloh stepped around the desk – careful to give wide birth to the bloodstains on the carpet – to stand in front of McNair's chair, looking down at the desktop. In a line along the top edge of the desk: photo of a woman around McNair's age Shiloh presumed was his wife; a young-looking woman and man together that might be two grown children, or one adult child and an in-law; another picture of the whole group together. She remembered the baseball team photo on the wall and the pictures on the desk confirmed her thinking of the day before: probably a grandchild was in there somewhere. The bowling trophy on the windowsill: friends.

That heaviness again, something she had never felt leafing through case files, studying the photos of the dead and mangled: that each of those inanimate lumps of meat had a voice, had ties to people who loved them and whom they loved.

This is why Dad didn't want me to see him. So, I'd only remember him...alive.

She wavered on her feet, almost let herself drop into McNair's chair.

"Shy, you ok?"

She had, for the moment, forgotten they were there: Ben, Karras, Whelan, and saw the worry on the faces of all three. She gave them an I'm-ok smile, then got back to business: "Any defensive wounds?"

"Only mark on him is the head wound."

"What was your thinking?"

"Since he'd been hit from behind and there's no signs of a struggle, my first thought was blitz attack. But that lasted about a minute because nothing else figured."

"Yeah." Shiloh's eyes were still wandering around the desktop. It was nothing but idle curiosity, but she noted that her father's file, which McNair had had in front of him, wasn't among the files and papers on the desk. *Must've filed it away.*

"He was hit here," Karras said gesturing at where McNair must've stood by the desk when he was hit. "But how? His back is to the desk; how'd anybody get behind him?"

"Could he have been hit, you know, someplace else 'n' maybe he kinda stumbles over there or somethin'?" Ben offered.

"No," Karras said. "The way he was bleeding, there'd be a blood trail on the floor. There's no blood splatter anywhere from the blow. He had to be standing near the desk, his back to it, when he got hit. And that doesn't figure either. You get hit from behind, you tend to fall forward on your face."

Shiloh shook her head. "Doesn't make sense."

"That's what I'm saying. And it gets weirder. Now, yeah, I have to wait to get the M.E.'s report, but what I could see of the wound, it wasn't like a club, like a bat or something. It was narrow and hard, round, like some kind of wooden or metal bar. But that's not the weird thing. The wound was almost perfectly horizontal," and Karras drew an imaginary line across the middle of the back of his skull.

"I don't get it," Ben said. "Why's that weird?"

Shiloh beckoned Karras over and to turn around. She pulled a pencil from a pencil cup on the desk and pretended to strike the back of Karras' head. "I hit you from behind, the wound is going to either be vertical or some kind of diagonal. The only way you get a horizontal wound is I'm on a stepladder or I'm eight feet tall."

"So, a guy comes in quiet, hits him up there..." Ben mused, "What're you lookin' for? An eight-foot-tall ninja?"

Something tickled at her, drew her eyes back to the desk. She'd been too distracted by those pictures of McNair's family to notice it at first, but there was something different about the mass of papers on the desk. There was a clear space of just a few inches along the side where McNair had fallen as if someone had pushed everything back all along that edge.

And something else. The way the wood, scuffed and scratched as it was, shone. Right in front of her, on a rare open stretch, she ran her finger along the wood, and it came away dusty as it had when she'd run a finger along the top of the outer office file cabinets.

Karras must've picked up that something was working on her: "What is it?"

She ignored him, went around to where McNair's body had lain, leaned in close to the desktop for a better look...and caught a faint scent. "These offices don't have their own bathrooms, do they?"

"No," Karras said. "There's a communal can on the floor."

She beckoned Karras over. "Take a sniff."

He did, immediately turned to Whelan. "Jake, go to the bathroom down the hall. Get a paper towel or some toilet paper, something, and bring me a shot of the hand soap. Use your gloves, don't touch anything you don't have to."

"What is it?" Ben asked.

"Smells like that cheap, industrial-strength antibacterial goop they use in public bathrooms," Karras said.

Then Whelan was back with a mucousy glob on a piece of paper towel. Karras and Shiloh each took a whiff and nodded in agreement.

"Jake, post that bathroom. Nobody gets in. Somebody on the floor has to go, tell them to use the coffee shop downstairs."

"Ok, I'm missin' somethin' here," Ben said.

A two-inch lip extended the desktop past the body of the desk, and the half-inch rim of the desktop was rounded. Shiloh ran her fingers along the underside of the lip above where McNair's body had fallen. "Right there," she said to Karras, and he felt for it, too.

"What's right there?" Ben was getting frustrated.

Shiloh wet her pinky tip with her tongue, ran it in the same place under the desktop lip, then held it up for Ben, smudged with red.

"You bring your techs back," Shiloh said to Karras, "The way this wood is scratched up, I'll bet they find traces of McNair's blood, that soap, and maybe even paper towel fibers stuck in the grain. You may have a homicide, Sergeant, but I don't think you have a murder."

"For Chrissakes, Shy," said an increasingly peeved Ben Cole, "Anybody gonna tell me what all this means?"

"The perp comes in," Shiloh began, "but it's not a break-in. McNair's not afraid of whoever it is, there's no fight, no signs of a struggle. Then I'm guessing there's a discussion, maybe it gets a little heated and our perp gives McNair a shove. McNair's an old guy, overweight, doesn't take much for him to lose his balance. He falls back, hits his head on the edge of the desk.

"The perp, he's not a pro, he didn't come here for a kill. He panics. He tries to clean up as best he can and all he's got available to him is soap and water from the floor bathroom."

"The blood underneath…"

"It's called adhesion. Our guy didn't realize that some of the blood on the side of the desk traveled underneath and stuck there."

"Now everything fits," Karras said. "Still doesn't tell us who or why."

"Can't help you there, Sergeant."

"But I'll differ with you on one point. I'm putting this to the D.A. as a felony murder. All the time our perp was cleaning up after himself, McNair was laying there bleeding to death. This prick let him die."

Shiloh nodded Ben into the outer office with her while Karras got on his cell phone to call back the forensics crew. "Block the door," she whispered to Ben who, despite obviously wondering why, tried to look casual as he leaned against the doorsill to McNair's office.

Shiloh went to the file cabinets, found the drawer marked "U-V-W," and as quietly as she could, slid the drawer open. She quickly looked at the name tags, had the drawer closed by the time Karras was done on the phone.

"Do you need me for anything else, Sergeant? I think I've done about all I can."

Karras took her hand. "Ms. Vail, you don't give yourself enough credit; you've been a huge help. If you ever want to change jobs…"

"Thanks, but I'd rather not do this, again."

Karras seemed to understand. He looked down at the bloodstains in a way that had Shiloh wondering if Karras ever wanted to do this again. A little heave of his shoulders, and then, "If I have to, can I…?"

"I'm only in town for a few days, but if you think there's something else I can do, don't hesitate to give me a call."

"Your dad would be proud, Ms. Vail."

Maybe, but I don't think he ever wanted something like this for me.

Out in the hall, Ben started to open his mouth and Shiloh, knowing what he was going to ask, quietly hushed him.

Then they were out on the sidewalk and the brisk November air felt good to Shiloh, she breathed it deeply, felt like it cleaned the morbidity of McNair's office out of her system. They started walking to where Ben had parked his truck down the block.

"Now do you want to tell me what that was about up there?" Ben asked.

"My father's file is gone. It wasn't on the desk; it wasn't in the file drawer where it was supposed to be."

Ben's walk slowed to a halt. "Fuck me... You think whoever killed this McNair guy...?"

"It doesn't look good."

"And you're not going to tell the cops?"

"Ben -"

"Because of that goddamned house? Jesus, Shy, this isn't just somebody rootin' around in your backyard. Somebody's dead! You think a house is worth it?"

"It's not just a house, Ben. It's where my father raised me and my sister and my brother, jackass that he is. It's where I grew up. Yeah, I know, that doesn't make sense, it's stupid, it's crazy, and I know sooner or later I'm going to have to tell the police about this other stuff. McNair's secretary is going to go over everything with them when they work up an inventory; they'll see the file is missing and I won't have to tell them. But that buys me a little time to try to figure out what the hell's going on."

"Well, lady, I didn't go to college, and I don't read a lot of books, but I agree you're being stupid and crazy. But..."

He nodded. He'd go along.

She felt bad about that because she knew he was only going along because he was Ben, and she was Shiloh and sometime in the past they had been Ben & Shiloh.

They climbed in the truck, and he kicked over the engine. "You want me to take you back to the island?"

She shook her head as she took out her cell phone.

"Who're you callin'?"

"Zoe. I want to see if she knows where my mother lives."

"Uh…"

"What?"

"I know where she lives."

"How do you know?"

"Your father told me."

"How the hell did he know?"

Ben squirmed in his seat; his face twisted as she could see him trying to figure out the best way to put it. "See, like, well, your dad… He kinda kept tabs on her."

Shiloh felt heat flushing her face.

"Look, it wasn't like some kinda stalker thing. He was always worried 'bout her, he just wanted to make sure she was ok. When she remarried, the guy she hooked up with, your dad even had me go by his place, make sure he wasn't some kinda dud. I know he felt bad 'bout the divorce."

"He told you that?"

Ben shrugged. "Sorta. Somethin' he said at the end. He was pretty doped up those last few days, 'n' he was in 'n' out. This one time, I don't know he was talkin' to me or just, you know, babbling…"

"What'd he say?"

"I don't 'member exactly, but somethin' like, 'Do you think she'll ever forgive me?'"

Ten.

Shiloh and Ben sat in Ben's truck for some time, parked in front of Delia's address. The building had been re-sided recently which gave it a clean, white, almost glowing look in the morning sun, but it took more than new aluminum to conceal the blocky, functional shape common to Munjoy Hill houses.

Delia-Vail-now-Delia-May and her husband had the top floor in a three-family on Munjoy Hill, the high ground on the Portland peninsula. Like most of the houses on the hill, it was old, pre-war from when there was only one war worth mentioning. But as Portland's fortunes had changed, the hill had begun gentrifying, a lot of the houses in the neighborhood – particularly those along the Eastern Promenade which ran along the bay shore - being upgraded and up-priced, the multi-families often turning from dowdy apartments to comfy condos with a price hooked to how good a view they had of Casco Bay.

Delia had married Arthur May some years before, Ben couldn't remember exactly when. Arthur had been a salesman on a car lot in South Portland and had done well enough that he'd been made manager…well, assistant manager, a detail, Ben said, he liked to leave off unless pressed. That wasn't good enough to put them on the Promenade, but they were far enough up the hill to have an IMAX-caliber view of the bay.

"Well," Ben said after a while.

"Yeah." But Shiloh still didn't move.

"Do you want me to come up with you?"

Shiloh shook her head.

"Change your mind?"

"I wish," she said and finally climbed out of the truck.

Shiloh wasn't sure if Delia didn't immediately recognize her or was just taken aback by her appearing at her door, but after a beat Delia's puzzled frown finally morphed into a wry smile. "Of course."

Shiloh was breathing heavily after climbing the two flights of stairs.

That got something close to a chuckle from Delia. "Try it when you got two armloads of groceries."

"I can imagine."

"So."

"Yeah."

"No 'Hi, Mom'? 'Hello Mother'?"

Shiloh said nothing. After a bit, Delia nodded an ok-fine nod, stood back and clear of the door, as much of a won't-you-come-in as Shiloh expected to get.

The condo was a collection of rooms tidily kept, tidily furnished with Bob's Discount kind of stuff, nice enough without being plush.

"I'm going to pretend to be polite and offer you something," Delia said. "Coffee? Tea? A drink?"

Shiloh shook her head.

"Well, I could use something," Delia said and disappeared into the kitchen. "You might as well sit," she called back.

Shiloh didn't sit. She could see a back room, something like a sunroom opening on to a deck. One side of the room was nearly all floor-to-ceiling windows offering a panoramic view of the bay.

"We can talk here." Shiloh hadn't realized she had actually entered the room. Nor had she heard her mother come in behind her. Delia nodded her to a sofa in the sunroom facing the bay and took a chair nearby for herself. She had a bottle of beer in one hand, had picked up a pack of Marlboro Lights as well. She held out the pack to Shiloh who nodded it away. "Good for you," Delia said in a way Shiloh couldn't tell if it was earnest or a dig.

Delia had never been an overly pretty woman; the word "handsome" would probably be the best description, her features not unattractive but unfortunately one degree off from being truly appealing; cheeks a little too sharply angled, sadly canted eyes just a hair too small and close set, nose a bit too round, and her dark hair – now heavily streaked with grey - refusing to obey a comb. Even though she had put on some weight since Shiloh's last remembered image of her, the weight hadn't softened her sharpness, just added a nearly perfect half-sphere to her middle where it pushed down the waist of her jeans.

Delia lit one of the Marlboros, took a deep pull and exhaled, considerately aiming the smoke stream off to a corner of the room. She waited for Shiloh to speak, and when she saw Shiloh was at a loss for how to start, smiled in a darkly amused way. "Considering we haven't said two words to each other since I left, I don't figure you're here for a hug from dear ol' Mom. How'd you know where to find me? Zoe?"

Shiloh weighed how much to say, then came to thinking there was no reason to hold back. "Seems Dad was keeping an eye on you."

"Really?" More curious than upset.

"The way it was explained to me, he was worried about you."

A slight laugh, phlegmy: too many cigarettes, too much beer. "That sounds like your dad."

"You seem to be doing ok."

"Arthur's a good man. Not that you'd be concerned if he wasn't."

It stung a bit because it was true.

"What do you want, Shiloh?"

"I saw Henry McNair the other day."

"Ah."

"I wanted to make sure I've got the story straight. He says -"

"I didn't want anything from your father."

"I don't often hear that. I work in a law office -"

"I know. Zoe keeps me up to date."

"What I was going to say was I'm more used to seeing an aggrieved wife gouge her ex."

Again, that unpleasant little smile. "That's how you think of me? You think I'm that kind of person?"

"I thought you were that mad at him. But no alimony, no settlement, you didn't take the house -"

"Why the hell would I want that house? You know the story on that house, right? What it used to be?"

Shiloh nodded. "But no money, no support -"

Delia turned toward the windows. It wasn't visible from their vantage point, but Delia's eyes were aimed in the direction of St. Aggie's Island. "That was between me and him."

"I don't think so."

"Why not?"

"Because my next question is why did you hate me so much? Was that your way of getting at him?"

She turned back to Shiloh, surprised. "You think I hated you?"

"You have to admit, there was a hell of a difference between how you treated Zoe and Jericho and how you treated me."

Delia studied the glowing tip of her cigarette for a few seconds, tapped the ashes into an ashtray on a nearby lamp table before nodding in agreement. She stood, leaving her beer, and stepped out onto the deck.

Shiloh followed. It was chilly up there, but the breeze off the bay didn't seem to bother her mother.

Delia closed her eyes, let the soft gusts wash over her, then she opened her eyes, took a last drag of her cigarette before dropping it to the deck and carefully stubbing it out with the tip of her shoe. "It probably doesn't matter now, but I was wrong about that. It wasn't about you. You just got, well... I guess you'd say you got caught in the crossfire. I don't suppose after all this time it would make a difference for me to say I'm sorry."

"Those cuts are too deep. Twenty years too deep."

Delia looked back out at the bay, a sad nod of agreement. "Yeaaaahhhh," she sighed quietly.

"Was Dad having an affair?"

"What?" She almost laughed.

"Did Dad cheat on you? I'm trying to figure out why you were so mad all the time and that's all I can come up with."

And now she did laugh. "Ya know, I honest-to-God don't know how to answer that."

"He was either seeing somebody or he wasn't, so it seems simple to me."

"You'd be surprised how un-simple it can be."

"Don't play fucking games with me, Delia."

Her mother's face went cold, turned to her with hard eyes. "I'm going to say something to you, then you're going to leave, and if we ever see each other again, bump into each other on the street, whatever, you're never asking me about this again."

"Are we negotiating?"

"No. I'm telling you flat-out. I'm not telling you a goddamn thing about this because I made a promise. Whatever you think of me, how I treated you, what was going on between me and your father, I made him a promise it would stay between me and him. And I'm gonna keep that because however shitty I treated you – and I did – I owe it to you. Don't ask for a clarification because this is all you get."

"Henry McNair is dead. He was murdered in his office last night."

For the first time since Shiloh had shown up at her mother's, Delia seemed to lose her mental footing, actually wavering on her feet.

"Are you sure?"

"That he's dead? Or that he was murdered? Yeah, somebody killed him."

There were wooden garden chairs on the deck and Delia - still stunned and unsteady - made her way to one. "Would you mind getting me my cigarettes?"

Her first impulse was to tell Delia, "Get them yourself," but the way her mother sat sagging in her chair, Shiloh felt just enough pity to go back into the sunroom and grab the Marlboro pack and the nearby lighter.

"Thank you," Delia said when Shiloh handed them to her. She lit up a fresh cigarette, sat back, let the nicotine do its work.

Shiloh sat in one of the other chairs. "Did you know Dad knew the Clearys?"

"Hm? Oh, yeah, sure. He and the son – well, I guess he's the old man now – they were old buddies. They were in the Navy together, them and some other dude, somebody who went in the cops with your father. Why?"

"I never knew that."

"After we got married…" Something worked on her mother, something which made her frown, then her face went slack, some kind of dismissal. "I didn't like them coming around."

"Why?"

A long pause, that frown again. "When they got together, they kinda regressed, know what I mean? Guys. It was like they were twelve, again. They would still get together in the city, but I didn't like them in the house. Why do you ask?"

"One of the sons – Sean Junior – came out to see me, said Dad and his father had done some kind of business together."

"I wouldn't know anything about that. Wait; this have anything to do with what happened to that lawyer?"

"I don't know. I'm just asking. Do you know anything about how Dad got the house on the island?"

Cruelly, now: "You mean after they threw the whores out? And disinfected the place?" She let that feeling go, her head easing against the backrest. She took another long drag of her cigarette. "He'd already been living there when we got married. So, again, I wouldn't know." She seemed to make some kind of decision, sat up, her face firm: "Look; I didn't know about anything your father had to do with Cleary, I don't know about any business he did besides being a cop, and I don't know anything about how he got himself a used whorehouse. And if you're thinking a wife should know those things about her husband, maybe you're getting an idea of some of the reasons we got divorced."

Which felt like a conclusion, so Shiloh stood, went back into the apartment heading for the door.

"This is gonna sound funny from me…" Delia had followed her daughter and was standing in the middle of the living room.

"What's going to sound funny coming from you?"

"Like I said, Zoe keeps me up on stuff. Sounds like you got a nice job down there in Washington. You look good. How're you doing?"

Too late for you to be a mother. "Seriously? Well, my dad just died so I'm feeling a little down right now."

"Ok, I got that coming. But I heard you weren't at his funeral."

Shiloh turned for the door.

"I felt bad for him," Delia said. "When I heard he was sick. Your father was a good guy. A nice man. But we never should've got married. I spent a long time, a lotta years being mad at him. And then I got to feeling bad for him. And about how I treated you. World looks different to you at a certain point, I guess."

"I'm told he felt bad about the divorce. You should know that."

"Really?" Skeptical. "How do you know?"

"A friend of the family, somebody you don't know, was spending time with him those last days. Something Dad said. He said, 'Do you think she'll ever forgive me?'."

Delia laughed, laughed so hard it triggered a smoker's harsh cough.

"What's so funny?"

The coughing subsided and Delia could finally gasp out a reply: "That you think he was talking about *me!*"

"You ok?"

Shiloh shrugged.

"I take it she didn't say much that was helpful."

"She did say she didn't hate me, just that she treated me like shit and felt bad about that."

"Oh." Ben frowned at the invisible design his fingertip was making on the Formica tabletop, and after a bit, "That's something, I guess."

"I believe the phrase is, 'Closing the barn door after the horses have left'."

They were sitting in a booth in the Miss Portland Diner, one of those old-fashioned aluminum-and-stainless-steel lunch car-styled affairs on the Back Cove side of the peninsula; a world and a mile or so away from the tony eateries dotting the Old Port. Ben had picked it – *God bless him, he's still trying the nostalgia route* – because, so he said, it was the only place left from "our days" that hadn't changed.

When Shiloh had come down from her mother's place, whatever the look had been on her face, it had been enough to actually draw a wince from Ben.

"How 'bout some lunch?" like he was offering her a Band-Aid.

"That's supposed to make me feel better?"

"No, it's supposed to make *me* feel better. I didn't have anything to eat this morning. You know; 'count a tryin' to look after you 'n' gettin' clonked on the head 'n' all."

It was an effective piece of guilting and Shiloh nodded her ok.

A waitress had handed them menus, but Shiloh let hers sit untouched on the table.

"Eat somethin'," Ben pushed.

"Not really hungry."

"Eat somethin'."

"Ok. Something light. They have salads?"

"Salad? You're gonna come to a place like this 'n' have a salad? I take you home in my boat 'n' we hit a rock 'n' sink, you want the last thing you ate to be a salad?"

She laughed. "Order me a cheeseburger."

When the waitress came back, Ben threw two beers on the order, too.

"Isn't it a little early for that?" Shiloh said.

"Sun's over the yardarm."

"Do you even know what a yardarm is?"

"Somethin' nautical tells me it's time for a drink. 'Sides, it's for medicinal purposes," and he gingerly touched the back of his head, made as if he was in great pain.

"How is your head?"

"I once saw a guy on the docks, cable snapped 'n' a trap swung 'round 'n' caved in his skull. I can live with this."

The food came, Shiloh pinched off little pieces of her burger bun to nibble, pushed her glass of beer around.

Ben watched her not eat, not drink, shook his head in disappointment. "You're gonna waste food like that, you're payin'."

"Ben, did Dad ever say anything to you about knowing the Clearys? Even when he was in his incoherent babbling mode?"

"Nope," he managed to get out around a mouthful of cheeseburger. "Why? Your mom say somethin'?"

"According to her, Dad and Sean Senior were old buddies back to when they were in the Navy."

"Really? Wow."

"That's what she said."

"Wow."

"You said that, and I really wish you'd swallow before you say anything else."

Ben swallowed, set his burger down, wiped his hands grease-clear on his napkin, took a sip of his beer, sat back, the vinyl bench cover crackling as he settled.

"Do you remember what it was like down here? I mean back when." Ben's eyes had an odd look; he was looking out at Bayside but a Bayside that wasn't there anymore.

The diner sat on Marginal Way which paralleled the west shore of the peninsula. When Shiloh had been a child, this part of Bayside had been – as carping editorials in the *Portland Press Herald* put it with nagging frequency – "blighted" with "low value industry"; repair shops of one kind of another, metalworking outfits, warehouses. But, like so much of Portland, it had been undergoing redevelopment pushing the area more toward the residential: new apartments, a CVS, a supermarket. Behind the diner was Route 1 but beyond that was now the green band of Back Cove Park and the Western Promenade with a view of Tukey's Bridge across the neck of the cove.

Shiloh could see it; he was looking back but to measure it against today.

After a bit, he pushed his plate with its half-eaten burger away, sighed. "I get it, now. I know I said it yesterday, but I was just sayin' that 'cause I know that's what you wanted me to say."

"What the hell're you talking about?"

A smile with a sad cant to it. "How you changed." He took a sip of his beer, set the glass down, turning it round and round with one hand. "Watchin' you at work up there in that lawyer's office - 'n' I see you gettin' ready to pooh-pooh what you did; don't do that. You were sharp up there, Shy. So maybe you're not a lawyer, or a whatchacallit, an investigator, but, damn, girl… I saw it: there's 'bout a thousand miles 'tween you 'n' me. I was just sayin' it yesterday, but I saw it today. You have changed. "

"So have you. Everybody changes over time."

"Oh, you're just bein' nice, Shy. If I changed, it's not like you. I just maybe got better at what I used to do, but I'm still doin' the same-ol'-same-ol'." He looked back out the window only now he was looking at the years ahead. "Ya know, I look at my ol' man, 'n' I know what it's gonna be for me. One day, everything'll hurt, everything'll be stiff, I'm gonna feel the cold out there on the water like I never felt it before. Lookit these," and he held up his hands. On his left, the pinky jutted out at a right angle to the other fingers. On the right, his fourth finger and pinky also wandered off away from the pack.

"They go every which way 'cause each one of 'em's been broke, this one -" and he flexed his right pinky "- more than once. I awready had surgery on my shoulder, torn rotator cuff. Dad's had surgeries on his knees, his back, almost lost the tip of his nose to frostbite once. There's times the catch was so bad we wondered if we were gonna lose everything.

"Maybe there's gonna come a day everything hurts so much I'm gonna wonder what was goin' through my head I didn't change course. Sometimes I'm out there when the weather turns, or it's so goddamn cold I can't feel my hands or feet, I'm thinkin' it then! But even sittin' here talkin' like this, I'll be damned if I can think what else I'd do.

"'N' I look at that, then I see how you were up there today...'n' I get it."

She felt it like a heavy hand on her chest; it was a eulogy. "I'm sorry, Ben."

He nodded the apology away. "Not like anybody did anything on purpose. Different roads is all. But lemme ask you; do you ever think back to... You know. Do you remember it? Do you ever miss it? Do you ever miss any of it?"

That heavy hand lifted and, in its place...a warmth. "Yeah. Yeah, I do. There are times when I think back to those days. When I do, I remember it all. And I miss it all. It was a special time, Ben. And if I could go back ... But you can't. It's like you read the last page in a chapter. Chapter ends, you turn the page, new chapter. Been a lot of chapters since then."

He nodded, understanding, then smiled. "Figures you'd say somethin' involvin' a book!"

She held up her glass of beer. "To good books."

"To good books."

He touched his glass to hers and they both drank.

Even in the Down Easter's pilot house with the heater on, Shiloh was feeling a chill. She looked aft at Portland, the view swaying with the lobster boat's bobbing as it crossed the bay. *From here it looks like it always looked…but it's not.*

And maybe that's where the chill came from, she thought, pulling her jacket closer around her. Something is lost, how do you not feel cold?

"Can I ask you somethin'?" Ben kept his eyes ahead.

She looked at his hands on the wheel, the splayed fingers, calloused and chapped, and thought of what Ben had said about ending up like his father. She looked down at one of her own hands, the slender fingers, manicured nails, milky silky skin that never went to bed without a dose of moisturizing lotion. *A thousand miles between us.*

"Can I, Shy?"

"That usually means a question that's going to hurt. But go ahead."

"Well… I'm tryin' to figure out how to put it. Is there, you know, somebody waitin' back there in D.C. for you?"

That's why you can't look me in the eye, and she smiled, glad he couldn't see it. "At the moment, no."

"But there has been."

"I have not led the life of a cloistered nun if that's what you want to know."

His windburned cheeks reddened, but he pushed on: "Any of 'em get serious?"

"One or two. One even looked like he might propose."

"What happened?"

"Same thing happened with all of them. Once they got comfortable, they started acting like guys."

He laughed. "I been workin' the docks long enough to know what that means. I have definitely seen what it is when guys start actin' like, ya know, *really* guys."

"In one case, it finally occurred to him – after a couple of months - to tell me he was married."

"Oof."

"What about you? You're not going to tell me you've spent all this time monastically pining for me?"

He made slight motions of the wheel to make an approach to the inlet on St. Aggie's. "I was actually engaged for a while. Couple years ago."

"What happened?"

He seemed to consider whether to answer or not, then, "She wasn't you."

He cut the engine, leaned back against the far bulkhead. The boat swayed gently on the waves. "I've spent a lotta time wonderin' why I can't let go, Shy, lotta hours out here runnin' it through my head. I know other people, they break up, they get divorced, somethin', maybe it takes some time, but they get past it. They – like people like to say – 'move on'." His head went side to side, puzzled at himself.

"But not you."

"'N' I wondered why that was. You know who explained it to me?" A broad smile. "Sandy."

"Sandy? Sandy-from-the-band Sandy? With the, uh…" and she held her hands up in front of her indicating a better-than-average breast endowment.

Ben laughed. "Yup, that Sandy."

It was Shiloh's turn to laugh. "And Sandy-Boff-Anything-With-A-Penis explained the affairs of the heart to you? Sandy who's tested more beds than Tempur-Pedic?"

False admonishment: "Ya know, you guys really had her wrong."

"So, she wasn't a skank? Tramp? Slut? She really didn't sleep with half the senior class?"

"Well, she did, maybe not half, but…"

"But?"

"It wasn't like you all thought. Sandy was a romantic."

"Please."

"No, seriously. She wanted to fall in love."

"And she did. Constantly."

"I'm not sayin' she had great judgment, but I'm tellin' you, that girl musta seen every Hallmark movie ever made! She could quote lines to you like it was Scripture! She just kept tryin' to make it come true for herself."

"And trying…and trying…"

Ben waved a reprimanding finger at her, so Shiloh nodded an apology. "Ok, so what did this grand romantic have to say?"

"She said I couldn't let go 'cause you and me're soulmates."

"I'm sorry, but what did Boom-Boom Sandy know about soulmates?"

"I don't think she knew much. I think it was something she heard -"

"In a Hallmark movie."

"Probably. But I looked it up. So, one of those old Greek guys, Plato, this is, like, back in those *Clash of the Titans* days -"

She couldn't help but grin at all that: *a thousand miles between us.*

"- somebody you probably read, he wrote this thing once where he said once upon a time, there wasn't men and women, just people, 'n' the people had four arms, four legs, 'n' two heads. Then one of the gods, I don't know which one, maybe it was Thor or somebody -"

"Wrong mythology."

"Anyways, this god, for some reason he gets pissed at people, so he splits everybody in half, 'n' half are men 'n' half are women. So, we each spend our lives lookin' for our other half."

"And you think I'm your other half?"

"I don't think it, Shy. Doesn't matter you don't feel the same like me. You could hate me. But that won't change you're my other half."

It had all seemed kind of funny in a cute way…up until then. She looked aft, past the transom to where the Down Easter's dissipating wake had melted into the waves. "In which case, I feel sorry for you, Ben."

He turned back to the wheel, turned over the engine. "Well, I feel sorry for me, too."

Ben pointed the prow of his boat into the inlet and, "Oh, fuck me."

Shiloh immediately recognized the cabin cruiser moored at the dock from the day before. And the figure on the after deck.

"Ahoy!" Sean Cleary, Junior called, giving them a broad wave.

"How much you want to bet he's here for you?" Ben grumbled.

"Sucker bet," Shiloh said.

Ben tucked his boat at the dock close behind the cruiser.

"You know, if you pull in in front of me, that'll make it easier for me to pull out."

Ben continued to concentrate on getting his boat snug against the dock. He cut his engine, tossed his lines up on the dock and jumped up after them to tie up.

"You need any help with those lines?" Cleary said.

"Nope."

Cleary turned to Shiloh. "I've been waiting a good part of the morning for you. Your sister told me you were in town. I knew you'd have to come home sometime." Then, as Ben helped Shiloh up on the dock: "You're Ben Cole, aren't you?"

"Yup."

"I think my father and your father had dealings some time ago."

"They did."

"As I heard it, things got out of hand. I'm sorry about that."

"Then you'd be ok with me tyin' you to my anchor and throwin' you in the bay."

"I wouldn't be happy about it, but I'd understand."

Thinking it might be wise to step in before things escalated, Shiloh asked, "I presume you're here to see me, Mr. Cleary?"

"Actually, it's not me. My father would like – and this is an invitation, not a demand – would like you to come out to the house. There's some things he'd like to discuss with you. Some of it seems to involve your father."

"Now?"

Cleary gestured at the bulk of the cruiser behind him. "Your chariot awaits. I'll take you across, you have your chat, I'll bring you straight back. You're gone maybe two hours at the most."

She turned to Ben. "What do you think?"

He turned his back to Cleary and dropped his voice. "On the one hand, I think there's bottom-crawlers in this bay I'd trust more."

"On the other hand?"

"Maybe you get some answers. Maybe. Some. I'll go with you."

Cleary must've caught that last bit or at least guessed it: "I'm afraid, Mr. Cole, the invitation only extends to Ms. Vail."

Which clearly made Ben uncomfortable. Shiloh set a hand on his arm. "It's ok, Ben. I'm sure Mr. Cleary Junior will be the perfect gentleman."

Cleary gave the kind of curt bow one only saw in old movies about the aristocratic set. "Perfect to perfection, Madam." Then, more seriously: "And, again, Mr. Cole, I am sorry about the past unpleasantness. If I'd've known that's where things were heading, I would've tried to stop them before they got that far."

Which only brought a sour face from Ben. "Watch him," he said to Shiloh, making sure it was loud enough for Cleary to hear, "He's a sweet talker."

"He is that."

Ben stepped back, a sign of go-ahead. "You gonna see me play tonight?"

It felt more like a request for reassurance than a reminder. "I'll be there."

Cleary leapt lightly onto the dock, held out a hand to Shiloh. "Shall we?"

She took his hand, he helped her aboard, then turned to untie the cruiser's mooring lines.

Ben stepped close to the cruiser, gave a wary look toward Cleary, then turned back to Shiloh. "Just remember what I said about the bottom crawlers."

Eleven.

"Shiloh, Jericho, Zoe. Interesting. All names out of the Bible, aren't they? Were your parents very religious?"

Shiloh had to admit, the wheelhouse of the Cleary cruiser was infinitely more comfortable than the one on Ben Cole's Down Easter: roomier, heated, with cushioned seats. Cleary invited her to go below to the cabin where she'd find a bar and an urn of hot coffee if she was so inclined. She was not.

"I always thought it was funny since I can't remember either of them ever going to church," Shiloh said. "They weren't even married in church. Or by a minister. I asked my dad about our names once."

"What'd he say?"

"He said considering him and my mom, it might be the only religion we got."

Which was worth a shared chuckle.

Sean Cleary, Junior may have affected the dress - if in more upscale fashion - of just another guy from the docks, but it was not completely a pose. Shiloh had been impressed at how he'd handled the lines of the cruiser before bounding back on board, and then tickled the throttle back and forth with one hand while handling the wheel with his other, carefully coaxing the cruiser out from the tight mooring in which Ben had quite intentionally boxed it.

As Cleary heeled the boat around toward the bay, he caught her respectful look. "Inside every superficial ass is some little real thing," he said. "Like the gooey center of a Cadbury egg."

He had, as he had promised, acted the perfect gentleman, showing her to her seat, inviting her to use the cabin, and if he sometimes carried it off with some self-mocking cheek, Shiloh did sense, as he'd said, there was something real buried somewhere inside the man.

"I did some Internet searching," he said. "'Shiloh' apparently means 'tranquil,' at least when it's given to a girl. You don't strike me as the tranquil type."

"Oh, I am tranquil. Until someone pisses me off."

"I'll keep that in mind. On a somewhat related subject... I know you've heard a lot of stories about my family. Like the one involving your friend Mr. Cole. You know him a long time?"

"Practically back to the womb. Anything he tells me; I take as credible. So, if you're planning on telling me that all these stories aren't true, that they're exaggerations, or they're just slanderous lies told by jealous competitors, and so on, well..."

"Some are."

"And some aren't?"

The cheekiness faded and he seemed to fall into a kind of sad resignation. "My grandfather," and it sounded almost as a sigh, "he's the one who got the family started in Portland. Irish immigrant. He was still a kid when he came over. Didn't have the proverbial pot to proverbially piss in. Grew into a crude man. Crude...and tough.

"He was still around when I was growing up. I always remember him smelling of cheap whisky and even cheaper cigars. There was this thing he liked to do… He only shaved every couple of days, so he liked to grab me and my brother, pull us on his lap and rub his face hard against ours. Was like hugging sandpaper. He thought that was funny as hell.

"Never finished school, had no use for the written word, but the man did have an instinct for business. He was like a bloodhound the way he could sniff out an opportunity to make a buck. But it was a killer instinct. He liked winning more than he liked playing fair. A lot of the Cleary reputation owes itself to how he did things."

"But your dad is different."

Even more sadly resigned. "He wanted to be…I think. Any time my father tried to rein in his father's worst tactics, Granddad considered that a sign of weakness. He did not tolerate weakness in his son. A kid shouldn't see his father get ripped a new one by *his* dad, and I saw it a lot. You grow up with that, it's hard to break the mold. It's something just to crack it a bit."

At which point Shiloh couldn't tell if he was talking about himself or his father. "Frankly, Mr. Cleary?"

"Sean, please."

"Ok, Sean-please. Frankly, I can't tell if you're trying to tell me your father's a saint or has become as big a sonofabitch as your grandfather."

"Maybe because I can't tell, either. I guess all I'm trying to say is, hear him out. Don't prejudge him."

"Frankly, again, Sean?"

"Please."

"I also can't tell if you're telling me all this because you want me to think you're an upfront and honest guy…or because you *are* an upfront and honest guy."

"I'm just hoping you don't prejudge me just because my last name is Cleary. I know I can come off a bit, oh…"

"Slippery? Slick? Facile?"

He laughed. "Never argue with a woman with a word-a-day calendar."

"Tell you what…Sean. I learned on my job, sometimes painfully, not to get ahead of the evidence; let the evidence tell the story. I'll wait for the evidence. Fair enough? For both you and your father."

He did seem genuinely pleased with that. "Fair enough."

Home for a weekend from her first internship at a Boston law firm, Shiloh had confessed to her father to being staggered by the amount of sheer bullshit that went on between client and attorney.

To which he laughed. Hard.

Something I learned as a cop, Sweets: everybody lies, her father had told her. *Everybody. Even good people, even when they're trying to tell the truth, they'll lie about* something.

Why?

Sweets, people lie for two reasons: to protect themselves, or to protect somebody they care about. But everybody lies about something.

The Cleary estate was a few heavily wooded fenced-off acres at the tip of a small peninsula. The story behind the house – at least the one Shiloh had grown up hearing – was that it had originally been built by a Greek immigrant who'd come to Portland after the Second World War and scored big in the fishing industry during its more robust days. He brought the rest of his family over from Greece, wanted a house big enough for his substantial clan, and designed one himself. Unfortunately, the Greek had more ambition than taste and the result was something between a Greek temple and a blockhouse: big, imposing, and utterly without grace or grandeur. The Greek gave the estate a measure of privacy by bordering the peninsula – except for a gap facing the bay – with cypress trees. Although the peninsula had no name on maps, the cypress trees which had, since then, grown into a rather stately curtain, got the locals in the habit of referring to it as Cypress Point.

There were a number of stories about how the Cleary family came into possession of the estate, none of them flattering, all of them, in one form or another, involving forcing the Greek family out and breaking their fishing business to do it.

Sean Cleary moored the cruiser at a small dock near the grounds behind the house. He helped Shiloh ashore and led her toward a semicircular solarium attached to the rear of the house. Inside the solarium, Sean left her while he went off to get his father.

The room was spacious, high-ceilinged with a Tiffany-styled dome, furnished with pieces of white, cushioned wicker. Despite the sun glowing through the floor-to-ceiling windows, the large room didn't warm easily, and Shiloh found herself pulling her flannel close about her.

"Ah, Miss Vail! Thank you for coming. I appreciate it, especially since there was no advance notice."

The voice was soft edged but not soft, clear, almost soothing. While Sean Cleary, Sr. was, as far as Shiloh knew, a peer of her father, they were night-and-day in appearance. As he had aged, her father's diet of crap, cigarettes, and a regular (if moderate) intake of cheap liquor and beer had done the damage one might expect - blotchy face, bloated body, aching joints. But Cleary Senior was slender, handsome even for his years, and where Shiloh's father's hair had become a wiry, thinning scraggle which hardly ever saw a comb after retirement, this man boasted a full, thick topping of white hair in a dignified rearward sweep. He was dressed to suit his looks: a thick, woolen shawl-collared cardigan over a starched white dress shirt, pressed corduroy slacks…but the shoes.

Not leather, but soft suede slip-ons, easy to manage, easy on the feet. The cane with which he walked, explained it. His left foot dragged slightly, and when he smiled at Shiloh, she saw the left side of his face didn't match the movements of his right. *A stroke.*

"I had a space on my calendar, so why not?"

A soft laugh. "Good one." He nodded toward the hulking figure she hadn't at first noticed standing in the shadow of the archway leading from the solarium to the house. Shiloh couldn't make him out well: the figure of a bouncer, broad in the shoulders but beer-bellied, a beard, dark hair pulled back in a short ponytail. Black T-shirt, black denims, black Durango boots. She knew the type; more than a few criminal cases had come through her firm featuring these kinds of characters. Rough types who wanted the world to know they were rough types. Sometimes it was a pose, sometimes it wasn't. Not being able to tell the difference was often what had some poor hospital patient bringing such cases to Shiloh's firm. You usually didn't know the difference until that point. "This is my other son, Aidan."

Shiloh gave him a nod of hello, but there was no motion of acknowledgment from the man in the shadows.

"Would you mind if we talk here?" Cleary Senior said. "It's getting to that time of day when this becomes my favorite room in the house."

There was just the slightest of lisps when he spoke. His tongue had, evidently, been touched by the stroke as well. And this close, she could see the lid on his left eye sagged, the eye was foggy. "No problem."

He nodded at her to walk along toward two peacock-styled chairs by a glass-topped wicker coffee table, the chairs angled to partly face each other, partly to face the arc of the solarium's rear which looked out through that gap in the cypress curtain toward the bay. "It's that amber light you get in late autumn. Come sunset, it's a better picture than television."

It was, she thought, a lovely view: Great and Little Diamond Islands to the left, Peaks to the right, backlit with that warm, almost orange light Cleary had referred to. She could imagine the panorama under a sky going fiery red to mauve to a deep purple leading to a star-filled night.

"It tends to get a little chilly out here, so I've had something prepared. Is there something else you'd like? Coffee? Espresso? Unless it's something exceptionally exotic, I'm sure we have the makings."

"Since you went to the trouble, whatever you prepared will be fine."

He beckoned to Sean Junior who'd been standing off to the side. "Sean, would you mind?" And then a flick of a finger toward the man in the archway. "Aidan, you can..." which was enough for him to retreat completely into the house, the sound of his boots slow and heavy on stone echoing back into the solarium. Shiloh half expected to hear the *chink-chink-chink* of spurs as he walked off.

"Please, sit." Sean Senior took the left-hand seat so his fully functioning right side faced her. "Excuse me," and he fidgeted over something uncomfortable in his pocket. He fished out a cell phone, set it on the table. "Damned thing. But business doesn't allow me to go anywhere without it."

"I understand."

"I hope this isn't presumptuous, but would you mind if I called you Shiloh? You see, I was around when you were a baby."

"I didn't know that. I don't remember."

"Yes, of course you wouldn't. But you've grown up as beautiful as I thought you would. Your father kept me up on how you were doing, and we were all always very proud of you. Your father was the first of us to have a child. I think that's why, in a way, we felt a kind of shared investment here -" and he touched his chest "- in how you did. We all watched you grow up, at least your early years, the years you don't remember. That's why I still think of you as 'Shiloh' and it's hard for me to get my head around 'Ms. Vail'."

"I understand. Feel free."

He paused, his eyes lowered, something touching him. Then he brightened: "So! How has your return to Portland been? I mean, considering the circumstances."

"It is what it is. Lot of changes."

"Too many?"

"Depends on your point of view, I guess."

"True." His cell phone vibrated, rattling against the table's glass top. He made no move toward the phone.

"Shouldn't you get that?" Shiloh asked. "You know; business."

"You're more important right now, Shiloh."

She nodded, acting flattered. "I suppose you want to talk to me about whatever arrangement you had with my father? The thing Sean spoke to me about yesterday?"

He dismissed this with a smile, lazily flapping a hand as if shooing the topic away. "Actually, no. That business was a long time ago, I was just tidying up some old paperwork. It's not important anymore. I'm sorry if it troubled you in any way."

"I haven't really had the time to give it much attention, so…"

"Ah, here we go!"

Sean Junior had returned carrying a silver tray. There were two mugs of steaming hot chocolate hand a tray of assorted mini scones. There was also a small, uncapped bottle of Baileys Irish Cream.

"That's real Swiss chocolate," Sean Senior bragged. He reached for the Baileys, poured a dollop into his mug. "I wasn't sure if you indulged, but I've found a shot of Baileys does even more to ward off the chill. And, in my case, the aches and pains that go with my years."

"Don't mind if I do," she said, and he leaned forward to similarly dose her drink.

"Sean, if you wouldn't mind…" and Sean Junior disappeared down the same archway as his brother.

Shiloh held her mug under her nose. The aroma was chocolaty rich. "I went to see my mother today."

"Ah, Delia," he sighed.

"I detect a lack of fondness."

"Delia didn't take to your father's old friends after she married Eddie."

"Old friends - see, that came as a surprise to me. And now you're telling me you were around when I was a baby. She tells me that you and my father went back to his Navy days."

He smiled broadly. "Oh, further than that! There were three of us; we came up through school together. We were so close, I used to call us the Three Musketeers, although some of our parents, well, you know the things young boys can get into. Some of them thought we were more like the Three Stooges. My father's preferred descriptive for us was 'knuckleheads'." Affecting a gravely voice and Irish brogue: 'Wha'd yoo knoockleheads git inna this time?'" He chuckled warmly at the memory. "How's the hot chocolate?"

"I'm having flashes of yodelers and the Alps."

"Good! The scones, they're made for me special by a baker in Portland. I had them done just for this meeting. At least have a bite."

Shiloh picked a blueberry scone and took a small bite. It was one of the better pieces of pastry she'd tasted in a while, nicely flaky inside with just a ghost of sweetness to it.

"Good?" When she nodded, he added, "Glad you like it. Now, as I was saying, the three of us, we all decided to join the Navy together. My father had some influence, he was able to see we were assigned to the same ship. Our idea, like a lot of young men in Maine then and now, was that there had to be a bigger and more interesting world than Portland, and this was our way to see it."

Shiloh gestured toward the waters of Casco Bay. "Sailing the seven seas."

Sean Senior chuckled. "Well, mostly just the one. We had visions of cruising the oceans of the world on a warship; a destroyer, a carrier, something suitable for young warrior adventurers. Instead, we were on a bucket called the *Charleston*. Amphibious transport, although most of the time we were with her, she was hauling all kinds of equipment here and there. We were the Navy's version of Mayflower Moving."

"Did you manage to see any of that big, wide world?"

"A piece of it. We did the east coast as far as New Orleans, some trips into the Caribbean. Once, we had to deliver some cargo to the Sandinistas in Central America. An actual military mission!

"We did get across the Atlantic once. Saw Greenland then Iceland, where I saw seals lounging on the docks at Reykjavik. Their barking kept me up at night.

"The best time was when we were docked in Portsmouth – that's England – for about a week. We didn't know if we'd ever get to Europe again, so we wanted to see as much of it as possible. We hit London, took the ferry to France, ran through Belgium and Holland. I'm sorry, The Netherlands, as I was corrected many times. The boys' favorite was London, probably because everybody spoke English which made it easier to talk to the ladies. Sort of. It was harder to understand than you might think."

She laughed. "But it wasn't your favorite?"

Sean Senior sat back in his chair, and his face went soft with the memory. "Oh, I enjoyed it all, but my personal favorite was The Netherlands. I used to think our fall colors were impressive, but the Dutch tulip fields... Shiloh, the colors were so vivid... Nature's quilt. So beautiful I almost cried. No exaggeration. I took pictures but it was impossible to do it justice."

"And after seeing the world, you all came back."

He shook his head, seemingly just as surprised at his decision as she was. "It was different for each of us. They missed home. It's funny; you don't think you will, you think you'll get out there and just want to keep going. But after four years, they wanted to come home. For some people, at a certain point, the familiar is a comfort."

"That was them. But you?"

His voice changed. There was a certain... Was it sadness? "It was always assumed I'd work for my father and then take over the business when he passed. And so..." He gestured at the house around them.

"And so. Not exactly breaking rocks for a living."

He smiled at that. "I suppose. Anyway, they joined the police, I went to work for my father, but we three stayed close."

"Until Delia."

He shrugged. "I can understand it. Look, she was a nice woman, a good wife and mother, but I've seen this with other wives, even with my own wife; the husband gets together with old friends, and they suddenly seem to forget they're adults with responsibilities. I can't say I blamed her. We still managed to keep meeting in town, which didn't seem to bother her as much; out of sight, out of mind, I guess."

"But after they divorced, I don't remember seeing you come around."

He nodded, admitting guilt. "I know. I guess we'd gotten in the habit of not seeing each other so much by then. We each got married, had our families, work... It got harder and harder to get together. But make no mistake; I considered your father one of my closest friends. See, we were like brothers. We grew up together, served together... It may sound like some kind of movie cliché, but it's true. When we did get together, even if it had been months since the last time, it was like we'd just seen each other the day before."

"You didn't come to the wake. Your son said you were too busy."

Another guilty nod. "I made myself busy. My wife died about five years ago."

"I'm sorry."

"Cancer." He looked out at the bay, the sun slowly going more soft gold than yellow as the afternoon wore on. "I know what that looks like, and I didn't want to see your father like that. My understanding is you weren't at the wake either."

It was her turn to look out at the bay's water. "It seems, Mr. Cleary, in that respect, we had something in common."

Cleary Senior's cell phone rattled against the glass again, and, again, he ignored it, giving her a smile saying she was his priority.

She took a sip of the hot chocolate, the warm fluid and the Baileys giving off its own glow as it went down. "While I'm enjoying hearing about my father's globetrotting days, and some day it might be nice to get together and I could hear more -"

He nodded, knowing where she was going. "I'd like that, too, but yes, yes, you want to get to the purpose of my having you here."

"I wouldn't mind."

He took a last sip from his mug, set it down where it lit on the glass top with a quiet clink. He sat back in his chair, turned a warm, sad smile toward her. "When your father got sick – and it broke my heart, Shiloh, because I knew where things were going – he and I would sometimes talk on the phone. About you, Zoe, Jericho. His main concern, as it always was, was the welfare of all of you. Your father, as I'm sure you know, was not a wealthy man. Toward the end…" And the memory seemed to pain him. He took a breath and pushed on: "When he could still think clearly, he asked me to see if there was something I might be able to do for all of you. He knew I was, as they say, well-fixed. I promised him… I *promised* him…I would." He paused, looking to see if she understood these were not just words, but there was something behind them. Then, "As you also know, the bulk of his estate is the house."

"Yes."

"I'd like to buy it."

"You want to buy my father's house?"

"I assume – and correct me if I'm wrong – that none of you have use for it. You're living down in Washington, I know your sister Zoe and her family have a place in South Portland, your brother, well, pardon me, but from what I know about Jericho, it's doubtful he could keep the place up.

"I know the housing market on the island is depressed. Terribly depressed. I would not want to take advantage of Eddie's children, so I've based my offer on what that house would bring in the best neighborhoods in Portland, say the East or West End, or Rosemont. Plus, ten percent. I have no problem with you conferring with a realtor to confirm my estimate."

Shiloh took a quick guess and thought that meant something in the mid-six-figure range…at the very least. It took her a few seconds to come back from that stunning math to ask, "Why?"

"Why that price? Or why do I want the house?"

"You've been buying up property all over the island."

A sly smile. "Yes, I know you've been to the Register of Deeds. My father built up a network of contacts in the city. I've inherited that network, even added to it a bit."

"You haven't answered my question. You were the one who originally built up the island."

"Actually, that was my father. Although it was my idea. When we were in the Navy, whenever we passed through Portland, we had to go past that island."

"St. Aggie's." They exchanged a grin over the shared knowing of the island's history.

"Yes, I thought you might've heard about that. That…house…was the only thing on the island in those days. I looked at the communities that had been built up on Peaks Island and Long Island and I thought, why couldn't the same thing be done on St. Aggie's? I pitched that to my father and…" He waved a kind of *voila* gesture with one hand.

"But now?"

"Well, it worked for a while. Then I suppose the novelty wore thin."

"I'm guessing you have something else in mind."

"A recreational area. Small golf course, water park, maybe some rides, maybe a spa. Something less pricey than what they have on Chebeague, or the way Peaks used to be before it went full residential. Your lot is the largest on the island, so, of course, it's important to the project. And because you're Eddie's children, your welfare is important to me, thus the premium offer."

It seemed a way too innocent explanation for the man's interest which in no way explained the break-in of her father's shed, Henry McNair's death and her father's missing file from McNair's office, all of which Shiloh couldn't help but think was somehow connected to Cleary Senior's interest in her father's house.

"There's a couple of hurdles, Mr. Cleary."

He nodded. "Always is."

"For one thing, the will has yet to be probated. My father's attorney told me that could take –"

"I know how long that takes in Maine, but, as I said, I have contacts."

"I'm sure you do."

"I could probably have the will probated as early as the end of the year."

She nodded, impressed. "And, of course, I'd have to talk it over with my brother and sister. The will gives us joint ownership."

"Of course."

"The biggest problem –"

An understanding smile. "Yes, the lack of a provenance on the house. As I said, I know quite a few people. Along with this offer goes my promise that any difficulties arising from the sale in that regard will be *my* difficulties. You sell me the house and any issues arising therefrom come with the sale."

"This is all very generous of you."

"As I said, Shiloh: we were like brothers. I told your father I'd do what I could, and this is what I can do. Think about it, talk about it with your brother and sister. If we can do this before the end of the year, I get some tax advantages out of that, but if not, however long as it takes you all to reach a decision is fine." He stood, pocketing his cell phone as he did so: the meeting was over. "I hope you'll let me do this for you. For all of you."

Cleary Senior had Shiloh follow him into the main house looking for Cleary Junior. As soon as they emerged on the other side of the archway into a cavernous main hall, she could hear raised voices, unintelligibly watery echoes in the unfriendly acoustics of the hall. She could make out Cleary Junior's voice if not what he was saying. The other voice was low, gravely.

She looked to Cleary Senior who had suddenly picked up his pace, his cane *clacking* faster on the marble floor, his face gone to a cold anger. He was aiming for a pair of partly opened oak doors. As they got closer, Shiloh could make out snippets of an angry back-and-forth.

Cleary Junior: "…not how we want to do business…"

Then the other voice she presumed to belong to Aidan: "…isn't business. You can afford to be a pussy about this, it's not your ass…the one's gotta make the trip to Warren!"

"…you think Dad…"

"Granddad wouldn't stand for this limp-dick bullshit…"

Shiloh and Cleary Senior were at the doors. He stopped, turned to her: "Would you please…?" beckoning her to go into the sitting room on the other side of the hall. After he saw her step into the room, he pushed open one of the doors with the foot of his cane.

"What's the hell's the matter with the two of you?" She was surprised at how that cottony voice of his disappeared in a clap of thunder. *"Isn't there's a grain of common sense between you?"* and he slammed the doors shut behind him.

After that, she heard only Cleary Senior's voice, no longer bellowing but loud and firm, the words unclear through the heavy doors.

Then…silence. A beat. Two. One of the doors opened slowly. Cleary Senior emerged first, looking still angry but drained. "My apologies," he said to Shiloh, beckoning her to come out into the hall. "If you ever have children, I would advise girls."

Sean Junior followed, red-faced and slumped.

"My son will take you home. Again, I'm sorry you had to witness this…unpleasantness. You'll let me know when you and the others reach a decision?"

"Soon as," Shiloh said and began to follow Sean Junior back into the solarium.

"Shiloh," Sean Senior called after her.

She stopped and turned. The old man seemed to search for words, gave up and settled for, "It was good to see you after all this time. You remind me of a happy time. Thank you…for coming."

"How'd it go?" Cleary Junior had been quiet, humbled she thought, as they'd climbed back aboard the cruiser, and he helmed them back into the bay.

"I'm wondering."

"About?"

"How much your father meant, or whether he's just the best bullshit artist I've ever met."

A rueful smile. "Sometimes it's both at once. I've been with him my whole life and I can't always tell."

"I especially liked the touch with the cell phone to make me feel important. That was cute. What was that mess going on between you and your brother?"

His face clouded. "Brother stuff. Look…" He made a point of not looking at her, of keeping his eyes fixed on the waters ahead.

"Yes?"

"If you're walking down the street and you see my brother walking your way, I advise you to cross the street."

They rode in silence for a bit. The sky over the bay was taking on those darker, more textured shades Cleary Senior cherished so much.

"Your brother," Shiloh ventured. "He was the guy who spiked one of the Cole family boats, wasn't he? And who broke into my father's shed the other night."

"What shed?" If it wasn't honest surprise, it was a pretty good facsimile.

"You're going to tell me you didn't know anything about that?"

"I rarely know what my brother is up to. I don't want to know. But if I had to guess, probably to both."

"Why does your father want my father's house so badly?"

"Didn't he tell you? He has this project -"

"Yeah, yeah, right, but there's a lot of crap going on that's not explained by somebody just wanting to buy a house. Do you know who Henry McNair was? He was my father's attorney. He's dead, and he didn't slip on a bar of soap."

"Christ..."

"Could that be your brother?"

His mouth opened, but then he shook his head, seeming not to know, not wanting to know, hoping it wasn't.

"What's going on, Sean?"

"I don't know. Really. All my father's told me about is this recreation thing he wants to build on the island. You should understand something: my father is faced with a dilemma wrapped in a paradox...or maybe a paradox wrapped in a dilemma."

"That was clear as a foggy day."

"You can tell my father has, um, well, health issues."

"Looks like a stroke."

"About a year after our mother died. Serious, but not awful, but it's gotten him to thinking about what happens after..."

"After he's gone."

"It was always assumed, without anybody saying anything, maybe just because I'm the oldest, that when the time came, I'd be the one to take over the business. That's why he sent me to U-Conn. It was supposed to help 'groom' me for that day. Since his stroke, he's been more forceful about it, showing me the ropes, teaching me who all the players are inside and outside the business, which strings to pull, which buttons to push. Truth is, I could step in tomorrow if I had to. Problem is, I don't want the job. But Aidan…"

"Aidan does. But your dad doesn't think he's up to it?"

"That's an understatement. He's pretty sure that not only will Aidan run the business into the ground, but wind up buried up to his eyeballs in legal troubles to boot. Aidan learned all the wrong lessons from Granddad. He thinks any way you get what you want that doesn't land you in jail – not because it was honest but because you managed not to get caught - is perfectly fine. He thinks that's…*manly*," which he accompanied with a grand eyeroll.

"Cain and Abel."

Another rueful grin. "Something like that."

"What is it you'd rather do?"

Sean Junior put on a dopey smile, began to sway at the wheel, turned into very un-PC archetypal lisping gay artiste: "I have alwayth felt I was meant for the dahnth," and he did an absolutely awful plie, so bad he almost lost his balance. "The bal-*lay* hath alwayth called to me," and he shot out a leg as if he was standing at the barre, "but fathah would have none of that! He would pothitively have dithowned me."

She laughed, so did he, then it grew quiet. "C'mon, seriously."

"I don't know. I grew up in a family where it was in the air: Cleary follows Cleary. It never occurred to me to think of anything else. What's so funny?"

"You'd be surprised how much you have in common with Ben Cole."

He puzzled over that a bit, then seemed to get it. "It's probably not my place to ask, but are you two...?"

"It's not your place to ask." But she decided to give him some slack: "I told you; we go back a long way. We're friends."

"I only ask because -"

"I know why you're asking."

"Would it ever be possible to sit someplace, like for coffee or a bite, where you could forget my last name is Cleary, and go from there?"

"I could always see you dahnce the bal-*lay*. I'm only in town for a few days. But...maybe."

Cleary Junior smiled. "I'll take maybe."

It was only late afternoon when Shiloh got back to her father's house, but the sun was already low, shadows long. Inside, there were no lights in the front room, but a low fire crackled and flickered in the fireplace, outlining Zoe sitting quite still in a chair. On the coffee table in front of her was her father's bottle of cheap whisky, a half-empty glass cradled in both her hands. Zoe's eyes were fixed on a package, a rectangular box maybe a foot tall sitting on end on the table. She seemed oblivious to Shiloh's entrance.

"You ok, Zee? What's the matter? What's that?"

"Hm?" She shook off her daze, took a sip from her glass. She gestured at the package. "Well, it's, uh...it's Dad. Came in on the package boat while you were out. Teddy brought it up. He also brought this." She held up a yellow hooded oilskin jacket that had been sitting on the floor next to her chair. "He says you're gonna need it. Looks like another storm's comin' up the coast." She let the jacket drop back to the floor, her eyes went back to the package.

Shiloh sat across from her. Zoe gestured toward the bottle, Shiloh shook her head no. "You didn't open it."

"I, uh…I couldn't."

Shiloh got out of her chair, brought back a steak knife from the kitchen. The mailing label had the return address of a "cremation service" in Portland. She cut away the packing paper, the tape sealing the box, and pulled out a plain, stainless-steel urn. It wasn't heavy; ten, twelve pounds at best, and she guessed some of that was the weight of the metal. She set the urn on the table and tossed the box and wrappings in the fireplace. The flames picked up at that, cast a rising glow on the metal cannister. She dropped back into her chair.

The two of them sat quietly for a moment, looking at the urn.

Zoe took another sip of her drink. "So that's it."

"Yeah."

Her sister frowned. "What're we supposed to, you know, what do you do with…"

"I don't know. He never said anything to you? "

Zoe shook her head.

"Me neither, and he didn't leave any instructions with his attorney."

"My sister-in-law keeps Sasha's ashes on her mantlepiece."

"Wasn't Sasha a German shepherd?"

"I know. I'm just sayin'."

"Well," and Shiloh pulled herself out of her chair, "until we think of something better… If it's good enough for Sasha…" She set the urn on the mantlepiece, stood there for a moment, leaving her hands on the urn, the rising flames warming her middle. She gave the urn a small pat and dropped back into her chair. "We still going to see Ben play tonight?"

Zoe drained her glass, set it down on the table and stood. "That's the plan. Hey, maybe Dad said something to him." She let out a long, tired breath and headed for the stairs. "I'm going to crash for a bit. I don't seem to do late nights as easy as I used to."

"Zoe, Sean Cleary – the dad – wants to buy the house. At some point, the three of us need to sit and have a discussion. And I saw Delia."

That stopped Zoe at the foot of the stairs. "And?"

"Can't say we mended fences."

Zoe shrugged, unsurprised.

"Hey, Zee, you ever been to Warren? Was wondering what's up there."

Another shrug. "People. Feral cats. How'd I know?"

"I mean is there anything up there worth seeing?"

"Only on visiting days."

"Visiting days?"

"Yeah. That's where the state prison is."

Zoe trudged up the stairs, and Shiloh reached for the bottle on the table and Zoe's glass to pour herself a drink.

Maybe because it had been the long day, moving from murder to estranged mother to an old friend of the family Shiloh didn't know they'd had, or maybe it was that shot of Baileys with Cleary Senior and a glass - well, two - of her dad's awful whisky, but she had dozed off in her chair. How long she'd been out, she didn't know. It was dark when she blinked awake, but it was November in Maine which meant it could've been anywhere from five in the afternoon to the middle of the night.

But then she saw it couldn't have been very long: the fire was still going although it was quite low, mostly iridescent embers.

She took her father's urn down from the mantle, set it down on the table, and slumped back into her chair. She poured herself another short drink, touched the glass to the urn in salute and downed it.

And then...

Thinking it wasn't a good idea but doing it anyway, she leaned forward, took the urn, set it between her legs and began unscrewing the lid. The lid free, she hesitated a moment, debating just how stupid a move this might be, then set the lid down and looked into the steel cannister.

In the gloom of the front room, the low light from the dying fire didn't reach inside the urn. There was just blackness. She shook the urn slightly, heard a sound like moving sand. She reached behind her to the standing lamp overlooking her chair, pulled the chain for the light, and tilted the urn to light the inside. Sounded like sand, and that's what it looked like - a few pounds of grayish sand.

She remembered Zoe's words: *So that's it.*

A lifetime. A lifetime and everything that went with it: laughs and tears, things done and not done, hugs and kisses and storming out of the house angry, a hundred memories, a thousand. *So that's it.*

She screwed the lid back on the urn, turned off the light, sat there hugging the urn close, and for the first time since Zoe had called with the news their father had passed, she let the sobs come.

Farmington was about an hour and a half up U.S. 2, a good way into the Maine boonies. Maybe forty-sixty minutes from the New Hampshire state line, depending on how heavy one's foot was on the gas.

The three of them – Shiloh, Zoe, and Anthony – sat abreast in the cab of Anthony's tank of a Sierra 3500. "What does he do with this thing?" Shiloh had asked her sister as she pulled her up into the cab alongside her, "Drive through walls?"

After they passed Lewiston, the highway narrowed down to a single, twisting lane each way and Shiloh realized how spoiled she'd become driving around the great metropolitan glob running unbroken from Boston to Washington: wide highways always well lit, if also always well packed. Even with his high beams on, Shiloh felt Anthony's lights didn't do near enough to cut into the night to suit her, especially at the speed her brother-in-law liked; Anthony's testosterone seemed to amp up considerably behind the wheel of his pick-up.

After Lewiston, they rarely passed another vehicle, and the small towns they cruised through were quiet, tired looking. The mills had kept this part of Maine alive at one time, but most of the mills were gone now, had been for years. Some towns had survived by refurbishing their centers with cozy eateries and quaint shops. Some just sat withering.

They took the bridge over the Androscoggin River at Livermore Falls, the spray from the falls picking up moonlight to create a softly glowing aura over the river. After the bridge, they paralleled the river for a bit, went past the crumbling hulk of one of the last of the big riverside mills which had been the town's heart, looking even more ghostly, more dead under the moon's pale luminescence.

Farmington was a college town, home to one of the regional campuses of the University of Maine. But it was a small campus, not enough to give Farmington what one might call a throbbing nightlife. "Downtown" was just a block in each direction around the crossroads of U.S. 2 and Maine 43 around which were a cluster of shops all closed up for the night, a single pizzeria, two churches, and five bar/restaurants.

"We've been up here to see Ben play before," Zoe said. "One time I got to talking to one of the kids from the school, asked him where he was from. He told me he was from some small town about an hour north of here. I said, 'I thought *this* was a small town.' He said, 'Nah, this is where we'd come on weekends!'"

One of the five drinking establishments – Tuck's, where Ben's band was playing – wasn't so much a restaurant with a bar, as it was a bar offering a couple kinds of burgers and finger foods.

Shiloh didn't think it so much a bar as a saloon. The façade was English pub, but the place was built like a bowling alley, long and narrow, not trying to look like anything more than a place you went to drink, with a bar running most of the length on one side, a handful of tables along the other, and a beer menu behind the bar ten times longer than the food menu. Men wearing Stetsons and spurs would've looked quite at home there, but, as an equal replacement, among the handful of listless drinkers, were a couple of dudes in leather and Durango boots to go with the Harleys parked at the curb.

One of the Harley dudes was talking about something with a guy in work twills. The only part of it Shiloh could pick out was from Mr. Work Twills: "I don't know nothin' 'bout that stuff. Ask me how long it takes to incinerate a cubic yard of wet trash, that's somethin' I can talk about."

Ben's band – just a three-piece of Ben on guitar; a lanky, tattooed kid on bass; another kid, stubby with an embarrassingly patchy adolescent beard working a minimal drum kit – was jammed into a small space between the front door and a wall.

The small crowd was a disappointment for Shiloh. The mood in the truck on the ride up had been melancholy to say the least as she'd recounted her visits to McNair's office, her mother, and her conversation with Sean Cleary, Sr. And then, of course, there'd been the urn. She'd been hoping a taste of bar party might pick them all up. She felt worse for Ben and his cramped trio, playing up a storm to a mostly empty barroom while also trying not to crash into each other in their small space. She said as much to Zoe.

"You wait," her sister said. "Come nine o'clock, they have a happy half-hour, and the college kids come flooding in here like a dam busted."

Which is exactly what happened.

After their first rounds, the young people were all, "Yeah!" and "Awright!" as Ben's group did an impressive job working through a nonstop mix of classic rock, country rock, and contemporary – a spread that, at one point or another, pushed the right buttons in everybody, from university literature major to Harley-riding road gypsy.

As Ben came to the end of his first set: "One more song before we take a break. This one's a request," and now he was looking directly at Shiloh.

I don't care what he said today, he's not giving up. But she wasn't angry about it. She wasn't quite sure how she felt as she tried to ignore the teasing looks from her sister.

Ben went into a cover of Niki Lane's "First High," a mid-tempo rocker about a woman going back to her hometown, but the lyrics were gender-free enough in their references that they worked just as well coming out of Ben's mouth.

Every "first" he touched in the lyrics brought his eyes back to Shiloh. *I shouldn't be looking back at him,* she kept telling herself, but then feeling if she didn't, it would be a colder response than she felt was deserved.

By then, she was a couple of beers into the night, a couple more than she knew was probably good for her for one reason or another. The beer and the mood in the bar loosened the reins on a lot of memories. It hadn't been that long ago – had it? – that she'd been one of these college kids, up for good tunes and cheap beer. She'd come home from college on vacations and sat in hot, crowded places like this watching a young Ben Cole and his motley band wail away, Ben in those days thinking he was another Dave Grohl, aping Grohl's windmilling guitar strikes, his equally imitative long hair stuck in strands to his sweaty face.

If I could go back… she had said to Ben that afternoon, if she could let the years and the distance and everything that went with them fall away, back to when everything – even love – was new -.

But you can't.

The set was over, Ben grabbed a beer from the bar, came to their table, introduced his bandmates. "What'd you think?" he asked Shiloh.

She pushed the memories away and gave him a smile. "Not bad."

"Not bad?"

"Ok, you guys were pretty good. Say, who made that request?"

"A little voice in my head."

They heard excited voices from outside spurring a movement of drink-carrying customers out to the street. Curious, Shiloh looked to Ben for an explanation.

"Couldn't be," he said, his face eager, anticipating. He took her hand, and she let him lead her outside.

Most of the drinkers were crowded at the curb, some wandering out into the empty street, all looking skyward at vast curtains of shimmering blue-green lights rippling through the night sky: the aurora borealis.

"We don't get it very often," Ben said, "and when we do it's almost always further north. You must be special — it showed up for you."

She felt him squeeze her hand. She looked over to him, the aurora giving his face an ethereal quality, something not of this place, but from a place out of time. He turned to look down at her, colored on one side by the warm glow from the bar's lights, on the other by the celestial hues from above, the weathering and windburn disappearing, and for a moment, the clock wound back.

She stretched up, not needing to say anything for him to bend a bit until they kissed.

PART FOUR:

True Things

Eleven.

"So, how do we do this?" Zoe asked. "Work top to bottom? Side to side?"

"This is where my paralegal organizational expertise comes into play."

"Ok, expert, what do we do?"

"I don't know, just grab a bag."

Shiloh was with Zoe in the attic. Since St. Aggie's was essentially a huge rock covered with just a few feet of earth, none of the houses on the island had a cellar. Consequently, attics, garages, sheds, even porches - especially enclosed porches - served as family warehouses.

The attic seemed as good a place as any to start going through the more disposable bits of their father's estate; maybe better since that wasn't the only reason to be poking through the bulging boxes and stuffed trash bags. Even though they'd interrupted the shed intruder, Shiloh had the feeling he hadn't found whatever it was he was looking for, yet he'd exposed enough stored junk that she had a fairly good idea what had been stowed there, so she could, for the moment, bypass it. The attic, on the other hand, was virgin territory.

As kids, they'd spent many a winter or stormy day up there, so many her father had done what he could, with his limited expertise, to make it a comfy play area, insulating it, dangerously heating it with cheap space heaters in the winter, running exposed wiring for a few bare-bulb light fixtures. One year after Christmas, he'd taken the strings of colored lights from their living room Christmas tree and strung them among the rafters, his only explanation after he was done a simple, "That's better, isn't it?"

Over the years, as the amount of *stuff* accumulated, there were enough boxes, trash bags, milk crates, plastic storage containers stuffed with clothes, toys, board games, old kitchen utensils, small appliances, pots and pans, house decorations for every major holiday, and old bedsheets covering odd pieces of banged-up furniture to make mazes, forts, and a walled off lounge complete with an ancient portable TV. The history of American home entertainment was jumbled together in one corner: stereo with milk crates of vinyl albums, 8-track player with carrying box of cartridges, cassette player with storage rack of cassettes, and a VHS player with more milk crates of VHS videotapes. The plastic playhouse shaped like a castle, which had hosted many a tea party with water-for-tea and Oreos, was still up there and intact.

"Do you think we can sell any of this stuff?" Zoe asked.

"Maybe to a museum."

They started working their way through the mess, separating items into piles: all clothes together, toys together and so on. Shiloh found a few boxes containing what must've been damned near every school project, paper, and report card they'd ever brought home, from a small child's construction paper Thanksgiving card with its drawing of a turkey built around the outline of a little hand, to their high school diplomas.

"Good God," Shiloh said, rifling through her childhood academia with what would become a recurring refrain, "didn't he ever throw anything away?"

There was an oddity to the way this stuff had been boxed which, after her visit to her mother, didn't surprise Shiloh. All of the school things belonging to Zoe and Jericho were boxed together; Shiloh's were boxed separately.

"Hey, uh, Shy?" From the teasing tone, Shiloh knew what was coming. "So, uh, ya know, like, what was goin' on with you 'n' Ben last night?"

"Nothing."

"Really? Nothing? 'Cause -"

"Too much beer, ok?"

"Really? Too much beer? 'Cause -"

"Not talking about it, Zee."

"He looked pretty good up there last night, don'tcha think?"

"Not talking about it!"

Truth was, Shiloh had to admit to herself, she didn't know what was going on between her and Ben that night. Nostalgia? Too much beer? Too much -. Too much what?

Thinking thankfully evaporated when she popped open a plastic storage bin and found her father's Class A police dress uniform. A musty smell came up from the wool, the cloth felt rough under her fingertips. It came to her, a picture of him, not toward the end of his career with buttons straining across his belly, unable to hitch the collar button around his swollen neck, but that time he'd come to her college graduation brandishing his new sergeant's stripes. She picked up one of the sleeves, her thumb caressing the brass cuff button.

"Did you spend much time with Dad?" Shiloh asked.

"After he got sick, I was out here a lot. But before that… It was hard, I mean after I married Anthony, and we got the house in South Portland. And especially after the kids were born… It's not like, let's take a drive out to see Grandpa, 'n' you hop in the car. Hey, you 'member – I think it was when you turned sixteen – he took us all down to Boston?"

Shiloh laughed. "Damn, we practically ate our way through Fanueil Hall!"

"Yeah! Yeah! What was that boat? We took a tour of that big ol' boat?"

"The *Constitution*."

"Of all of us, I think he was the one got the biggest kick out of that! Like a big kid on that boat!"

Then the laughing faded. Zoe sat on the dusty floor near where Shiloh was kneeling over the uniform bin. "Shy?"

There was no teasing tone now.

"Shy, why do you think he was different with you than with us?"

"Don't start that, Zee."

"I'm not tryin' to say somethin', Shy. I got kids, I know you love 'em all, but sometimes you get a feelin' for one, well, you feel different for each one -"

"Zee -"

"I'm just sayin' I always wondered why it turned out the way it did."

Shiloh let the sleeve drop back into the bin, pulled the cover back in place. "Because it did."

Shiloh stood, dusted off the knees of her jeans. Everywhere she looked there was something which brought back a memory; the attic was a museum of memories, and what she was now finding, so many of those memories brought with them questions which would never be answered because the answers were lost in those ashes in an urn on the mantlepiece downstairs.

She walked away from the piles, not wanting to touch those memories and questions for the moment. She went into the "lounge" – a wall of boxes and bags around a legless futon and some folding garden chairs with rusted metal frames. She plopped on the futon. She closed her eyes for a long moment, opened them and saw Zoe sitting across from her on one of the garden chairs, leaning forward, elbows on knees, fingers knitted together…waiting.

"I don't know if he ever said anything to you," Shiloh said, "but he told me to leave. I don't mean like he was kicking me out, nothing like that. Even back when I was looking at colleges, he told me to look out of state. He said it would be better for me."

"That's what I mean, Shy. He never even talked about college to us."

"Don't ask me why. There were times he was talking to me; I had no idea what he was talking about." They both smiled at the memory. "Remember? Dad would say something, like he was this wise, old sage, you'd give him a blank look – 'Dad, what the *hell* are you talking about?' – and he'd give you that look -"

"This one!" and Zoe mimed putting on a serious face while laying a hand on an imaginary body. "The hand on the shoulder -"

"Yes! Yes!"

Now imitating their father's grave-for-the-moment tone: "'Someday, Sweets, you'll understand'."

The laughter felt good. But as it always did, it passed.

"A lot of those 'some days' have passed, Zee, and I still don't know what was in his head half the time. I don't think Jay was sorry to see me go."

"Well, you know: Jay."

"Yeah, Jay. Maybe that's why he talked to me in a way he didn't talk to you two. Or am I wrong? Does Jay ever speak to you about our youthful bonding days? Running around the island together? Like those three kids in *To Kill a Mockingbird?* Because we didn't have them, Zee, and maybe that's why it was different with me."

Zoe nodded, understanding, but Shiloh could tell, not quite.

They sat silently for a moment, both of them sifting through resurfaced memories.

Then, Zoe said, "You were the only one who sat out there when he was having one of his moods."

"I was the only one who *wanted* to sit out there when he was having one of his moods."

Zoe grinned. "That's true. I remember one time I said to Jay, 'Me and you should go out there.' So, we go out to sit with Dad, Jay sits there for maybe a minute, then he gets up, goes, 'Well, I'm bored,' and goes inside to watch TV."

"God, what was it Mom called them? Dad's moods? She had a name for them."

Now Zoe was laughing, again. "She used to say, 'Oh, look out, one of your dad's clouds is rolling in!'"

And Shiloh was laughing, too. "Yeah, that's right! His 'clouds'! Then he'd pour himself a drink, that Godawful stuff, and go sit out on the porch for a while."

Then Zoe wasn't laughing. "What was that about? Did he ever say?"

It was coming back to Shiloh; sitting on the portico's front steps next to her father, his eyes fixed on something beyond the horizon. Sometimes he would put an arm around her, pull her close, his cheek rubbing against her hair. "When I got older, I just figured he saw a lot of crap on his job, that it was his way of decompressing."

"Maybe," but Zoe sounded unsure. "Ya know, after they made him retire, he still did it, went out there with his clouds, but it was more than one drink. I don't mean he was turning into a drunk or anything, nothin' like that, but it used to worry me, two, three drinks."

"He missed the job."

"I guess." Then, "I think he missed you."

"Zoe, I called, we FaceTimed -"

"I know, I know… but you know it's not the same."

Shiloh had nothing to say to that because she knew it was true; it wasn't the same. She grunted her way to her feet, took a deep, sighing breath, gave Zoe a look saying, We have to get on with this. Zoe nodded and they went back to sifting and sorting.

There was the Keurig she'd bought her father for a birthday, still in its box, never used. And the train set for under the Christmas tree he could never get to work properly. The polyester Santa Claus suit he -…

"Hey, Zee? Remember this?" and she held up the Santa suit.

"Oh, yeah! I 'member Mom waking us up to see him clomping around in the living room pretending to be Santa 'n' all we wanted to do was go back to bed. She was so pissed at us -"

"But was that Dad? I seem to remember…"

Their faces wrinkled as they searched back in time.

"I want to say it *was* Dad," Zoe said, still fishing through old, faded mental images, "but…"

"Yeah."

"Maybe this'll help. Look what I found!"

It was a looseleaf binder done up as a photo album. Someone had hand-wrapped the covers with silver foil wrapping paper, stuck a cloth square on the front on which was embroidered *Our Day*.

It was a make-shift wedding album.

The two of them shared a seat on an old hard plastic picnic cooler as they leafed through the album.

After some of the lavish spectacles she'd witnessed in Washington, Shiloh had almost forgotten how comparatively modest most Maine weddings were. The photos on the cellophane-wrapped pages were taken at the house. Her father wore his Class As, her mother a simple white dress, the "reception," such as it was, seemed to be a simple buffet of cake and soda and beer laid out on their dining room table.

"Damn," Zoe sighed, "did you ever see them that happy?"

"Not that I remember."

They leafed through the pages, reminiscing about their since-passed grandparents, the aunts-in-law and uncles-in-law and cousins they hadn't seen since their parents' divorce, and then there were some pictures of their father, obviously feeling his beers, clowning around with...

"Oh my God," Shiloh muttered and set a finger on a vaguely familiar face. "I swear that's Sean Cleary. Senior."

"Are you sure?"

"It was a long time ago, but it does kind of look like him."

She tapped another figure. He was a burly man in a policeman's uniform, built like a football lineman if on the short side, but with a wide face built for laughing. "Little Miss," she said under her breath.

"What?"

Shiloh shook her head, unsure where the phrase was coming from, only that seeing the burly man seemed to spark it. "I think this was Santa Claus."

Zoe looked closely at the photo and the same thought seemed to come to her. "Maybe. Mayyyybe. Do you know who he was?"

There was another picture of the three of them: her father in the middle, Sean Cleary, Sr. on one side, the big man on the other. She remembered what Cleary Sr. had said to her:

There were three of us…We were so close, I used to call us the Three Musketeers…

Shiloh peeled the cellophane off the page, flipped the photo over hoping there might be a note about the picture.

Nothing.

"Do you remember him, Shy?"

Little Miss…

"It's in there somewhere," she said, tapping her head, "but damned if I can pull it up."

"I'm kinda surprised he kept this," Zoe said, "You know; considering."

"Maybe he didn't even remember it was still up here."

She could see Zoe wanted to talk about it more, probe things, but Shiloh closed the book and put it aside. It was just a volume of more questions without answers.

They had most of the attic organized and Shiloh had begun at one end of the attic beginning to subdivide the piles into more specific groupings while Zoe was still poking around a last mound of bags and boxes jammed into a far corner, stuffed into the low space where the rafters came down to the edge of the floor.

"Hey, Shy! You think this could be something?"

Behind that last pile of stuff, Zoe had found a footlocker tucked as deeply against the slanted rafters as it could fit. A padlock held it shut. "You think we should open it?"

"I'm the executor, so I'm going to make an executive decision: go find me something I can bust this sucker open with."

A few minutes later, Zoe was back with a heavy screwdriver. Shiloh jammed the shaft of the screwdriver behind the footlocker's latch. *Let's see if all that money I spent on gym memberships was wasted.* Sitting on the floor, her feet braced against the footlocker - "C'mon, you little fucker…" – and with one last grunting pull she popped the entire lock assembly – latch, lock, padlock – free.

"Remind me not to arm wrestle you," Zoe said, as she lifted the footlocker's lid. "Holy shit! Shy, lookit this!"

Zoe disappeared behind a scooped-out cloud of shiny white silk. She stepped back and held a knee-length wedding dress against her front. "God*damn,* if I'd known this was up here, I coulda saved myself ninety-five bucks when I got married!"

It was, upon first glance, a simple piece; no fluff to the skirt, no puff to the sleeves, no train. Shiloh picked herself up from where she'd still been sitting on the floor, still breathing heavily from breaking the lock. Close up, Shiloh could see the only extravagance was pretty brocade work across the chest of the dress. The brocade was uneven enough to show itself to have been done by the hand of an amateur. Whoever owned the dress had decorated it herself.

And it was small. Delia had never been a full-figured woman, but neither had she ever been petite enough to fit in this dress. Shiloh went back to the wedding album.

"I wish there was a mirror up here," Zoe said. "I don't think I coulda fit in this, though. I'm not sure my big toe would fit in this. Why the hell would Dad keep Mom's wedding dress?"

Shiloh brought the wedding album over to show Zoe. "He didn't. That's not the same dress."

Which froze Zoe for a second. She set the dress aside and took the photo album for a better look.

"What's that?" Shiloh held up the dress showing two gold rings, one larger than the other, held to the breast of the dress by a single white thread. Wedding rings.

"Was there anything else in there?" and Shiloh nodded at the footlocker.

"Just this." Zoe reached into the footlocker and came out with a large, white, gossamer bow with trailing twin tails. "I don't know what this is."

"The fabric is organza. It's supposed to go here," and Shiloh touched the back of her head.

Wanting to get a better look at the rings, Shiloh started to tug at them to snap the holding thread…then decided she shouldn't. She stood under one of the bare light bulbs trying to get a better look inside the rings. "There's an inscription. In each of them."

Engraved in cursive inside the larger ring was *Tu as les clefs…*

And inside the smaller ring: *…mon coeur.*

"That's French, isn't it?"

"Looks like," Shiloh said.

"What the fuck, Shy."

"Yeah." But she already had her phone out, flicking to Google Translate.

"Well?"

"The big one says something like, 'You have the key,' and the other one says, 'of my heart'."

"That doesn't sound like Dad. Or Mom for that matter. What the *fuck*, Shy?"

"Are you just going to keep saying, 'What the fuck?'"

"I mean, well, what's this mean?" although Shiloh was sure Zoe had a pretty good idea what it meant.

"I think, for now…" Shiloh carefully folded the dress as she placed it back in the footlocker, thinking there were more questions than ashes stuffed in that goddamned urn.

She closed the lid on the footlocker, knelt down to slide it back into its place against the rafters, but its bottom caught on something. She felt around behind the footlocker to see what was hanging it up.

There was a small space between the rafters, and between edge of the attic flooring and where the rafters extended past the floor to make the roof eaves. Shiloh pulled the footlocker back out for a better look.

Where there should've been a space where she could see through to the downstairs ceiling, she saw a plank of wood. "Zee, you have a flashlight?"

In a few minutes, Zoe was back with a flashlight. The plank was hinged at the back, and there was a latch and padlock on the front. Shiloh crept closer into the tight space and saw that the plank was actually the top to a rectangular wooden box, obviously and crudely hand-built to fit in the space between the rafters, and the attic floor and the ceiling below. But it was built so roughly it didn't quite fit, the lid sticking up above the attic floor by a fraction of an inch; just enough to catch the bottom of the footlocker.

"What the hell is that?" Zoe asked.

"Let's find out."

Unlike the footlocker, the box's construction was poor enough it didn't require much effort to pop the latch free.

"What's in there?"

Shiloh answered by reaching in and dragging out the contents. A fistful of photographs. And a shallow plastic container, like the kind for dip, holding what appeared to be charred bits of paper.

Shiloh and Zoe knelt down beside each other while Shiloh spread the photos out on the floor. She shuffled them around to form a reverse chronology, recent to oldest, which allowed her to keep recognizing the people in the pictures even as they regressed into their smooth-faced, trim-waisted youth.

Together, they were a mosaic portrait of her father's life before his marriage to Delia, years before Shiloh Vail had ever greeted the world.

Forty years ago, or more, her father had graduated as a police officer. This was when potential officers did their training on the Thomas College campus in Waterville, decades before there was a dedicated academy at Vassalboro.

There were pictures (Shiloh assumed taken by her father's parents) of two seated rows of two dozen or so officers in the uniforms of various local departments and the state police in an auditorium; a senior officer making a speech at a podium; a congratulatory banner hanging along one wall of the auditorium.

But then the more personal photos. There was her father, an impressive figure in his uniform in those days, even striking (she had scant memories of him looking so well groomed), one arm around another officer, the burly man – the suspected Santa Claus. He was looking less burly and more muscular in those pictures. Her father's other arm was around a slender figure in civilian clothes: Sean Cleary, Sr. Pictures of the new graduates goofing around with their non-cop friend: pretending to arrest him; to frisk him; their guns (hopefully empty) pointed at him as he shrunk back in Victorian theater-caliber faux fear.

Then earlier: the Navy. A picture of the burly man standing at a 45-degree angle to a ship's deck, the frighteningly rough seas rocking the ship in the background. The three of them dressed only in T-shirts and "skivvies" (she'd heard her father use that word fishing around in his dresser for fresh underwear) crowded onto a bunk in hear-no-evil/see-no-evil/speak-no-evil poses. She flipped the photo over. In handwritten block letters were:

Athos - corresponding to Sean Cleary, Sr. -

Aramis - for her father -

Porthos - the burly man)

There were three of us…The Three Musketeers…

Other photos of them from around the ship, on the dock in Iceland - she presumed, going by what Cleary Sr. had told her - pointing at the seals basking on the planks.

And then the photos of their sprint through Europe: the burly man pretending to match his watch against Big Ben; her father posed in the foreground, so it looked like he was opening London Bridge; Sean Cleary fleeing a flock of pigeons in Piccadilly Circus he'd somehow managed to antagonize. A picture from France, the three of them at a streetside cafe, noses in the air as they sipped from espresso cups with pinkies out. And then the explosive colors of the tulip fields of The Netherlands, Sean Cleary in the foreground, hands to his face, mouth agape, eyes wide in cartoonish wonder at the sight.

Still earlier. Portland High. Her father and the burly man in the uniforms of the Portland Bulldogs, the school's football team. Another picture of the two of them pretending to weigh down Sean Cleary with pads, helmets, tennis rackets, a hockey stick, even an athletic cup hanging from the hockey stick.

Zoe let out a long, contemplative breath.

"What, Zee?"

"Oh… Dad was old so long you don't think he could ever be this young. Why do you think he hid these up here? All locked up? 'N' this dress…"

Shiloh shook her head. She opened the plastic container. The charred pieces were intact enough that she could tell this wasn't burned paper.

Photographs.

People lie for two reasons: to protect themselves, or to protect somebody they care about.

Which lie were you telling, Dad…and why?

She went back to the photo of three young Maine men clowning on a ship's bunk as they went off on their great adventure to see the world…at least some of it. She set a finger on the burly man: *Porthos.*

Who the hell are *you?*

Twelve.

The McDonald's on St. John's Street was a good distance from police headquarters on Middle Street, too far to walk and that's how Shiloh wanted it. Karras spotted her as soon as he came in the door from the parking lot. She beckoned grandly at the menu over the counter. "Whatever you want! It's on me!"

"Gee," Karras said with a smile that wasn't really a smile, "you're gonna spoil me."

She made a gesture of helplessness with her hands. "The longer I'm up here, the more I realize I'm operating on a budget."

"Lucky me."

Then they were sitting across from each other at a small table, Shiloh sipping on a Diet Coke, Karras munching his way through a Big Mac and large fries.

"I thought," he said after clearing his palate with a hefty slurp of his own giant-sized non-diet Coke, "all you Big Law types had your martini lunches in nice, fancy restaurants."

"First of all, martinis are for the old folk. The preference among young professionals these days are things like cosmos, pina coladas, bellinis... And, yes, Big Law lawyers like a nice lunch at a nice place. Big Law paralegals, on the other hand, eat cheap take-out salads at their desks as they try to plow through all that work the Big Law lawyers dump on their desks on the way out to their nice lunch."

"I seem to have been seriously misinformed."

"Watch less TV. I feel my arteries closing up just watching you eat all that."

"I burn it off at the gym. Well, most of it. Some of it. Actually, my plan is to die of a heart attack before my daughters are your age, so I won't have to watch them deal with a bonehead like your Mr. Cole."

"Ben means well. It's just sometimes he can be a bit of a -"

"Bonehead."

"Well...yeah."

"Want a fry?"

"No." But she took a fry. Then a second one, giving Karras a so-sue-me look of surrender. "Sergeant, I need a favor."

"Uh-oh." He put his burger down.

"What do you mean, 'uh-oh'?"

A small burp. "Excuse me, but you just gave me an ulcer. It's been my experience that when someone asks a police officer for a favor, it's usually for something neither one of them should be doing. Why don't you just take some more fries instead?"

"You're awfully cynical."

"Your father should've told you it goes with the job."

"He did."

"That we're a couple miles from police headquarters -"

"One-point-seven, I clocked it."

"- and talking here instead of at my desk isn't doing much to ease my anxiety."

"Look, I did you a favor, I'm just asking for a small favor in return."

"'Small favor'; that's another red flag and my anxiety is increasing."

"You violated investigatory protocols when you brought me into the McNair crime scene."

Karras winced.

"All I'm asking for is a much smaller violation of protocols."

He winced, again. "Which protocols?" with a face of painful expectation.

"Personnel."

Now puzzled. "Personnel should be able to tell you anything you need to know about your father."

"Yes, but they won't tell me diddley about any other police officer."

She saw Karras shift from puzzled, to wary. "Like who?"

Shiloh reached into her breast pocket and brought out one of the photos from the attic: her father and the burly man at their police training graduation. She set it on the table, touched a finger to the burly man. "Him."

Karras cleaned McD's special sauce off his fingers with a napkin before picking up the photo for a closer look.

"Who's 'him'?"

"Porthos."

"Say what?"

"It's a joke. I don't have a name."

"That hardly narrows it down."

"He went through training and graduated with my father. This was back when they did the training at Thomas College."

"Dinosaur days."

"The classes look like they were pretty small, and only some of the graduates went into the Portland P.D., which should narrow it down a bit. I'm presuming they came into the department together."

"So, you want a name."

"And how I can get in touch with him. If he's still alive, he's getting a pension and there'll be an address to go with it."

Karras set the photo down on the table, nudged it back toward her like he was afraid it would bite him. "Why do you want this guy?"

"I have information which suggests -"

"You may not be a lawyer but, Jesus, you know how to sound like one."

"Which suggests they were close friends at one point, but they haven't been in touch much recently. He may not even know my father passed."

Karras' eyes narrowed and it looked like he was staring so hard at her he was trying to see into her brain. "You're not on some kind of anti-cop crusade where this winds up all over the news, I get fired and maybe my tires get slashed?"

Shiloh laughed. "This is purely personal. My father never talked much about his life before he married my mother."

"That seems a little weird."

"More than a little. This guy goes back to those earlier days. I'd like to hear about those days."

Karras took a moment, running it all over in his head, and then, obviously not completely satisfied with what he'd heard, muttered, "Alright. Can I...?" He took out his phone and took a picture of the photo. "But if I locate this guy, before I give you his information, I'm going to get in touch with him and ask if it's ok. That's a non-negotiable condition."

"I'm ok with that." She went back into her breast pocket and set her business card down on the table. "That's got my cell phone number. Soon's you find out anything, let me know." She started to slide out of her seat.

"You know what's funny?"

"I can always use a good laugh."

"What's funny is you haven't asked me anything about how we're doing on the McNair business."

She slid back into her seat as Karras picked up his burger, took a healthy bite.

"I just assumed if there was any news, you would've let me know."

"Nice sidestep."

"I thought you'd like it. So, Sergeant, how're you doing on the McNair business?"

"Nice of you to ask. We're still plowing through his client list, people involved in his cases. It's a lot of names. But here's another funny thing: Mrs. Rutherford – his assistant? – she did manage to inventory his files. One – only one – was missing. Want to guess which one? Your father's. Isn't that funny?"

"Hysterical."

"Somebody was after your father's file and killed McNair in the process."

"Sergeant, I can't think of anything that would've been in that file worth the trouble. The only things in there would be stuff like a copy of his will, paperwork on his divorce... I can't think of anything of interest to anybody."

"The will –"

"I'd already shared the will with what's left of the family. There wouldn't've been any need for any of them to go to McNair."

"So, you're telling me it's one big fat coincidence."

"I'm telling you I don't know what anybody would want with my father's file. Call me if you can find that other police officer."

"Why do I have the feeling there's something you're not telling me?"

"Because you're a cynic. Sergeant, I would never do anything to get on your wrong side. We have a date, remember?"

"A date?"

"Yeah, in a couple of years. You want me to teach your daughters how to deal with bonehead boys."

Route 2 nipped through the edge of Wilton just 10 to 15 minutes short of Farmington. Shiloh made a left off 2 onto Main Street. What she saw of the commercial center of Wilton reminded her of Zoe's conversation with one of the university kids: that Farmington was the entertainment metropolis the kid went to from his even-smaller town. Wilton looked to be one of those "even-smaller" towns.

Wilton's main drag consisted of a motley collection of a dozen or so small shops, some of them vacant. There was a pizzeria/sandwich shop and a Chinese take-out place because small as Wilton was, it was big enough that these were almost a requirement. There was a craft brewery, craft breweries – or at least Shiloh had surmised from the massive beer menu at Tuck's – fast becoming Maine's new signature industry. There was a New Agey-looking cupcake bakery because rural corners of the state harbored the last vestiges of hippy culture. There was an outdoor ice cream shack which even this late in the year was still open, because it has to get pretty damned cold in Maine before it's too cold for ice cream. At the head of the strip, sitting on the banks of Wilson Pond, was the four-story hulk of what had once been the Bass Shoe factory which had been Wilton's economic heart until the Bass family pulled the plug in the late 1990s. Since then, some – and just some - of the building's floors had been turned into a mix of apartments and commercial space. A rather nice Italian restaurant was in what used to be the factory's boiler room, and had a dining patio overlooking

Wilson Stream which, long before even the oldest current resident had been born, had provided power for the factory.

Shiloh followed Main Street past that sleepy stretch of stores, turning onto Pond Road which unsurprisingly wound around the pond. She could tell which houses were owned by commuters and which were owned by the purely local by how well kept up a house was. Commuters had the better-paying jobs because there was little in Wilton of the kind of work which could provide the revenue to properly maintain the rambling homes overlooking the water.

On the far side of the pond were a few of what Mainers call "camps." Shiloh had often had to explain to her D.C. acquaintances that a Maine "camp" wasn't something with tents and Boy Scouts. They were, she would tell them, "Vacation homes for people without money"; a small second house, sometimes little more than a comfortable shack, or a trailer parked on a plot of land and used for weekend getaways, vacations, hunting and/or fishing trips.

The location Karras had given her was for a camp with an enviable location – a quarter-acre right on the water with what, during the fall foliage season, would've been an eye-popping view of the tree-lined pond. But, as it had been the entire drive up from Portland, the sky was covered by an unbroken sheet of gray clouds, and foliage season had come and gone leaving the trees around Wilson Pond bare and starkly skeletal against that slate sky. This camp consisted of a rust-streaked trailer, a forty-footer – what the trade calls a "destination" trailer since it's supposed to be a home away from home, although in Maine, it was often just *the* home. Its undercarriage was partly hidden behind a dirty plastic lattice collapsing in places, its window screens clotted with several seasons of uncleared black flies.

The driveway had been graveled once, but much of the gravel had been washed away by past rains leaving a tire-scarred path of mostly mud. At the bottom of the drive was parked a Ford pick-up looking like it hadn't moved in quite some time, and a mud-spattered minivan.

Shiloh parked behind the van, climbed out, peeked in the van's windows. Two child seats in the back, children's toys scattered on the floor. In the front passenger seat, a jumble of empty plastic bottles and boxes for prescription medicines, boxes of gauze, antiseptic wipes, nitrile gloves, a small oxygen tank with attached breathing mask.

She went to the door of the trailer, but rather than chance the iffy-looking pile of cinderblocks acting as stairs, she reached up to rap on the storm door.

The inner door opened, then the storm door swung out, and Shiloh caught a whiff which reminded her of her father's bedroom: a mix of antiseptic, ammonia, gauze. The door had been answered by a tall, long-limbed woman with a heart-shaped face. Young, maybe late twenties or a tired-looking early twenties. She wore a blue hospital scrub top mottled with still-wet water stains and dried tiny handprints in what might've been finger paints or food condiments...or maybe both. She wore nitrile gloves, and her dark hair was pulled back in an unraveling bun.

As soon as she caught sight of Shiloh, her mouth curled up in a dimple-producing smile, her large, dark eyes almost disappearing behind her cheeks. "I'm betting you're Shiloh! Hey, Dan!" she called into the interior of the trailer. "She's heee-eeeere!" She reached down to help Shiloh up the stairs, realized she was still wearing gloves and pulled them off before re-offering Shiloh her hand. "I'm sorry, I was just cleaning up. Seems like I'm *always* cleaning up. I come from home after cleaning up after my kids and then I have to clean up after *this* guy! It's like I have three kids! Well, four, counting my husband!"

The smell was stronger in the trailer but there were other flavors to it: dish soap from the bubble-filled sink in what barely qualified as a kitchenette, and the aroma of tomato sauce, boiled pasta, and coffee still hovered in the air from what Shiloh assumed had been a late lunch.

"C'mon, Dan!" the woman called. "You're keeping this young lady waiting!" Then, to Shiloh: "Ever since you called, he's been, 'What should I wear? What should I wear?' He wants to make a good impression. You'd think he was going on a date. Why don't you sit, make yourself comfortable." To the right of the counter that set off the kitchenette was an open dining/living room space. Scattered across the small dining table Shiloh recognized Medicaid, Medicare, and Social Security forms. She stepped by the table to place herself on a U-shaped bench seat under the picture window at the front end of the trailer.

"I'm just gonna finish up in here," the woman said, pulling back on her gloves as she went back to the dish-filled sink. "Oh," and she froze with a thought. "I'm sorry, I'm not thinking. That's a long ride up from Portland; are you hungry? Did you have lunch? There's still pasta left over from lunch. It's no trouble to warm it up for you."

Shiloh nodded a polite no-thank-you. "I picked up something on the road."

Now peeved, the woman turned toward a dark hallway that led to the back of the trailer. "Daniel! Did you get lost?"

There was a flash of light at the far end of the hallway as a door opened. The brief lighting gave Shiloh a quick look: the hall ran past a stacked washer/dryer and what she guessed was the door to a closet-sized bathroom.

"See, that's how it works." The voice was gravelly, not so much soft as weak. There was a figure in the lit doorway now, shambling slowly down the hall. "She starts with 'Dan'. When she gets to 'Daniel', you can tell she's ticked at me. If she gets to 'Mr. Foy', I'm in for a spanking. Which might be kinda fun."

"Disgusting," the woman at the sink muttered, She turned to Shiloh: "He's disgusting, isn't he?"   Another turn: "Dan, you are disgusting."   But Shiloh heard no serious condemnation in it.   They sounded more like a long-married couple who enjoyed poking each other; it was their way of saying, *I like you.*

Daniel Foy finally emerged from the hallway.   Shiloh, for a moment, didn't recognize him.   This was supposed to be the burly man from her father's photographs.   But the bulk had long ago left him, eaten away, leaving the flesh behind, now hanging in loose folds like softened butter.   The man who had once played high school football, sailed the Atlantic, and been a city cop for decades now looked as frail as a pile of twigs.   His hair was a thinned, uncombed frazzle, his eyes watery, and he had walked down the hallway with one hand on the nearest wall as if unsure of his balance.   It all seemed explained by what he carried in his free hand: a purring oxygen concentrator.   A plastic hose connected the machine to the nasal cannula in Foy's nostrils.

Shiloh thought back to her father's last months, Sean Cleary, Sr. and his stroke, and now Daniel Foy.   *Good God, didn't any of these guys take care of themselves?*

What Foy wore seemed in about the same depleted shape.   The baggy sweatpants, loose-hanging Portland P.D. sweatshirt, and the open cardigan he wore over it were all faded, ragged around the edges. He shuffled forward in cracked leather slippers.

"That's what you wore?" the woman said as he entered the kitchenette, her face cartoonishly appalled.   "All this time – 'What should I wear? What should I wear?' – and *that's* what you wear? For a *guest?*"

"I choked," he said dryly.   "That's what happens when you don't pick for me."

"Jesus, Dan, you should've at least had me shave you."

He wasn't hearing her now. He'd gotten to where his bleary eyes could fix on Shiloh.

She felt, for some reason she couldn't define, that she needed to stand, to let him see all of her, and she did. He was looking at her the same way Sean Cleary, Sr. had looked at her just before she'd left his estate: *You remind me of a happy time.* Foy's mind seemed to go to the same place, and for a second Shiloh thought those watery eyes might produce tears.

"Dan?"

"Mr. Foy, are you alright?"

He waved both their concerns away, waved at Shiloh to sit back down. "This," and he pointed to the young woman, "is Miss Moon. I'm sorry: *Mizzzz* Moon. She's what's called a home health aide. She does not aid. If she was aiding, she'd be doing things that make me happy. Instead, she seems to think it's her job to keep me alive as long as possible against my will by doing things that do not make me happy."

Ms. Moon gave a grand eyeroll. "Oh, God, here he goes."

Foy shuffled over to where Shiloh was sitting, sat at one end of the bench seat where he could still get a full look of her. "Pardon me for staring, Little Miss," he said after a bit.

Something went warm in her at that: *Little Miss.* She found herself smiling. "You used to call me that, didn't you? 'Little Miss'?"

All those loose folds on Daniel Foy's face slid into a jowly smile, yet there was something sad about it. "Little Miss. Yup. That was my name for you."

"And weren't you Santa Claus once?"

And now he laughed, although it was cut short by a wheeze and a cough.

"Dan?" and Ms. Moon started to come to him, but he waved her away.

It was one cough, it passed. "You remembered that?"

"My sister and I were going through the attic. We found the Santa Claus suit…and I sort of remembered."

He took a moment, seeming to bask in her remembering, then his face sagged again. "I know I said it on the phone, but I'm sorry about your dad. I mean, *really*…." And then he faded, shaking his head. The words weren't there.

"I know."

He passed through the feeling. "How'd you find me?"

"I saw Sean Cleary."

"Seanie! That's what we called him."

"He didn't mention your name, but he did say there were three of you that went back a long way. He made it sound like the three of you went back to the womb."

"Just about," and he chuckled. Then a little more serious: "Did he say anything else about those days?"

"No. His primary interest seemed to be in buying my father's house."

"Hm."

"What?"

But Foy just shrugged, then he seemed to find a comforting thought. "I was glad they were talking again."

"They hadn't been talking?"

Foy sighed. "For a lotta years. Something happened, I don't know what, they wouldn't tell me. Seanie would say it was just something between them, Eddie would say it was something personal. They didn't talk for years. That hurt 'cause we'd all always been so close. I was glad to see they reconnected, mended fences as they say, but sorry it took Eddie getting sick."

"Cleary didn't tell me anything about this."

Foy shrugged. "We were all good friends, even when they weren't talking. I know 'cause I was in the middle and they were both always asking me how the other one was doing. I guess that's how Seanie wanted you to remember us." Then something warm came to him. "Seanie always asked about you, how things were going with you."

"When was this? That they had their falling out?"

"Oh, hell," and Foy's face wrinkled as he tried to pull the memory up. "It was a while ago, ten, fifteen years maybe. It was around the time your father got his lieutenant's bars. Broke my heart 'cause, like I said, we were all so close. I'm glad we were all back together for your father, you know, the way things were going with him being sick and all." Then he smiled. "You were telling me how you found me."

"Like I said, my sister and I were going through the attic, and we found some stuff tucked away. Like my father was hiding it."

"Some stuff."

"There was a wedding dress."

Foy shook his head, smiling. "Jesus, he kept that?"

"There were two wedding rings with it. There was something inscribed inside. In French."

"Something like, 'You have the key to my heart'?"

"Something like that."

Again, the shake of the head, as if disbelieving…and the smile.

"There was another box. Pictures of the three of you." She reached into her breast pocket and set down a photo on the bench seat next to Foy. It was of the three men in the Navy, crammed together on a bunk: the one with the names of the Musketeers written on the back.

Foy picked up the picture, his eyes went soft. He turned it over, grinned at the inscriptions, then went back to the image. "Can you believe I ever looked that good? And look at all that lovely hair!"

"You'd look a hell of a lot better if you combed the hair you have once in a while," Ms. Moon called from the kitchenette. "Maybe dressed like you weren't picking clothes out of the Goodwill bin."

Shiloh set down another photo, this one of Foy and her father on graduating from their police training. "You trained at the same time. I figured you came onto the force at the same time. That's how I ran you down. All the pictures in that box, it was all stuff from before my father married my mother. He never talked much about those days."

Foy nodded, unsurprised.

"I also found this." She reached into one of her coat's deep pockets and brought out the shallow plastic container which had been with her father's old photos. She set that down on the bench by Foy. "That's not burned paper in there. That's what's left of photographs."

Again, the unsurprised nod. "You don't know what they are?"

She shook her head.

Foy sighed. "They're pictures of your mother. I remember Eddie telling me about this, how Delia watched to make sure he burned them."

"Why would my mother make my father burn pictures of her?"

And now the saddest of sad smiles. "That's not what I said. I said Delia made your father burn pictures of your mother."

It took Shiloh a second because the words initially didn't make sense. But as their meaning fell into place… "Delia…wasn't…"

"Delia is not your mother, Little Miss. And that's not the half of it."

Thirteen.

Shiloh didn't faint. It was something else. A kind of detachment; a feeling of being there yet not there, present but not present, falling away without moving. Things seemed miles away even though she could see they were only a few feet distant, voices seemed far off, watery the way they'd sound echoing down a long corridor. If she focused – and it was difficult to focus – she could sift through the wavering sounds.

Ms. Moon, voice raised: "It's already getting dark and it's getting cold. You'll get pneumonia!"

"Then I croak, and you get a vacation paid for by Unemployment."

"What I get is having to hunt down another crabby old bastard and break him in. Besides, it's supposed to rain!"

"We could use the air."

"That little machine of yours gives you all the air you need."

"*Real* air."

"What am I going to do with you?"

"Pillow over the face while I'm asleep would be nice."

"Fine! Go freeze!"

"If you're that worried about it, maybe you should start me a fire."

Then some kind of exasperated grunt/groan, a door slamming.

An arm reached down from a million miles away, then there was a hand in front of her, beckoning, and finally a clear voice, Daniel Foy asking, "Want to help an old man down the stairs?"

As she took his hand, everything seemed to properly set itself again, she could feel herself coming back into the here and now.

"You alright, Little Miss?"

She could only manage a nod, got to her feet, wavered for a second.

"You sure?"

She nodded, again, led Foy to the door, went carefully down the cinderblock steps more unsure of her own footing than Foy's, then turned to help Foy come down, one step at a time, not moving forward until both slippered feet were sure on a stair.

"Where we going?" Shiloh asked.

He nodded her toward a spot about halfway down the gradual slope between the trailer and the water. There were some wooden garden chairs set around a firepit where Ms. Moon was scratching around with a small hand rake, clearing out old bits of charred wood and matted damp leaves. "You're a pain in my ass, you know that?" she called back to Foy.

"I proposed to her, ya know," Foy told Shiloh as he held her arm while they walked slowly – a shuffle, really – toward the firepit.

"He proposes to me at least three times a week," Ms. Moon said.

"She says she won't marry me because she claims she loves her husband and her two little brats."

"I love that," Ms. Moon said: "*'Claims'*."

"I could make you happy," Foy said. "I've had plenty of practice."

"That's one of your problems. All that practice and you never got it right."

Ms. Moon stood back from the firepit. She had set some balled up pages of old newspapers at the bottom, made a tent of kindling over them, then a cross of logs over that. She set off the paper with a long-necked lighter. "I don't know how good this stuff'll burn. This wood's been sitting out for the longest time. Some of it's so rotten it almost came apart when I picked it up."

"How could you not love a woman who knows how to build a fire?" Foy said. He had Shiloh lower him into one chair, beckoned her to pull another one close to him.

Shiloh sat, the chair creaked and groaned. She wondered if the chair's wood was as weather-rotted as the logs in the fire, but as she settled into her seat, the creaking stopped, and the chair held, though it didn't feel like a firm guarantee. The kindling had caught and was already sending off some subtle waves of warmth.

"Anything else, your majesty?" Ms. Moon said, bowing in front of Foy.

Foy held up a regal hand. "Some coffee might be nice." Before she could complain, "Not so much for me," he offered in justification, "but for my guest. And you should bring me my special medicine."

"Christ, Dan, you gonna do *that* now?"

"What's it gonna do? So, I die an hour earlier."

With a resigned sigh, Ms. Moon headed back up to the trailer.

Foy watched her go. "God, she's great. If I was forty years younger and had met her two marriages ago…" He looked at Shiloh with a smile. "Timing, Little Miss, is everything."

Finally, and welcoming the feeling, Shiloh found it in herself to laugh. But then she remembered why she was here.

The logs had begun to burn, the heat from the fire felt good against the chill coming with the late afternoon feeling of the day going gray.

"My dad bought this property," Foy said, his eyes wandering around the heavily wooded lot and settling on his trailer. "His plan was to build a nice little camp out here when he retired. He was a mechanic with Public Works. One day he was working on some supervisor's car, he's under the hood, has a heart attack. He was lying on that damn engine almost an hour before someone noticed he wasn't moving. I inherited this. Then *I* thought it would be a good idea to build a nice little camp out here."

"What happened?"

Foy chuckled. "Two divorces and medical bills. I'm lucky I have that thing," and he nodded at the trailer. His shoulders heaved up and down like he was getting ready for some great effort. "So, Little Miss."

"So."

"Your father never said anything, made you think...?"

"Nothing. Nothing in the will, didn't leave anything with the lawyer. Nothing. Not a clue. Not until I started digging around in the attic."

"And when you went to see Seanie..."

She shook her head.

"Really." Foy seemed both surprised and impressed.

"You thought he'd say something?"

"We did promise your father."

"But you thought Cleary would be the one to break the promise?"

Foy frowned, like he was working on the best way to make his point. "Seanie's head didn't work like ours. Those names he wrote on the back of that picture? The Three Musketeer names?" He laughed. "He had to explain them to us. He read a lot."

"Reading a lot. That's a pretty low bar for branding somebody as a — Well, what *are* you branding him as?"

The frown again. "It's not that. Like I told you, we were close. Look, we came out of the Navy, your dad and me joined the force, Seanie went to work for his dad. Different roads is what I'm saying. And you always hear stories about the Clearys, but you never know how much of that was the old man – Kieran – and how much the rest of 'em are keeping it up. I'd hear this stuff and I'd think, well, not Seanie. Still, you never know, right? But he kept his word on this. That's nice to hear."

"You said you *both* promised. But here we are."

Again, Foy looked around the grounds, seemed to be thinking, *How did we come to this?* "Here we are." Then nothing for a long while.

He'll come to it when he's ready. Sometimes, Shiloh knew, you just had to wait for a witness to find their moment.

Foy took a deep breath. "This was when your dad was really sick, but he could still think clear. We hadn't seen much of each other these past years. Neither one of us was in shape to travel a lot. But we used to talk on the phone, then we got to talking a *lot* when he got sick. And when he got bad, he wanted me to promise. I said, Eddie, best my conscience'll let me do is I won't reach out to her. But if she finds me – and I figured if you were as smart as he was always saying, you'd find me – if she finds me, I'm telling her everything. That's the best I can do."

"And he accepted that?"

A phlegmy chuckle. "What was he gonna do? Sue me from the Great Beyond?"

They heard the doors of the trailer, then Ms. Moon was there with a folding tray table carrying two steaming mugs of coffee and a bottle Shiloh instantly recognized as the same awful brand of whisky her father had kept. Ms. Moon was also carrying a heavy blanket over her shoulder. She set the table down between them.

Foy thanked her and she responded with a flat, "Screw you." She threw the blanket across his lap, pulled it up and tucked it around his chest. "Keep this on." She turned to Shiloh with a not-quite-mock fierce face. "You, make sure he doesn't take that off. He catches pneumonia and I'm holding you responsible."

"Yes'm."

Then back to Foy, wagging a finger in his face. "And I hear one raindrop hit the roof of that tin can of yours and I'm dragging you inside by what's left of your hair, I don't care how much you squawk about it." She stormed back up to the trailer, muttering something about what a pain in the ass Foy was, why did she keep coming out here if he was so intent on killing himself, etc.

Foy watched her slam the trailer doors behind her with a smile. "God, she's great, isn't she?"

"You two are like an old married couple."

"If either of my marriages sounded like that, I'd still be married."

Shiloh decided on a gentle nudge to get the conversation back on course. "Mr. Foy -"

"Danny. There was a time when I was looking forward to being called 'Uncle Danny'. I'm not gonna make you do that, but if you could: Danny."

She was good with that, it felt…right. "Ok. Danny -"

He held up a hand to stop her and pointed to the whisky bottle. "If I were you, I'd take a shot of that."

"Oh, God, it's the same toxic waste Dad drank."

Another chuckle. "I know." He fumbled around under the blanket and came up with a pack of Camels and a Bic lighter.

"Should you be doing that?"

Foy took a first, savored drag…and coughed. "You gonna start on me, too? At this point -"

"I wasn't thinking about pushing your termination date as much as I was thinking of the oxygen and being more worried you'd blow yourself up."

He shrugged, unconcerned. "Worse things could happen."

The sharp aroma from the cigarette; she remembered that same smell hovering almost permanently around her father. "Same awful weeds as my dad. His rotten cigarettes, his cheap whisky."

"Maybe I shoulda married him. You can do that now, right?"

"You would've made the cutest couple," and that was good for a small laugh from both of them.

Then Foy grew serious, focused. "Before you start bugging me with a lot of questions, do us both a favor. With love I say this: shuddup and let me tell this, ok? It's a long story, kinda complicated, and you start throwing questions at me and I'm gonna lose my place. So, take a belt, Little Miss, 'cause I guarantee you, you're gonna need it."

She poured a shot into her coffee mug, Foy nodded at her to do the same for his. She handed him his drink; they touched mugs with a small *clink* and took a sip. Foy's went down with lip-smacking satisfaction. Shiloh, on the other hand, wasn't any more used to this flamethrowing stuff than she was when Zoe had served it to her.

After Foy stopped laughing/coughing at her gag reflex, he took another drag on his cigarette, then seemed to settle in his seat. "Seanie tell you anything about the house on St. Aggie's? His big plans and all that?"

"Why does he want to buy the house so badly?"

The glowing tip of his cigarette went this way and that in a warning wave. "What'd I just tell you? We'll get to the house. So -"

"Shuddup," and she mimed padlocking her lips shut.

"He told you about how he talked his father into wanting to build on the island, something like Peak's? Just nod your head. You know what the house was? You can say."

"A whorehouse."

"I prefer, 'House of Ill Repute'. Not as harsh. Even though if you were interested in that kind of thing, Aggie's had quite a good reputation."

"Your Ms. Moon is right: you *are* disgusting," but it was delivered with a smile.

"By the time the old man, I mean Seanie's dad - Kieran -gets around to wanting to start putting money into this thing, Eddie and me are with the force maybe not quite two years. Not rookies, but still new guys, low on the totem pole, as they say. Seanie's dad, Kieran, I don't know what you know about him, but that guy was plugged into the city pretty deep. Connected to all the – what's the phrase? Shakers and movers?"

"Movers and shakers."

"Same difference," Foy said with a shrug.

"Yeah, I've heard the Clearys had -"

"And still have."

"And still have a lot of pull with the city."

"Ok, so Seanie says something to his old man, and Kieran says something to somebody else, and me and Eddie get the job of getting the ladies to vacate the premises, as they say. Seanie rigged this 'cause he thought he was doing us a favor."

"How -"

"How is that a favor? Well, like I said, we were the low guys. Portland isn't the kind of place gives a beat cop a lot of opportunities to shine. Seanie figures we pull this off, get the ladies out without a fuss or mess, it's points for us. Now me, I could give less of a -. Oh, uh, sorry."

She laughed. "I'm over twenty-one, Danny. *Well* over. And I work around a lot of lawyers who think they're tough guys because they play racquetball every week, so they talk like they're in a Quentin Tarantino movie. You don't have to police yourself for me."

Foy took another pull on his cigarette which set him coughing, badly enough that Shiloh grew alarmed, started to rise but he waved her back down, that he was fine. He flung the cigarette into the fire, looking disappointed at having to give it up, soothed his throat with a couple of swallows from his mug. He cleared his throat, Shiloh waited for him to get his breath.

And then, "Now, Eddie, he always had more ambition than me. Not in a bad way, but he always wanted to be good at what he did. Even when we were in the Navy, by the time we got out, he had stripes, I didn't. You're gonna feed me, give me a warm place to sleep, give me beer money, I'm fine pushing a mop. Now we're in the cops, he was the same way. Me, I'm happy in the cruiser asking kids on the corner why they're not in school."

"But not Dad."

A smile, looking back with admiration. "That wasn't Eddie's way. So, he's thinking this thing with the ladies on the island would get us some good attention. We put our heads together, we figure we're going to do this in stages. Go out there first time, say something like, 'Hey, ladies, the city wants to build something on this rock and they're gonna need you to take your business elsewhere.' Some of 'em leave, most of 'em don't, so you go back: 'Hey, ladies, we're serious, you really need to look for some other place to go.' Each time, some of 'em leave, too many stay, and finally you go out there to the ones who're left and it's, 'Yo! No kidding now! You don't get your patooties outta here as in this second, next time we come we're bringing troops with us, gonna throw you and your stuff in a boat, take you over and dump your asses on the Portland docks'."

"Is this how my dad got the house? "

A reminding look of warning.

"Ok, I'll wait. What is it?"

Foy had started to say something, then stopped. His eyes grew soft. He looked out toward the water, gray going black under the darkening sky, but some of the wind-tickled wavelets sparked briefly, picking up light from the firepit. He turned back to her, not just to face her but Shiloh got the feeling he saw something in her, something that brought out the same sad smile of remembrance she'd seen on Sean Cleary, Sr.

He turned away, lowered his head, closed his eyes, and when he spoke, his voice was so soft she barely heard him: "Evangeline."

"Evangeline. She was one of the women?"

After a bit, Foy finally lifted his head. "Evangeline Donnadieu. Don't even know that was her real name, but that's the name she wanted to live with."

The whisky started to churn in Shiloh's stomach. "Did my dad -"

Foy beckoned her to hold off. "It was kind of the same old, sad story you hear a lot from women in that situation. When we met her, she couldn'ta been more than nineteen. Funny; I didn't think of it 'til now, but she'd only been at the house maybe as long as Eddie and me had been on the force: almost two years. Her family lived out in the boonies somewhere in Quebec."

"A Quebecoise." Shiloh already knew where this was going, and she could tell Foy knew she knew, but they were both committed to a laying out of the full story. She took a heavy sip from her mug. Foy had been right; she needed it.

"I guess that's the proper word."

"She spoke French."

"She spoke French."

"Tu as les clefs mon coeur."

Again, he signaled her for patience. "Don't think you know," he warned, "because you don't." His gaze turned toward the fire; its flickering light reflected in his eyes.

"Even though she didn't like to talk about it, it must've been pretty bad at home. You picked up bits and pieces from things she said, you figure her father musta knocked her and her mother around. She didn't like to wear short sleeves, even when it was hot. 'Cause when she did... You're a cop in Maine, a lot of domestic abuse calls; I know what scars from cigarette burns look like," and he tapped a line along one arm, showing where he'd seen them. "And she didn't say it; again, you just kinda picked up on things, but I think her dad did more than just bang her around if you know what I mean."

She did, and she could feel her face warm at the same time there was a cold knot in her stomach with the understanding.

"Eddie used to tell me sometimes she'd talk in her sleep. It was in French, so he didn't know what she was saying, but she'd wake up in a sweat. One time she screamed so loud in her sleep she woke them both up."

They were sleeping together.

But, again, Foy could see her thinking running ahead, and a firm, warning finger came up. "Don't. Wait."

She nodded her acceptance of the terms but that didn't quiet the racing thoughts in her head.

Foy went on: "She runs away from home, sneaks herself across the border, winds up in Portland. She's what? Seventeen at the time? Doesn't speak much English, didn't finish school, she's got no papers, no skills..."

"Which is how she winds up at Aggie's house."

"Like I said: an old, sad, familiar story." Another pause but this time Shiloh could see it wasn't about trying to figure out how to say what he had to say. In the warm yellow and orange light of the flames, she could see him cherishing a memory. "Thing was, first time we went out to the island, to the house, and we're talking to all the girls, first time Eddie talked with Evangeline, you saw something click between them. I mean, you could *see* it! And every time we went back out there, they'd talk, you could see this thing between them was a bit more each time. Her bad English, Eddie's got a year getting C's in high school French, still you could see this thing…

"When we finally cleared out the house, Eddie helped her find some cheap dump in Bayside, this was before they started fixing up that part of town. Helped her find a job waiting tables in some dive, crappy job but paid enough to keep her fed. "

He smiled knowingly, anticipating her suspicions. "Ya know, you're a cop, you hear stories about cops and girls who, well… Cop has a crush, or he thinks he's Sir Lancelot and wants to save her, his wife isn't interested anymore, and he thinks it's more than just what it is, or it's her, she's looking for a way out of the work."

"Which one was this?"

His smile grew a little wider. "None of them. You hear about this from anybody else and they tell you different, pardon my language, Little Miss, but that's bullshit. I was there. I was there for it all, I saw them together. This was real and it went both ways.

"See, Evangeline, all the stuff she'd been through – the stuff back home, her time at Aggie's house – somehow it didn't touch her; not here," and he touched a finger to his chest. "She had her scars, and not just the ones you could see, but that was never her. If you met her and didn't know anything about her, Little Miss, you'd think she was the sweetest, nicest person you could meet with a face like an angel to go with it."

"Sounds like *you* had a thing for her."

Foy sighed deeply, then another smile, the wry kind of a child caught doing something he wasn't supposed to do. He nodded. "Yeah, I did. I think Seanie did, too. She was that kind of person; how could you not love her? That's the kind of person she was.

"But you could see, like they were wearing a sign; Eddie was it for her. From the beginning, they just always looked like they belonged together."

She could hear Ben Cole's voice: *Soulmates.*

"And I think she could see it in me and Seanie, how we felt, and that's why she was always asking us to come along, whatever they did. It was the four of us most of the time. I guess that was her giving us, like, whatchacallit? A consolation prize. It was Eddie and her, like it was supposed to be, you could tell that right off the way they connected, so the best Seanie and me could be, was try to be the best friends to both of them we could.

"She always wanted to be something...*more*. Kinda like your dad, ambitions, but different. I think she felt bad she never finished school. She read like a fiend, as much as Seanie. He was always bringing her books. That piano still at the house? That was there from Aggie's days, but Evangeline had your dad get her some piano books and she tried to learn how to play that thing. She wasn't very good, never got very good, but God bless how she banged away at that thing, trying, and we applauded like she was playing at Carnegie Hall. She tried learning how to paint for a while, that was another thing.

"It was like she was always trying to put things between what she'd done and what she wanted to be. See – this is funny – her and Eddie, each one of them never thought they deserved the other, and they were always working to try to be something they thought the other one deserved.

"Well, no surprise, one day she turns up pregnant."

Shiloh had seen it coming, but that didn't stop the chill from running through her once Daniel Foy put it into words, said it aloud. Even with the fire at its highest, she pulled her coat more closely around her.

"Eddie wanted to marry her. She pushed him off, thought that would mess him up with the department. 'Sides -"

"Besides, she wasn't legal." Shiloh was surprised at how small her voice sounded.

"So Seanie said something to his dad, his dad said something to somebody else, and then she had papers saying she was legal. And Keiran saw they got the house on the island, said it would be good for his project people would have a cop in the neighborhood."

"I'm surprised she'd be comfortable there. You know, considering..."

"Yeah, you'd think that. But see, where she lived in Quebec, she never saw big water until she got to Portland. Even when the house was still, you know, she liked being by the water. She liked it so much we had the wedding right out there on those rocks by the house, Seanie knew a lawyer could do it. I never saw either of them so happy.

"I was jealous, Little Miss, 'cause I knew I was never gonna find anybody to make me as happy as Eddie was. Don't get me wrong; I loved my wives, both of 'em, at least at the beginning, but nothing like what Eddie and Evangeline had. Hell, I don't know *anybody* had what they had. So, all the time she was pregnant, Seanie and I would go out there. We'd all work with her helping her improve her English, helping her study for her GED. She was always talking about going to college after the baby, that maybe they'd travel, see something besides this little piece of the world. She sounded just like us before we went in the Navy! There's got to be more to the world than this!

"The four of us would sit out on that big porch you got watching the sun go down and she'd have us talk about all the stuff we saw on the other side of the ocean when we were in the Navy. She'd make this thing for us… Oh, hell, what was the word? Verrines! It's like a parfait but with food instead of ice cream. Or sometimes she'd fix them up like a dessert; something for her friends, just sitting out there, shooting the bull, watching the sun go down.

"And then she had you. Man, if they were happy before…" He shook his head, looking as if even he, a witness, couldn't believe what he'd seen. "Made you feel good just to be around them." He turned to Shiloh, and she could swear tears were building up in the corners of his eyes. "God, how she loved you, Little Miss. For her, you were like everything behind her was gone, never happened, starting all new." And it was clear, now, they were tears. "Aw, Christ," he muttered, turning away, wiping at his eyes.

Shiloh stood, walked toward the water, letting Foy have the moment to himself. If there'd been a clear sky, there would've been a rising moon, stars, it would've been a twilight, but the cloud cover just had the day sliding from gray to black, except for the glowing circle from the firepit, the come-and-go stars of the firelight on the water.

"So, what happened?"

When he didn't answer right away, she turned. Foy was still, seemed to have sunk deep into the blanket, his face a glum blank.

"Why'd she leave him, Danny?"

He smiled weakly at her, the same kind of smile a tolerant parent gives a child who thinks the horizon line is the edge of the world. "She didn't. She didn't bounce back from the delivery. Tired all the time, kept getting sick. Eddie finally talked her into going to a doctor." He turned away, looking back into the fire. "Some kind of leukemia. She was four months dying, Little Miss. We were all dying with her, but nobody hurt more than your dad. He would've stayed with her all the time if he could, but he could only get so much time off from the job. We would spell him, Seanie and me. Besides, if he'd stayed there like he wanted, I think he would've gone crazy. It was bad enough as it was.

"He would try to put on a good face in front of her, and she was trying to do the same for him, but she was better at it. She made him promise that, you know, after, well, she said he still had a lot of life left to live, not to spend it moping. She made me and Seanie promise we wouldn't let that happen. For your sake. That's what she told us all: you deserved a dad to be there for you.

"She wanted you with her all the time, even when it got to where she couldn't get out of bed, like she was trying to cram everything into the time she had left. She told Eddie, ok, all that stuff we talked about we were going to do together, she told him to make it happen for you." A long, deep sigh. "And then she was gone."

Shiloh looked up into the blackening sky. *Not one fucking star. The other night, the sky lit up, but for this, not one fucking star.*

And for some reason, that made her angry.

"It killed us," Foy said, "but your dad... Jesus, I never saw anybody so broke up about anything. It got so bad, I started thinking maybe I should take away his guns. I think the only thing kept him going – and we got on him about this, reminding him what he promised Evangeline – was not leaving you alone. No matter how bad he felt, no way he was gonna leave you like that."

Fourteen.

Shiloh went back to her seat. She could almost feel the closing darkness falling on her like a chilling cloak. Her coffee had gone cold, but she took a healthy swig, less for the coffee than the whisky dosing. "Delia."

Foy pulled himself up in his chair, as if the hardest part was over. "Well, Little Miss, I gotta say that was kinda our fault, me and Seanie. See, Delia had a civilian job at headquarters. I think she'd always had a thing for Eddie. Maybe a year goes by after Evangeline… 'Eddie, you gotta get out there, again, that's what Evangeline wanted, your daughter should have, you know, like, a real home'. Looking back, we shouldn't have pushed it so hard."

"Did Delia know about Evangeline?"

"In the beginning, she knew your dad had been married before, obviously, because there you were. Only later… I don't know how she found out the rest. I wouldn't be surprised Eddie finally told her, her always asking what his problem was. Thing is, one way or another, she found out."

"I went to see her. She didn't say anything about any of this. Said she promised my father."

"I'll give her points for that. But she was tough to be around. I think she looked at me and Seanie as reminders, and that didn't sit right with her. After a while, she didn't say it outright, but she made it pretty clear we weren't welcome."

And then, after what seemed like a few moments of inner debate about whether to say something or not, Foy shrugged as one internal side surrendered to the other. "You should know; your father never blamed Delia for the split. We talked about it when it happened; he took it on himself, said he knew he'd never been right with her. And while she didn't make me a fan, I gotta say, it had to be tough for her. Everywhere she looked… He never got rid of that piano, right? And I'll bet he's still got those paintings Evangeline did. Man, if she'd ever found that stuff you found in the attic, she wouldn'ta divorced him; she'da *killed* him. Woulda been like cheating on her with a dead person. And then there was me and Seanie…"

"And there was me."

"And there was you. When they decided to get married, they thought – hell, we *all* thought, it'd be better you thought Delia was your mother. What was the point telling you about a mom you were never gonna know?"

"She never said anything. All this time."

"Like I said, I give her points for that. Maybe it would've all worked out better if your dad could let Evangeline go."

"You managed to let her go, though, right?"

That sad smile, again. "Not really. I just learned to live with it. See, it was easier for me than for your dad; she was never mine like she'd been Eddie's."

She took another sip from the cup but neither the drink nor the fire seemed to be doing much good, and a shiver ran through her. "Danny, I don't want to ask, but I have to: did my dad ever love Delia?"

His face wrinkled in thought. "I think he told himself he did. Maybe he did. He had two kids with her, right? But it wasn't the same, and no way Delia couldn't see that. Eddie could never really let Evangeline go. And I think that's why he treated you the way he did."

"Because I was Evangeline's daughter."

"It was more than that, Little Miss. You were something of Evangeline that was still here."

She got out of her chair, again, so much was running through her head she needed to burn off that energy with pacing. She walked back and forth along the edge of the firelight.

"I'm gonna say something to you, Little Miss, and you better take it in. Anybody ever says to you, and God forbid you say it to yourself, that your mother was a whore… Don't you ever let me hear you use that word about her. She ran off from a bad place, did something so she didn't starve and that's all it was. She was…the best of us 'cause there was nothing but good in that little body. And she loved you to pieces."

Shiloh stopped her pacing, looked off into the woods that were now turning into a single dark curtain. *Jesus Christ, I don't even know what I'm supposed to feel.*

"C'mere, Little Miss. I got something for you. Come back here and sit down."

She did. Foy didn't move right away, just smiled in a silly little way at her. Then he reached inside his cardigan and set three photographs down on the tray table.

It was her parents' wedding day. Standing by the water on the rocks near her father's house, the sun behind them painting the sky the Kodacolor pinkish-red of dusk, were the four of them: Daniel Foy in an ill-fitting suit, her father in his uniform, Evangeline, Sean Cleary, Sr looking rather spiffy in a tailored suit. The second photo was just of Eddie and Evangeline, the two of them smiling at each other, and the look on her father's face… Shiloh knew what Foy had meant when he said he'd never seen Eddie Vail so happy.

The third photo was just of Evangeline. She was a small woman, almost delicate, still carrying a little baby fat in her cheeks, but her face…

"I've seen pictures of you that age. You coulda been her sister," Foy said quietly. "And you look like she woulda - …" Another one of those sentences Foy couldn't find it in himself to finish. "Take those," and he nodded at the photos. "Those're yours."

It took a moment for Shiloh to find her voice. "I…couldn't take…"

"I been holding 'em for you, Little Miss, 'specially ever since Delia had your dad burn all the rest of 'em. It's ok; I still got some for me."

She picked them up, carefully, by the white edges. She put the one of just Evangeline on top, stared down into it, looking for…*something*…but not knowing what.

This was my mother.

She felt a sting in her eyes, her vision blurred. She felt Foy's hand on her forearm, a gentle squeeze. She nodded that she'd be ok and, still careful, slid the pictures into her breast pocket.

"You better be getting back," Foy said. "I can smell rain coming. 'Sides, I wouldn't admit it to Ms. Moon, but I'm getting cold."

"Danny, I don't know when -"

"You don't owe me another trip, Little Miss. I know you're going back to Washington soon. This is a long way for you. Chances are, by the time you ever get a chance to come back for a visit, I won't be here."

Which hit her with a pang.

"It's ok, Little Miss. I got to sit here and talk with you and see you all grown up. All the time you were in college, and then you got the job in Washington, we were all so proud of you! It's everything Evangeline - …" He faded off again, then, "I got to tell you about your mom. It was kinda like seeing her, again.

"I just got one thing I'd like to ask. It's a big thing, and it's ok you take a pass. See, I don't have much family. I got a daughter from my first wife lives with her family down in Scowhegan who doesn't talk to me, and my boy, he calls once in a while, but he works in a shipyard all the way down in Norfolk, and that's it, that's all I got."

"What're you asking me, Danny?"

"I'd take some comfort knowing you'd come to my funeral. 'Cause you're as much family as I got. Ms. Moon'll have all the information, you know, when the time comes."

She rose from her chair, leaned over the old man and kissed him on his unshaven cheek. She took in the familiar smell of Camels and bad whisky and for a second her father was there with them. "I'll be there…Uncle Danny. And…thank you."

Shiloh saw Ms. Moon standing in the doorway of the trailer, waiting. Shiloh waved to her, signaling they were done. She started to leave, then, "Danny… Where's my mother buried?"

"She isn't. She was afraid if there was a grave, that wouldn't be good for your dad. She was cremated, that's what she wanted. Like she asked, one day when Eddie was finally up to it, the three of us went down there on the rocks, same place where they got married, same time of day, and your dad spread her ashes out on the water. We used to say the currents would take her all the places she wanted to see. You say that kind of stuff to make you feel better about what you lost."

"Does it work?"

"Not really. But it's all you got."

Fifteen.

The rain was coming down in wind-driven sheets by the time Shiloh drove into Portland. She tucked the photos Daniel Foy had given her inside her bra hoping that would be enough shelter from the rain as she ran from the Casco Bay Garage to the ferry slip, all the time thinking about the oilskin jacket Teddy Granier had brought her and which was still sitting warm and dry back at the house on St. Aggie's.

The storm wasn't as rough on the bay as the one which had greeted her on her trip to the island a few days before, but she could feel it growing worse. There were few passengers on the ferry, none on the upper deck, probably because the rocking always felt worse up there. She was content to sit there alone, not feeling the rocking, not hearing the rain pelting against the large plexiglass windows, or the howl the wind picked up whipping around the wheelhouse. Her head was lost in the photos Daniel Foy had given her.

She had reached inside her coat to dry her fingers on her flannel shirt before she slipped the photos out of her bra, again holding them carefully by the edges. She held the pictures away from her so they wouldn't catch any of the water off her sodden jacket or from her hair hanging in dripping tendrils.

All three photos had been taken out on the rocks by the water near the family home. She knew those rocks, knew what it felt like to stand there, feel – even taste – the tangy ocean breeze, so she knew what it had felt like for Evangeline and her father and the others. They would've had to have spoken up to be heard over the water sloshing in among the rocks, and there would've been gulls circling overhead calling to each other, hoping the proceedings would have something to do with edible castoffs.

She knew what it would've felt like. Yet…

She settled on the photo of Evangeline alone.

My mother.

But the woman, despite their resemblance, despite their blood tie, remained a stranger, unconnected to her.

I should feel something, even though some coldly rational part of her taunted her with a *Why?*

Her father, Delia, Foy and Cleary, Sr. had been right; what good would it have done to tell her about this pretty petite young woman whom she would never meet, about whom nothing would remain, about whom Delia would go to great lengths to try to erase. For Shiloh, Evangeline's picture meant no more to her than a photo from the wedding announcements page of any local newspaper, a picture in *Portland* in a feature about cute local seaside weddings, something from a wedding boutique magazine.

My mother. I should feel…something!

She turned to the photo of her father and Evangeline. She may not have known her mother, but she knew her father and now so much was answered about him. Evangeline explained her father's life, everything from where they'd lived to how he'd treated his different children. And in that, the things Daniel Foy had told her rang like cathedral bells...

I don't know anybody *had what they had...*

The measure of the depth of that feeling was how badly her father had hurt when it ended...

I never saw anybody so broke up...

She didn't know Evangeline, couldn't know her, but she could know what she'd meant to her father...

From the beginning, they just always looked like they belonged together...

...and there was a pain that went with that knowing.

She ran a finger down the image of Evangeline, knowing it was a pointless gesture out of bad movies, knowing she would feel nothing from it. But realizing how much her father must've loved that woman she never knew, measured by how it had shaped him and how he had treated the child he'd had with her, she did, finally, feel something; not a sense of loss, because one can't feel loss for what one never had. But a different kind of loss...

God, I wish I'd known you.

By the time the ferry pulled into the slip at St. Aggie's cove, the storm had escalated to the point where it even punched through her ruminations. She tucked the pictures back safely – hopefully – against her breast, lowered her head against the blowing rain and headed home. But at the foot of the walk to the house, she stopped, turned, looked toward the ocean.

It was full-on dark, now, and she heard the surf more than saw it, but in her mind's eye... There. There on the rocks was where they had stood, Eddie Vail and Evangeline Donnadieu, when they promised themselves to each other. The storm was throwing the sea against the rocks, coming out of the dark and bursting in foamy detonations. She found herself walking toward the rocks, taking a few steps out among them…*Trying to feel what they felt.*

But the cold spray from the exploding surf was a poor answer.

She turned toward the house, shaking her head, surprised at her own romanticism. The cold, wet showers had been a kind of natural mocking: *What'd you expect? To get a warm and fuzzy feeling inside? 'Oh, gee, it's like I'd been there!' Grow the fuck up, lady!*

Her head had been bowed against the blowing rain which was why it wasn't until she'd reached the front steps that she saw the front door of the house standing open. There was no good reason for that so she ran the last few steps, calling out before she'd even reached the doorway: "Zoe! Zoe!"

As soon as she could see into the front room, she knew there'd be no answer. Seat cushions had been overturned and slit open, furniture moved, the living room rug rolled back. She could see into the dining room: the drawers on the sideboard pulled open, some pulled clear and dropped to the floor, the top of the upright piano was still propped open.

Oh, Christ, Zoe.

She knew, before she looked, the rest of the house would be in the same shape. An odd-shaped piece of paper stuck in the frame of one of the paintings bracing the fireplace told her there was no need to check; whatever the object of the search, it hadn't been found.

It was the envelope which had carried the letter to her from Henry McNair. On the back, in bold, penciled block letters, emphatically all capped, was written:

BRING PAPER YOU KNOW WHAT

BY MIDNIGHT GODDARD MANSION

COME ALONE NO COPS OR

U FIND SISTER ON ROCKS

She had no doubt this was the work of the Clearys, was even more certain that around her was the handiwork of Aidan Cleary.

"What the fuck do you want?!?" she shouted into the empty house.

Ok, clear your head. It was hard. Fear – no, *panic* – over Zoe. And anger – no, *rage* – at this invasion.

And feeling lost.

Since that first night when someone had been rooting around in the shed, the Clearys had been after something in this house. They hadn't found it in the shed, it was clear it hadn't been found in the house, and she and Zoe hadn't seen anything in the attic that could be remotely of interest to anyone – not even in their father's secrete cache.

Clear your head.

She did something she would never advise anyone else to do who needed to get their head focused. She got out her father's horrible whisky, sat on one of the shredded sofa cushions and took a swig. Then another. Closed her eyes.

Ok, where could you look that Aidan would've missed? Where would it never occur to him to poke his nose into?

As she had in Henry McNair's office, she opened her eyes, stood, and took in the scene. Aidan Cleary had gone for the obvious: furniture, rugs, drawers, the piano.

But he didn't know Dad. Didn't know him.

It wasn't a question of where would *someone* hide a document; it was *Where would* Dad *hide something?*

A document. It would be rolled or flat or folded. The way the house had been torn apart, rolled, which took up space, was probably a thin possibility.

So, folded or flat. Folded or flat. And a place which would only speak to her father.

Daniel Foy came back to her:

That piano still at the house?...God bless how she banged away at that thing, trying, and we applauded like she was playing at Carnegie Hall. She tried learning how to paint for a while, that was another thing.

Aidan Cleary had tried the piano.

Evangeline had also tried to learn how to paint.

Shiloh went to the painting hanging to the left of the fireplace, a bowl of fruit. She took it down, peeled off the brown paper backing.

Nothing.

She went to the other: flowers in a vase. Took it down, tore away the paper backing.

A single sheet of paper. She didn't have to read the heading to know what it was; she'd seen enough of these forms in her job to recognize it immediately: a police incident report.

She scanned it quickly and that was enough to stir the whisky in her stomach and send her running out to the front porch where she bent over the railing, welcoming the cold rain on her fevered head as she threw up.

She didn't quite pass out, because when her vision cleared, she found she was still on her feet, still bent over the porch railing, even if her legs had gone a bit jelly-like. She turned her face to the cold rain, opened her mouth to let it in, rinsed and spat, then turned back to the house.

Inside, she shucked her soaking coat, letting it fall to the floor, scooped up the oilskin hoodie from where Zoe had left it on the floor by her chair. She pulled on the jacket as she ran up the stairs.

First, to her room, which had been tossed like the downstairs. She took Daniel Foy's photos from her bra and slipped them carefully between the classic books in her reading nook; the books, she now knew, her father had ordered for her to honor his promise to Evangeline.

Then she went to his office, afraid yet knowing what she'd find. Her father's long guns were, thankfully, still in place, held there by the lock bar. But the desk drawers were all pulled out. His badge was still in its place in a top drawer. His revolver was not.

The ferry was gone. She could see its lights disappearing into the rain and dark as it scurried back to Portland.

She ran to Teddy Granier's store. The store was locked up for the night, but she could see Granier inside mopping the floor. She banged on the glass door. He looked up, saw her and smiled, ambled over.

Shiloh took a quick look at her phone for the time: 8:03.

Granier opened the door. "Hey, Shiloh. I'm closed but if you need something -"

She pushed past him, wiped the rain from her face.

"Are you awright,?" he asked.

"When's the next ferry?"

"Won't be one. They cancelled the last run 'cause ah the storm. Fact, the last one isn't even gonna finish his circuit -"

"Teddy, I have to get into Portland."

Granier's face moved to concern. "Somethin's wrong."

"I can't talk about it, Teddy, but I have *got* to get to Portland!"

He shook his head. "Short ah somebody crazy enough to take you on their boat -"

Fuckfuckfuck... "Do you have Ben Cole's number?"

He nodded and took out his own cell, punched up the number for her. He shook his head again even as she was dialing Ben. "He'll come out here for you, Shiloh, but I don't think that's a good idea."

"I don't have a choice, Teddy."

"Maybe, but you two go out there in this mess, good chance tomorrow people gonna find out you two drownded out there."

She was already running down the dock at the first sight of Ben's boat and was waiting for it by the time it nuzzled up to the pilings. Even before he could come out of the wheelhouse to tie up, she'd jumped onto the afterdeck, slipping on the wet surface and falling painfully on her ass.

Ben helped her up and into the wheelhouse. "What the hell's goin' on?"

"I told you; it's an emergency, I have to get into Portland as fast as possible."

"And you can't talk about it."

"And I can't talk about it.

He didn't hesitate, took his place at the helm, one hand on the throttle, revved up the idling engine and brought the boat about, heading toward the bay.

Even in the cove, the water was rough enough that Shiloh realized just how bad an idea this was, and how possible Teddy Granier's warning of winding up "drownded" was. But *The good thing about not having a choice is you have no choice.*

When they cleared the cove and got out into the open water of the bay, the rough water of the cove felt comparatively like paddle boating across a pond. The Down Easter rolled left, rolled right, crawled up a wave then slid down its back.

The gyrations weren't doing much for her already stirred-up stomach and that must've been clear to Ben: "You feel like pukin', I got a bucket below. You lean over the side in this and I'm gonna lose you."

"I'm fine," but it came out as a gulp. "Ben, do you have a gun?"

Ben did a double-take worthy of the best silent movie comedies. "Ok, enough! You tell me you got an emergency, need to get into Portland, and here we are, chance we're gonna wind up at the bottom ah the bay. Then you ask me I got a gun. Don't you think I'm entitled to a – Hold on!"

The boat suddenly shot upward, then dropped, then a foamy wall of sea slammed against one side of the boat so hard it began to roll sideways, so steeply Shiloh was vaulted from her place and only stopped from crashing into the opposite side of the wheelhouse by Ben's one-armed catch. He let her slide to the floor. From there, she watched him fighting the wheel, nailing the throttle to the max. The boat stayed nailed to the sharp list.

She wasn't afraid of dying just then though it seemed clear that was a possibility. Her fear was what would happen to Zoe. And as she looked to Ben trying to navigate a jungle of vomiting surf and whipping wind, *Fuck me, I killed him. I killed them both.*

But then the boat seemed to settle. It still rolled left and right, bow up, bow down, but not in any threatening way. She pulled herself back to her place against the side of the wheelhouse, realized she hadn't been breathing and was now gasping for air. "You ever been in weather like this before?"

Ben had, with a veteran's equanimity, returned to an almost eerie calm at the wheel. "Yeah…but not by choice." He gave her a you-owe-me smile.

She resigned herself to having to open up to Ben. "You know the Clearys have been after something hidden in my dad's house."

"You found it."

She nodded. "And they want it."

"You gonna tell me what it is?"

"No."

"Is there some big reason you haven't told them to go fuck themselves with a baseball bat?"

"They have Zoe."

"Shit."

"It's a swap, Ben. I give them what they want for Zoe. I have to be at the Goddard Mansion by midnight. Or Zoe..." She shuddered and it wasn't just from being wet and cold.

"I'm going with you."

"Can't. They told me no cops, come alone. It's Zoe, Ben, I'm not going to risk it."

"Christ, Shy, you don't know -"

"I know what they said and what happens to Zoe if I show up with company."

She looked at her phone: 10:09.

At the Portland docks, she was out of the boat while Ben was still tying it up. He called for her to wait. "My truck's right there on Commerce Street. It's closer than your garage."

"Ben, they said -"

"I know what they said. I'll stay in the truck when we get there, I'll stay out ah sight. And if things go bad, I'm right there. Hell, Shy, do you even remember how to get out to the cape? You're telling me we got no time to screw around, so..."

Shiloh looked at her phone: 10:47.

It took her just a few seconds to do the math and mentally measure distances. "Ok, let's go."

Sixteen.

Fuckfuckfuck…

11:03.

Fuckfuckfuck…

The blood-boiling irony for Shiloh was that Ben Cole could've sailed to Cape Elizbeth from St. Aggie's in twenty minutes or so. Problem was, there was no place along the rocky cliffs or boulder-strewn shores to put in. Ship Cove would've been even better, almost putting them in the Goddard Mansion's backyard, but its shallow depths and the storm-stirred seas would've ripped the bottom out of Ben's Down Easter if he'd tried to beach there.

Fuckfuckfuck…

11:15.

This meant having to drive around the bay, into South Portland and through the town of Cape Elizabeth. The only thing breaking in their favor was, because of the storm, the streets were mostly empty, allowing a rocketing ride of violated speed limits, and rolling stops through STOP signs and red traffic lights made all the more nerve-wracking by the driving rain, too much for the truck's wipers to keep

242

up with. Visibility was so bad Ben seemed to be driving as much by memory as by what he could see through the blurred windshield. Shiloh watched through half-shut eyes, mentally whipsawing between *Movemovemove!* and *Watchitwatchitwatchit!* as Ben zoomed his way through intersections, any oncoming traffic invisible and ignored through rippling films of water.

11:32.

Shore Road, parallelling the coast. Through the naked branches of the trees along the Cape Elizabeth streets, a flash. Shiloh first thought it was lightning, but there was no thunder, and then it came again, cutting through the night and waves of rain as it had since it had gone electric nearly a century before: the lighthouse at Portland Head.

Shiloh had Ben pull the truck to the curb behind a row of trees running along the park's wrought iron fence, short of the gate to Fort Williams Park. She had him kill his lights and the engine. They sat for a moment in the dark, the rain pounding down on the truck cab roof, heavy enough to be constant, like static.

Shiloh checked her phone. It was 11:52. "Well."

"Yeah."

"I'll walk from here."

"Hey, Shy…"

"What?"

"I know this isn't a great time for this, but I'm remembering when you and me used to come up here -"

"You're right, Ben," she snapped, "your timing is incredibly sucky. Could you pick a shittier time to reminisce?" She reached for the door handle.

"It's just – Wait, Shy, wait."

"What?"

"You're asking me to sit here and watch you walk into the lion's den, know what I mean? You know how hard that is for me?"

It hadn't occurred to her; she'd been focused on Zoe and the time. But now she saw it. Still, it didn't change things. "I know, Ben. But you promised."

Maybe he said something, or it was just some kind of grunt; she couldn't tell with the noise of the rain, couldn't see his face in the dark cab, but it sounded like some kind of resigned assent.

"Ben, I have to say this. You show your nose in there and it so much as gets Zoe a scratch, and I'll throw *you* down on the rocks. No joke."

She could barely make out his head nodding. She flipped up the hood of her oilskin jacket, opened the door.

"Shy…" He reached over, rummaged around in his glove compartment, and handed her a Mini Maglite. "You know, for…"

It wasn't *for* anything; Shiloh knew this wasn't about the light. It was the need to do something, anything, because it was that hard for him to sit and do nothing. And that required an equivalent gesture on her part. She leaned over, gave him a kiss on the cheek, and stepped out into the rain.

"Shy, if you're not back in thirty minutes, I'm calling the cops."

She didn't argue. She figured if she wasn't back in thirty minutes it was because she wasn't coming back at all. She shut the door and headed into the park.

Fort Williams Park was ninety acres of walking paths, greens, playgrounds, and tennis courts along the bluffs of Cape Elizabeth. It stretched from Portland Head Light at its southern border, to the remains of the Goddard Mansion at the northern end. The entry road led to a parking lot by the mansion. A walk paralleled the road before it turned away, leading up to the main entrance of the house.

Between the rain and the night, she couldn't see the mansion, couldn't see much of anything. There were the rhythmic flashes from the lighthouse at Portland Head, but they did nothing to light up the grounds of the park. The wind was blowing hard off the ocean, throwing the rain in her face. She kept her head down, using Ben's Maglite to light the walk just in front of her. As she passed by the parking lot, she took a quick look for parked cars to see if anyone else was in the park. Nothing.

Wait.

A subtle flash at the far end of the lot, under some trees, a weak reflection of the lighthouse pulses: the gleam of rain running down metal. She swung the light over: a large, black SUV. If she was dealing with Aidan Cleary – and she had no doubt she was – she also had no doubt, confirmed by the car's bulk, it would be something ostentatiously macho and expensive, like a Denali or Escalade.

She turned the light back to the walk. She was now close enough to make out the vague outlines of the derelict old house. She slowed her already deliberate pace, made a show of flashing the light in the direction of the house, wanting to make sure it was clear to any observer she was alone as instructed.

John Goddard had made his money in lumber in the mid-1800s, enough so he felt like rewarding himself with an elegant home with a horizon-to-horizon view of the Atlantic. Unlike the Greek who had meddled in the building of the architectural monstrosity at Cypress Point the Clearys now owned, Goddard had been smart enough to stick to his lumber business and let the builders build. The result was a handsome two-story Italianate structure of Maine stone. By the standards of the various mammoth DuPont and Vanderbilt houses, it was comparatively modest in size. The mansion had changed hands several times before it got into the hands of the Army in 1900, serving as quarters for the officers and noncoms manning the coastal artillery batteries sitting atop the bluffs guarding the entrance to Casco Bay. But by the end of WW II, the batteries were obsolete, and by the early 1960s, so was the fort. All that was left now were concrete foundations for some of the gun emplacements and a couple of observation bunkers.

As for the mansion, by the 1960s, it was in such bad shape it was considered unsafe. The interior was intentionally burned out and gutted, the cellar filled in, and now all that was left was the roofless shell.

The house sat on a slight grassy rise; its structure tailored to the slope. The main body of the house, with its square tower rising a full story above the roof line, sat at the crown of the rise, then another section of the house was further down the slope with a drop of a few feet from the main body. There was another drop to level ground for what at one time had been a stable, and which later evolved into a garage.

Shiloh tried to remember the layout inside the stone shell. Ben had been right; they had come out here in the old days, but she'd been out to Fort Williams long before that, with her father and Jericho and Zoe. She doubted there was a kid who'd grown up in the Portland metro area who hadn't been out to the park, the boys playing around the bunkers and gun emplacements pretending to fend off invaders, while the girls – at least she and Zoe – pretending they were princesses and the Goddard Mansion their palace.

But she and Ben… Sometimes during the day to walk the park, sit on the small beach of Ship Cove, to wander around the ruin trying to think what the intact house must've looked like, wonder how rich you had to be to own a place like that, what they would've done with such a place as their own.

And there were other times when they'd been out there at night, and that's where Ben had become her first.

Sometimes with her girlfriends back in D.C., after a few drinks and the conversation drifted in that direction, Shiloh would look back on that time – look back on it fondly – and say the first time should always be with someone you thought you were in love with.

"'Thought'?" they would say.

She would shrug. "Well, it was true at the time. But that was a long time ago."

What Shiloh remembered of the interior was nothing but open space. Not a lot of moves open to her if things went badly.

As she drew closer to the mansion, the Maglite gave her some good news…and some bad news.

The good news was the mansion had gone completely derelict. The interior was now overgrown with grass, shrubs, vines climbing the walls, even small trees, especially at the base of the square tower rising up out of the main body of the house along the back wall, all of it offering opportunities for concealment. The bad news was the reason for the overgrowth; evidently, sometime after Shiloh had left Portland, the mansion had been considered no longer safe for visitors and all the doorways and ground floor windows were blocked with chain link fencing. Once she was inside, she would be penned in.

Seeing the fencing, she stopped. Where was she supposed to go? The instructions she'd been left now seemed frustratingly vague. Then, from the interior of the house, a voice:

"Don't just stand out there in the rain. Come inside and stand in the rain. The front door, there's a hole in the fence." The voice echoed and amplified inside the stone walls, bigger than life, like the storm itself was talking to her. She recognized it; she'd last heard it in a yelling match with Sean Cleary, Jr. at the house at Cypress Point.

She found the gap where the fencing had been peeled back from its post. She paused for a second…

Ok, girl, here we go.

She slid through but stayed in the doorway, a wide, peaked entry designed for long-gone cathedral doors. She stayed in the arch, swept the interior space with the Maglite.

"Sorry for the poor accommodations, but I didn't have a lotta time to prepare for the party." The voice was coming from her right, the lower section of the house.

"I don't feel like being funny," Shiloh said and started across the floor, always looking, planning a move…just in case. The foot of the tower was to her left. The lower section of the house was recessed from the main body maybe a good ten feet, creating a wall of exposed brick between the sections to her right. But if she needed that cover and got to it intact, then what? The only way out was the hole in the fence at the front door, but by the time she could reach it…

He must've sensed her apprehension. "Relax your tits, lady, if I was gonna do somethin', I woulda done it when you were a sittin' duck out front."

Shiloh moved to the break in the floor, where it dropped down to the lower section of the house. She swept the Maglite around and found Aidan Cleary standing in a low doorway in the rear of the house which led out to the bluffs over Ship Cove. Rain slithered in shiny trails down his leather duster, his beard glistened in the light with droplets. He was wearing a wide-brimmed hat, something like an old-fashioned fedora, rain running off the brim in a glittering veil over his face.

"Do you mind?" and he made a gesture she knew meant her light. She didn't turn it off but dropped it from his face…

Oh, God…

…and it fell on a body at Cleary's feet. Her heart jumped a beat, Shiloh thinking for a second it might be Zoe, but it soon became clear it wasn't. Although she couldn't see the face, the rain spreading blood from an ugly wound to the forehead instead of washing it away, she knew who it was.

Flare of a match. Shiloh didn't know how Cleary managed it in the rain, but he got a cigar lit, the rich aroma drifting her way in the gusts finding their way inside the stone hulk. The end of the cigar pulsed like an angry heart.

"You know what time it is? You cut it close, lady. Ya know somethin'? You been a royal pain in my ass ever since you come back to Portland. You coulda saved us all a lotta trouble you just give that thing up."

"I didn't even know what you wanted until I found it tonight."

"Seriously? Your pop never told you?"

"Seriously."

She thought she heard something like a chuckle. "Well, keepin' secrets seems to be somethin' dads do."

"My sister."

"Got my brother all turned around, you did," and for a moment, the hatted head bowed toward the figure at his feet. "Then again, this kinda soft-headed guy, it didn't take much."

"My sister."

"She put up a fuss, she's got some dents on her, but she's someplace nice and dry. She's ok and you'll both stay ok long's we get our business done."

"I brought it. But it's not on me."

The cigar tip pulsed more rapidly. "Well, now, that's gonna be a problem."

"For both of us. See, I have a trust issue. I'm wondering if once I turn this paper over to you, well…" And she washed the Maglite beam over the body of Sean, Jr.

Another nod toward the body. "This got nothin' to do with *our* business. It was probably a long time comin'. Pop's gonna be real pissed 'bout this. But then, he's always pissed at me 'bout somethin'."

"I'm also thinking about Henry McNair."

Even across the space she could hear a loud sigh, but more one of impatience than regret. "That wasn't supposed to happen. But nothin' ties me to that."

"Anything tie you to breaking into my shed the other night?"

"Prove it." It wasn't a challenge; it was a flat statement that it was unproveable.

"What about when you came back?"

"Came back?"

"The night you clubbed Ben Cole, I'm guessing because you didn't want him to see you sneaking around the house again. Or maybe that was just a little bit of revenge for his dad not selling out to your grandfather."

Cleary didn't say anything for a while, the cigar tip flared like he was taking a long pull on it. Even through the dark and rain, she could make out the silhouette of his hatted head tilting, like a puzzled puppy. "What the hell're you talkin' about? Today's the first time I been out to your place since that night in the shed." The glowing tip of the cigar flew like a shooting star across the lower mansion as Cleary tossed it away. "Look, lady, you can untighten your ass 'cause here's the bottom line: there's nothin' tyin' me to anything. You gimme that paper and I got no reason to worry 'bout you, 'cause you won't be openin' your mouth 'bout tonight. See, I'm holdin' on to that paper, and you squawk 'bout this, the whole world's gonna see what you got there. I don't think you want that. Like I said before; if I wanted somethin' to happen to you, it woulda happened by now."

He let her mull that for a bit, and when she finally came to see the sense of it all, she nodded. "I don't suppose I have much choice other than to trust you."

"Seems like."

"So how do we do this?"

Another chuckle. "First off, I don't believe you don't have that paper on you, so -"

The crack of the gunshot rebounded sharply off the stone walls. The partial wall to her right wasn't close, but it was the nearest cover, and she ran for it, dropping the Maglite, her body tensing as she moved, waiting for the next shot to thud into her body.

A next shot didn't come.

She threw herself behind the wall, jamming herself into the corner where two walls came together, burying her face against the brick, waiting for Aidan Cleary to come finish the job.

Nothing.

She risked a peek around the edge of the wall –

Another shot whined off the bricks above her head. Stone flecks rattled down on her oilskin hood, close enough to chase her back to her hiding place, gasping.

A third gunshot. No sound of a strike nearby. And then...

"Shy? Shy! It's ok, you can come out."

Ben Cole.

Still wary – because a bullet impact near one's head will do that – Shiloh snuck a look around the corner of the wall. There was still a figure in the doorway below, but the silhouette was different. She picked up the Maglite where she'd dropped it, swung the beam toward the doorway. Ben Cole was standing over now two bodies in the doorway; Aidan Cleary lay face down at his feet. Ben held a large revolver in his right hand.

Shiloh felt herself sagging. It came to her how much she'd been fueled by adrenaline since she'd climbed out of Ben's truck, and now it was easing off and she was melting inside.

"I'm sorry, Shy, I couldn't just sit there in the truck. But I stayed out of sight, I really did! But I heard him, Shy. You know he wasn't gonna keep his word. That family never does. I heard the shots, there's a hole in the fence here, I jumped him -"

She waved at him that no further explanation was necessary.

Sean...

She moved quickly, now, climbing down to the lower level, pushing past Ben, kneeling by the body of Sean Cleary. There was a broken brick nearby. The rain had washed it clean, but she was guessing that had been Aidan's weapon. She reached for Sean's neck, felt around for his carotid. His skin was cold, he must've been laying there from before she'd gotten to the park, but there was the slightest throb in the artery; a pulse, but a faint one. "Ben, you have your phone? Call 911. We need an ambulance."

"For who?"

"Sean. He's still alive."

"You're kidding."

"Call 911, Ben!"

"Why? He's a Cleary! They're all rotten bastards!"

"If you're not going to do it -"

"Jesus fucking Christ, Shy, fine!" He took out his cell phone, stepped away, his back to her.

She turned to Aidan. No pulse. She scanned around the body with her light. "Ben, where's his gun?"

"His gun? I have it. I told you; I jumped him. We wrestled around, I got his gun away. He came at me, Shy, I, you know…"

She nodded.

Something's not right…

She looked from Aidan to Sean, the blunt object wound in Sean's forehead.

Ben must've seen her shaking her head: "What's the matter?"

"If he had a gun, why did he bash him like this?"

"Didn't want anybody to hear the shot?"

She nodded; that made sense. "You better give me your gun."

"Why?"

"The police are going to want it."

"Yeah, sure. I'll give it to them when they get here."

She turned back to Aidan, ran the light up and down his body, didn't see any signs of a bullet impact.

How could he miss me with that first shot? I was standing out there practically glowing in the dark in this bright yellow get-up, holding a light… Didn't even hear it hit close. But when I was hiding, he just missed my head…

Aidan Cleary was heavy, hard to roll, but she managed to get him on his back. Her light settled on his face. There was a jagged hole the size of a silver dollar in the middle of his forehead, and before the rain could wash it away, she saw his face was splattered with blood and gray matter. She reached around to the back of Aidan's head. She hadn't seen it when he was face down because his thick hair had been matted down by the rain, but now she felt it: a small entry wound.

She felt sick.

She stood and backed away from the two bodies. "Why don't you give me your gun, Ben? I'll hold it."

"I don't think I'm gonna do that."

She felt it in the air, the change between them.

"What are you thinking, Shy?"

She pointed down at Aidan Cleary. "That's an exit wound, Ben."

"So?"

"So, I'm trying to figure out if you two were fighting for the gun, how did you get it to where you could shoot him in the back of the head?"

Ben stepped back further into the house, putting space between them. "He was gonna kill you, Shy."

She lowered the Maglite. She didn't want to see his face. "The first shot was you, wasn't it? Then the second one, that was you wanting me to think he was after me. And the last shot was supposed to make me think that's when you got him. You better give me the gun, Ben."

A sad, resigned chuckle. "Goddamn, why'd you have to be so damn smart?"

"When we found you on your boat the other day, you said somebody attacked you… You did that to yourself. I didn't think much about it at the time, but it wasn't that big a bump."

Shaking his head, almost laughing now. "So damn smart…"

"On your boat, I asked you if you had a gun and you never answered me."

The laughing stopped, and now, not anger, but desperation: "For Chrissakes, Shy, I saved your life!"

"No, you didn't. He wasn't going to kill me. He didn't need to. You, you've been playing the white knight all along. What'd you think? You come to the rescue enough times and that's going to get all the old feelings back?"

"That night you came to hear me play -"

"I got caught up in a memory, Ben, that's all. I'm sorry, I shouldn't have let it -"

"Goddammit, Shy! I *killed* for you! I killed for *us!*"

"What 'us'? There is no 'us'! There hasn't been an 'us' since I left Portland. And it was dying before that."

Was that a sob she heard through the rain? Then, weakly from Ben, "Soulmates."

"I'm sorry, Ben."

He started to bring the pistol up.

"Please, Ben…"

"If you hadn't gone away. We were supposed to be together. If you had stayed here…"

"Ben, we have to find Zoe."

"…it could've stayed the way it was."

She heard the clicks of him cocking the revolver and her middle went cold.

"They say, if not in this life…"

Shiloh Vail closed her eyes, waiting for one darkness to be replaced with another one, one that would never end.

"…then the next one. I'll see you on the other side."

Her body spasmed at the shot. She remembered from past cases that sometimes, when a bullet passed through soft tissue, the victim didn't even realize they'd been shot. Her legs went weak, she fell to her knees, painful as they hit the concrete. She sat back on her heels…waiting…

"Shy, you ok? C'mon, lemme help you up."

A hand under her arm, pulling her to her feet.

"Oh, crap, Shy, I think you hurt your knees. I see blood on your pants."

She opened her eyes. It was her brother's voice. He held her by the arm, guided her to the ledge between the sections of the house, propped her there. In his free hand, she saw her father's gun. Laying out there in the middle of the floor was Ben Cole.

And then…she laughed. A lazy, tired laugh, not of humor, but what comes when all the tenseness, all the expectations of the horrible evaporate. "Jay, what in hell are you doing here?"

He leaned against the ledge next to her. "Teddy."

"Teddy Granier?"

"God bless that guy. I got a call. He said you were being stupid – well, that's not how he said it, but he was talkin' 'bout you wantin' to cross the bay in this mess, he figured somethin' wasn't right. He ran up to the house to see if Zoe knew what was goin' on -"

"And she wasn't there."

"Said the place was all tore up -"

"He found the note. The gun, Jay?"

"I called this afternoon to give you more shit about the will, sorry -"

She waved that away.

"Zoe told me you were out, I figured I'd sneak out there and get dad's guns. I told you I wanted his guns."

"You told me."

"I couldn't find the key for the rifle rack -"

"So, you took his pistol."

"You gonna give me shit 'bout that?"

"Maybe later."

They could hear sirens coming down Shore Road.

"And then I guess Teddy called the cops."

"You better give me the gun, Jay. The police are going to want it."

"Oh, yeah, sure."

She took the pistol and dropped it into her jacket pocket. She didn't want it in her hand.

Jay walked over to Ben Cole's body. He looked down, shaking his head. "Fuckin' Ben Cole, man." It wasn't a condemnation, just puzzlement. And something else.

He looked over to his sister. "'Member I was givin' you some kinda shit day after somebody broke into the shed? You know; 'bout, uh…"

"I remember."

He came back to his place by her against the ledge. "You were right. I'm gonna carry this a long time, aren't I?"

"So, I've been told. A long time."

PART FIVE:

Eulogies

Seventeen.

Through the rain-blurred windows of the police cruiser, the Goddard Mansion parking lot was a fireworks display of flashing blue and red lights from other cruisers and a pair of EMS rigs. The yellow slickers of the Cape Elizabeth officers floated through the rain and darkness like ghosts. A portable light tower had been set up inside the mansion. Silhouetted against the brightness of the lights she could see EMTs bringing out bagged bodies.

Shiloh, in the rear seat of the cruiser, pulled the blanket given her by one of the EMTs closer around her but she couldn't stop shivering. The cruiser driver, now one of those scurrying around the parking lot securing the scene, had thoughtfully left the engine running and the heater turned up full, but it didn't help.

In a way, the cold was a blessing; it numbed her, kept her mind off the events of the night because she knew if her consciousness drifted, there was a good chance her head would explode.

One of the cruiser's rear doors opened, letting in an unwelcome blast of the cold, wet night air, and Sergeant Karras, carrying two take-out cups, slid in beside her. He handed her one of the cups and quickly closed the door behind him. "Oof, ugly out there. One of the guys made a coffee run. I thought you could probably use something hot."

She took a sip, and it was almost hot enough to scald her tongue. As good as the coffee felt going down, she still couldn't stop shivering. "I can't get warm."

"Shock," Karras said. "It'll pass. How're you doing?"

"Seriously?"

"Right, sorry, stupid question."

"I hurt my knees."

"You want me to have one of the EMTs look at them?"

"One did. Iodine and Band-Aids. He gave me this blanket. I can't get warm."

"I know. Most people I know who've been through something like this, I tell them there's people to talk to. But I figure you know that." Which was his polite way of reminding her.

"My sister."

"You guessed right. We found her tied up in the back of Aidan Cleary's Escalade parked over there," and he nodded in the direction of where Shiloh had seen the SUV sitting earlier.

"How is she?"

"A little bruised up, but she should be ok. A car is taking her over to Mercy. Nothing some iodine and Band-Aids can't fix." When she wasn't amused by the reference, he went on: "They'll check her out, probably keep her overnight just to keep an eye on her for a while, but it looks like she'll be fine. I'll see she gets home tomorrow."

She nodded her thanks. "Sean Cleary."

Karras let out a long, sighing breath, took a lingering sip of his coffee.

"That bad?"

"We won't know anything for sure until the doctors look at him, but I didn't see the EMTs looking happy when they saw that dent in his head. That'll be him now."

Shiloh looked out the window toward where Karras was pointing: a blurred image of one of the EMS rigs starting to roll out of the parking lot, its siren winding up.

"Any idea what he was doing here?" Karras asked. "Aidan had a rep as a bad boy, but Sean…"

Shiloh took another useless sip of her coffee. "My guess is he was trying to stop his brother."

"Stop him from what? What the hell went on out here?"

Shiloh watched the doors on a second EMS rig being slammed closed; two body bags had been loaded. The rig pulled out without a siren. No need.

"You're Portland P.D.," Shiloh said. "What're *you* doing here?"

"Your friend Teddy Granier."

Shiloh smiled to herself. *Ahh, Teddy.*

"He remembered me coming out to see you, ran me down through the department and told me about this screwy note he found at your house. I called it in to Cape Elizabeth…but I thought I should be here."

Shiloh made a move of her head, something to show him she appreciated his concern.

"I haven't forgotten my question."

She looked out through the windshield, the water on the glass glowing with the light from the cluster of spotlights inside the mansion. She could see flashes inside the walls from the cameras of the forensics techs. "Aidan Cleary had some idea there was something he wanted hidden in my father's house. He took my sister and wanted to swap her for it."

"What was it?"

She wrapped her fingers around the coffee cup, but they still felt numb with cold. "I don't know. He never said. Whatever it was, he tore the house up and didn't find it. Neither did I."

"Then I guess we'll never know."

"We'll never know."

She could feel Karras' eyes on her. *He's looking for the lie.* After a few moments listening to the rain, she heard Karras let out what sounded like a resigned, long breath. *He'll live with it.*

"What about my brother? I saw them taking him away."

"Just to get a formal statement, then he'll be released. What he told us checks out with what you told us. I think he should be alright on the shooting. There might be a problem with the gun since he didn't have a permit, but I'll talk to the DA's office. Under the circumstances, they might let it slide, or at least knock it down to some kind of slap on the wrist."

"Thank you."

"Sorry about your friend, that Cole guy."

"Yeah."

"Ya know, I've been on my share of domestics. It never ceases to amaze me what shitty things people will do to, for, and about someone and say they did it because they love 'em."

"Yeah."

Shiloh looked over at him, found him staring at the plastic lid of his cup, shaking his head slowly, side to side. "What is it?"

"Those brothers, the Clearys. Like I said, I've been on domestics, but still, a brother doing that to another brother... I've got two brothers and a sister, and I'm not always nuts about 'em, been times we don't even talk, but still..." He shook it off and she could see him suddenly brighten, smile at her. "But your brother, man, that was something, right? *Your* brother saved your life!"

Maybe it was because she was so drained physically and mentally, or maybe it was just that kind of idea, but Shiloh found herself laughing. "Yeah, he did! And take it from me, Sergeant; that sonofabitch will never let me forget it!"

Eighteen.

By the time Shiloh had reached Cypress Point and driven through the gates of the Cleary estate, the storm was in its last, exhausted stages, the rain reduced to a sporadic mist, the winds down to gusty breezes. The long driveway ended in a lollipop circle in front of the house. Shiloh rolled to a stop at the foot of the wide front stairs. She could see the silhouette of Sean Cleary, Sr. standing in the open doorway, leaning heavily on his cane.

She didn't climb out of her car right away, sat for a good long time. Cleary gave no sign of impatience.

Neither one of us wants to do this, and we both know it has to happen. We both know we're going to hear things we don't want to hear…have to hear.

Shiloh finally pulled herself out of her car but still made no move toward the house. The way she and Cleary stood facing each other… Gunfighters at high noon? Jousters ready for a run at each other? Or two tired and mutually respectful opponents? With Cleary's face in shadow, she had no clearer idea of her own standing.

She could hear the little, bursting breezes off the bay moving the cypress branches about in weary sighs. The rain might have eased but

265

the night was still wet and cold, still clinging. After the nestling warmth of her car, the change had her shivering again. She pushed past Cleary into the entry hall, making a point of not looking directly at him. It seemed important to her not to show weakness, not to show… Not to show what?

It hit her: what to show, what not to show, what to feel… She had no idea about any of it.

She heard the front door close behind her.

"You look tired," he said. He sounded just as tired. "Would you like to lay down for a bit? We can always talk later. I can get you some dry things to wear."

She said nothing, kept her back to him. Cleary walked past her to stand by the open doors to a room off the hall; the room where she'd heard Aidan and Sean, Jr. fighting the last time she'd been out to the Cypress Point house. "I have a fire going. You look like you could use it. Make yourself comfortable, I'll be with you in a minute."

Again, averting her eyes, head bowed inside her oilskin hood, she walked past him, heard him leave.

It was some kind of study: wood paneled, bookshelves on either side of the wide fireplace, woven rug in the Persian style over a hardwood floor, and in front of a span of large, leaded windows, a massive oak desk.

There were deep-cushioned chairs by the fire, an equally comfortable-looking settee, but she didn't sit. Again, there was that feeling it was necessary to concede nothing, accept no friendly gesture or hospitality, because…

And that's where she came up dry. *Because of what? What the hell is that about?*

There were photos set out along the mantlepiece. Sean Cleary, Sr. with his wife, his sons, in different combinations at different ages. She looked deep into the photos of Aidan and Sean as young boys. She couldn't tell, at that age, which was which; just two sweet-faced little kids with matching smiles of two missing front teeth.

The radiating heat from the fireplace was lulling, reminding her it had been a long, horrible night, and she felt her legs going soft. She slid her oilskin jacket off, let it fall to the hearthstone, shuffled to the nearest chair and let herself drop in it. The warmth of the fire came over her like someone pulling a snuggly comforter up over her. Her eyes burned, lids growing heavy.

"I have spare rooms."

She forced her eyes open. Sean Cleary, Sr. was standing in the door to the study. He cut a figure in marked contrast to the well-groomed man she'd met on her first visit. He'd pulled a heavy robe on over clothes rumpled as if slept in. His hair was an uncombed tangle, the shadow of the coming morning's stubble on his chin. His limp was more noticeable, it seemed like every movement, however small, required great effort. He was as drained as she was.

That's when this need for distance became clear to her. It was less a need than a precaution because she had yet to determine if Cleary, Sr. was friend or foe. Maybe both, maybe neither, maybe something else. She remembered something one of the elders at her firm had said to her on an occasion when she was frustrated over what was beginning to look like endless negotiations over some matter.

"I can't tell who the good guys are in this anymore," she had said.

"Sometimes there aren't any good guys, there aren't any bad guys," the old gent had said. "Life is messy like that."

Cleary handed her a manila folder. The typed name on the tab read, VAIL, E.E.

"I found that in Aidan's room," he said. "I thought you would want it back. Would you like a drink?"

Shiloh took the file, sticking it next to her against the arm of the chair, as she shook her head no.

"I could use one." He shuffled toward a liquor stand in a corner of the room.

"I've been to see Daniel Foy."

"And he told you?"

"I know who my mother is."

"Ah." His head bobbed, nodding that he thought this was a good thing. "Did he tell you you look like your mother?"

"He did."

He turned, fixed her with his one good eye, a brief sad smile.

That look; it brought to mind something he'd said when she was leaving after their first meeting: *You remind me of a happy time.*

"Did you send Aidan to Henry McNair's office?"

He seemed pained she would think that of him. He shook his head and continued on to the liquor stand. "His idea and up to his usual standard, I'm afraid. I think he thought if he found something useful in that file, I'd have more respect for his methods. I didn't even know he'd gone there until he told me afterward."

"What happened?"

Whatever Cleary was mixing at the liquor stand, he downed most of it, then topped off his drink and started back toward the fireplace, a crystal tumbler in his hand. "I've been trying to hold onto the idea that what Aidan told me that night was the truth. He said he hadn't expected to find Mr. McNair in his office at that hour. He demanded your father's file, Mr. McNair refused, things got heated and Aidan gave him a shove. Mr. McNair lost his balance, and…"

"If it's any consolation, that fits what the police found. I doubt that'll be any consolation to the McNair family, though."

"When it feels appropriate, I'll see if there's something I can do for them."

"Think that'll help you sleep better?"

Clear dropped heavily into the settee facing the fire, took a deep sip of his drink. "Doubtful."

"Have you heard anything about Sean?"

Cleary took another pull on his drink, slumped in his seat, his eyes on the fire, the glow of the flames getting picked up by Cleary's eyes, which were wet. "It's still early. He's in a coma. They won't know if there's any brain damage until he comes out of it." He took a long, shoulder-heaving breath. "If he comes out of it." He turned to her; yes, his eyes were glistening, even the fogged one. "He went out there to stop Aidan, you know."

"I thought as much. I am sorry about that. Aidan said something to me... He said he thought this was years coming."

"Cain and Abel."

"Cain and Abel."

"You were hurt." He gestured with his glass at the bloodstains on her knees.

Shiloh nodded it away. It was nothing. She reached into the breast pocket of her shirt and drew out a single piece of paper neatly folded in quarters and opened it. The heading was:

POLICE INCIDENT REPORT

She read: "'Subject obviously under heavy influence of alcohol and drugs, verbally confirmed this to reporting officer. Subject states he met woman at bar in the Old Port. Claims not to know her name or remember which bar. States they had more drinks, then invited her to his boat. Took boat into Casco Bay and let it drift. States they did more drinking and also used cocaine. States he made advances of a sexual nature. She refused and an altercation followed. Claims not to recall if argument grew physical, but she lost her footing, fell and hit her head. Subject states she appeared to be dead. Subject panicked and dumped body over the side.'"

When she looked up from the paper, Cleary's glass was empty.

"He was only seventeen," he said, his voice empty.

"Drinking on a false ID no doubt."

"Of course." A sour smile. "He was a Cleary. Isn't that the kind of thing we do?"

"I'm looking at the date on this. My father was a sergeant. He wouldn't've taken that call. It would've been a patrol officer, or maybe handed off to a detective. But not him. I'm going to assume Aidan called you, said 'Daddy, can you help me out?' and you called my father."

Cleary's smiled turned to bleak amusement. "No. He called *my* father."

"Kieran?"

"I'm sure Aidan thought the way his grandfather handled things would work out better for him."

"What the hell did your father say to my dad to get him to bury this?" and she fluttered the report.

That awful smile grew wider. "Nothing. He didn't have to." He chuckled at some awful, black inner joke. "My father... God... He struggled to read the funny papers, but I always thought if he'd put his mind to it, he could've been a master at chess. My father understood the long game. He was always doing, um, *favors* for people he thought could help him, or might be able to help him sometime in the future. Then when something came up, he'd give them a call: 'Hey, hello, Fred, how're you doing? I'm fine, but I'm having this zoning problem down in Bayside that's giving me pains. Say hi to the wife and kids for me'."

"But they knew they owed."

"They knew."

"Kind of a 'Will no one rid me of this meddlesome priest' kind of thing."

Cleary nodded, impressed and amused at the reference. "The paradox, in Eddie's case, was your father was an honorable man, and that forced him to do a dishonorable thing."

"He knew he owed."

"Eddie got to marry Evangeline, to give her his name, to give *you* his name. They had a life together in the house my father gave them. All of that was because of my father." He looked off, his one good eye focused on something not there; Shiloh thought maybe it was that happy time. Then his face clouded as he came back to the present. "I know it hurt Eddie to do this. I hadn't seen him hurt like that since Evangeline died."

"So, Kieran called him, and my dad filed a false report."

"She was drunk, lost her balance, hit her head and fell overboard; that's how it was recorded. You may not believe this, but when my father told me what he was doing, part of me hoped Eddie would tell my father to go to hell."

"Part of you."

"Aidan was my son. You see, when your child turns out, well, like Aidan, it's hard not to wonder, as a parent, how much is your fault? And if it's even partly your fault, what's your obligation? Looking back, though, I wish..." There was something else, and Shiloh could see Cleary stuck on it, choking on it.

"What is it?"

Cleary closed his eyes, then took a deep breath like he was steeling himself. He opened his eyes, still moist, fixed on the fire. "A few days later, the currents washed the woman into the harbor. They sent the body to Augusta."

"For an autopsy."

He nodded, impressed she knew how things worked in Maine. Then, he seemed to collapse inside himself. "They found water in her lungs."

"Oh, God..." and Shiloh felt an icy spike run down through her body. "She wasn't dead when Aidan put her in the water."

"Again, I want to believe Aidan when he said he honestly thought she was dead. He was drunk enough, stoned enough, it's possible. God, how I want to believe that. Still... When Eddie heard..." Cleary's face twisted as if the pain he felt was physical. "By then, his report had been filed almost ten days. If he'd confessed then, he not only would've lost his job and faced departmental charges, but there was a good chance he'd be looking at criminal charges as well. It wasn't about concealing a death, now, but concealing a homicide. And still I think, if Eddie had been on his own..." Cleary's face wrinkled as he considered what the alternative lifelines would've been like.

"What do you mean?"

"Like I said, your father was an honorable man. And his obligations made him do dishonorable things. This wasn't about what he felt he owed my father. It's what he owed Evangeline. If he told the truth and wound up in prison... He'd promised Evangeline he'd take care of you. Delia had already left him. Leaving you orphaned like that..."

Now it was Shiloh's turn to feel the pain. She looked back at the incident report. "This date... As I remember, it wasn't long after this my dad got his lieutenancy. Kieran rig that? What was it? A bribe? A payoff?"

Cleary looked at her, shook his head as if she were a child asking why the sky wasn't green. "Chess."

"Come again?"

"It wasn't any of that. It was my father upping the stakes of going public for your father. If he came out with the truth, well, a disgraced sergeant is one thing, but a lieutenant in the department, that's a much bigger deal. If the truth ever came out, it would *look* like a payoff, and that would be even worse.

"I wouldn't've put it past Eddie to fall on his sword except he wouldn't leave you, your brother and your sister to deal with that kind of disgrace. Eddie didn't talk to me for years after that. I didn't blame him, but it hurt. We didn't talk until he got sick."

"Did they ever find out who the woman was?"

"No. No fingerprints on record, no matching missing persons reports. I even hired a private detective, but…" A shrug.

They sat quietly for a while, listening to the crackling of the fire. Cleary looked at his glass, seemingly surprised it was empty. He let it fall to the floor, bent over, put his face in his hands. A groan of, "Oh, God…God…"

Shiloh felt no anger, no pity. *Life is messy.* She flicked the incident report with a finger. "Why would he keep this?"

"Insurance, I think. In case we ever felt like asking for another such favor."

Shiloh flicked the paper again. "What am I supposed to do with this?"

Cleary sat up, seemed to regain his composure with a deep breath. "Give it to the press. Send a copy to every household in Portland. Hire a skywriter and spread it in the skies over the city."

"Is this some kind of reverse psychology thing? Do anything with it so I won't do anything with it?"

A sad little chuckle. "It doesn't matter. There's no one left to hurt, Shiloh. My father's gone, Eddie's gone, Evangeline is long gone. And my son is dead."

"There's you."

That same, rueful chuckle. He wasn't laughing at her but the larger cosmic joke of it all. "The only concrete thing you have tied to any of this is that document in your hands with your father's signature and which was hidden in your father's house. That reflects more on your father than it does me. There'd be rumors I was involved, of course, because there are always rumors about the Clearys. But it'd just be one more ugly Cleary story on top of an already tall pile of ugly Cleary stories."

He used his cane to push himself off the settee with a grunt, went to the fireplace, pointed to the photos on the mantle. "If you think I'm coming through this unscathed; my son is dead. My other son..." A pained look and shake of his head. He turned to her. "And years ago, this cost me a friend. No, a brother. Eddie Vail. I think I've paid for my sins."

"Debatable." She hauled herself out of the deep cushions of the chair, swayed on her feet for a moment until they firmed up under her. She walked to the fireplace, stood across from Cleary. She started to reach the incident report into the flames.

Cleary's free hand came up to stop her. "Are you sure? Eddie couldn't get himself to go that far."

"Like you said. At this point, there is no point." She let the paper slip from her fingers into the flames. The heat carried it upward for a bit before the edges glowed and caught fire, then it settled down onto the logs, turning black and curling up until it disintegrated in ashes.

Shiloh scooped up her oilskin jacket from the hearthstone and headed for the door.

"The offer on the house still stands," Cleary called after her.

She stopped and turned. "You're still going ahead with your project on the island? Your damned spa?"

Cleary shook his head. "One builds for one's children. As you said: at this point, there is no point. But I promised your father; I told you the truth about that."

"You know, Mr. Cleary, over the last couple of days, I've heard a lot of people talk about a lot of promises made and a lot of obligations kept. It seems all any of it has done is make for a lot of heartbreak. So, I'm going to break the chain." She held her hands out, as if letting a captured bird fly. "I free you! You don't owe us a goddamned thing! Keep your money."

"Are you speaking for your brother and sister?"

Obligations. *Ahhhh, shit.*

"I'll toss it to them," she said. "They can do whatever they want. But me…" Her hands flapped against her sides, the gesture of someone at a loss of knowing what the good call would be. She turned for the door again.

"Shiloh." Cleary had taken a few steps into the room, toward her. "Don't hate your father. He was one of the best people I've ever known. It's just sometimes you get pushed into a situation where all your choices are bad…and worse."

There was nothing to say to that, so she turned for the door, pulled on her oilskin jacket and left.

Shiloh pulled her car into the Casco Bay Garage, found a spot on the upper deck, killed the engine and let herself sink into her seat. She felt…done. *Getting almost killed will do that.*

It would not have taken much for her to let her eyes close, let sleep come, and considering what all was caroming around in her head, a bit of unconsciousness would've been a welcome break from the last twenty-four hours. But sleep would have to wait.

From the deck, she could see out into the harbor in one direction, the Old Port in another. This was where, a hundred years ago – or so it felt like – she had stood with Ben Cole looking out over a waterfront on its way to becoming something she barely recognized.

Ben Cole.

The name came to her with a moan attached. She closed her eyes and could see him twanging away at his guitar in Tuck's trying for a Hallmark moment thinking a few well-chosen pop songs would be enough for a resurrection. That bounced into another memory: that night at the house, just Shiloh and Zoe, Ben and his guitar, and stories about long-gone days. Laughs.

How the hell does that end in a body bag?

The rain had stopped but the storm was pulling a sky-covering train of dark, swirling clouds northward after it. There had been no daybreak, just a transition from night to a lightening grayness, leaving Portland, the waterfront, the bay drained of color. She didn't have to open her car door to know a bone-chilling damp went with that slatey air.

There was a Starbucks on Commercial Street just opening and Shiloh grabbed a cup of black coffee before crossing to the docks, hoping to catch the ferry serving the western bay islands on its first circuit of the day. The ferry was at its dock, engine in a rumbling idle. Shiloh couldn't see more than a handful of people lined up to board.

It wasn't just the ferry. Commercial Street – in fact, what she could see of the Old Port – was empty, the docks were quiet, no boats going out other than the ferry. This whole part of the peninsula seemed lifeless under that scudding, grim sky.

But then she heard the bells calling to the faithful from the churches up on Munjoy Hill. That's why the empty streets: it was Sunday morning. Whoever in Portland wasn't still asleep was at prayer.

Shiloh went back to the same upper deck seat she'd had the day before – *Jesus, was that just yesterday?* – sagged against the plexiglass window hugging her coffee cup close. She peeled the plastic lid off the cup, held it close to let the warm vapors wrap around her face.

There had been a feeling when she'd first walked back into the St. Aggie's house days earlier, of seeing it all with fresh eyes, checking what had always been there but never noticed because, growing up, it just *was*. Like the piano, the paintings by the fireplace. The way her father fathered his different children. She now had that same feeling looking back afresh at her life, only now seeing just how many pieces had been missing from the picture, seeing answers to questions she'd never felt the need to ask.

It came to her that maybe she'd never *really* known the people she'd *thought* she'd known her entire life: her brother and sister, Delia. Her father. And then there was the mother she'd never known: Evangeline.

And yet...

And yet, Shiloh could see how Evangeline had shaped her daughter's life in almost every way by how Eddie Vail had raised his oldest daughter in a manner he thought would honor his obligation to -. No, not obligation. To honor his *love* of Evangeline, a feeling he apparently carried, hidden away and camouflaged, all the way to his death bed.

Ben Cole had told her that one of those days on his sick bed, delirious, her father had babbled something about, *Do you think she'll ever forgive me?* She had thought, naturally enough, her father had been talking about the split with Delia, but now she knew. This was about *her*.

Or maybe, she thought...*Evangeline?*

St. Aggie's was drawing closer. Everything over the last few days had been about obligation, and as the island grew bigger in front of her, the brick house now visible on its little rise, Shiloh saw there was another debt to pay: what to tell Zoe and Jay. What did she owe them?

She remembered something else Ben had told her. She pulled out her phone, opened up YouTube. She found a recording of Tom Paxton singing "The Last Thing on My Mind," held the phone to her ear and listened to his soft guitar and gentle voice telling of a parting with no goodbyes to a love given badly.

Ben said he'd only sung it to her father that one time, and it was the only instance he'd seen her father cry. Again, she wondered if it'd been for her…or Evangeline.

Well, she thought, and for the first time that dark, cold morning, felt a warmth inside, *maybe it was for both of us*.

Nineteen.

She told them everything.

It hadn't even been much of an internal debate. All Shiloh had to do was run through once what her sister and brother had been through the night before to feel she owed them the truth; all of it.

She was surprised to find them waiting for her at the house. As soon as the doctors had done their antiseptic dabbings and bandaging where needed, and assured Zoe she'd suffered no serious damage, she'd signed herself out of the hospital; she'd wanted to be at the house when Shiloh got home. Zoe got her own surprise as she crossed the hospital lobby, seeing Jay stretched out across several seats, asleep. As soon as the Cape Elizabeth police had released him, he'd gone to the hospital to wait for her.

He'd gotten her home by "borrowing" - meaning he hadn't asked, and Shiloh could even hear the qualifying quotation marks as he told the story - a skiff from a "friend", who was probably just someone he barely knew unlucky enough to own an accessible boat, to get his sister back across the bay to St. Aggie's. The two were still trying to reassemble the house from the mauling it had suffered at Aidan Cleary's hands when Shiloh showed up at the door.

Zoe put on a pot of coffee, got out their father's throat-searing whisky, then they sat on torn seat cushions while Shiloh told them everything Daniel Foy had told her. She showed them the photographs Foy had given her. And then, the harder part: telling them Sean Cleary, Sr.'s story.

They said nothing. Zoe teared up, and when Shiloh's eyes also began to sting, Zoe sat next to her, a comforting arm around her sister.

But through it all, Jericho's face… Shiloh had never seen that look on him before. No matter the situation, no matter the event, Jericho had always been one to react viscerally, instantly, and often primally. But this time, it was as if the processing machine in his head was working overtime to analyze and digest and understand the new input. It almost made Shiloh smile; she had never seen her brother being *thoughtful*. Still, she had no doubt about what the output of all that mental processing would be. But that was fine; it was hard not to think he'd earned it.

When Shiloh finished, she sat back in her chair, beckoned Zoe for a refill of coffee and whisky, then waited for a reaction from Jay who appeared to still be processing.

"Go ahead, Jay."

"Hm?"

"Go ahead. Take your shots."

"Whaddaya talkin' 'bout? What shots?

"I owe you, Jay. You want to take a few shots at me, how I'm not really your sister which I'm sure you find gratifying, go ahead. And you always wanted to take Dad down a few pegs. You've got the ammunition now. You earned the right."

That look of thoughtfulness passed to consternation and then disappointment. He shook his head, made some kind of grunting noise. "Ya know, I don't got some fancy-ass college education, but it hits me that for someone who's supposed to be so goddamn smart, you don't know when to shut the fuck up." He rose from his chair, went to the mantlepiece, took down their father's urn and headed for the door.

Shiloh and Zoe exchanged a puzzled look and then followed Jay outside.

They followed him down the walk and out onto the rocks; the same rocks where Shiloh's father and mother had stood and exchanged vows unnecessary because the commitment and belonging had long been in place before being legally recognized by the state of Maine. They were the same rocks where her father had stood with his best friends – his brothers – and poured the ashes of his beloved Evangeline into the sea.

It was late morning and the gray shroud over Portland had finally broken up, letting the sun through, revealing a limitless azure sky. The gulls gathered over them, a halo of white wings, and that they were only there because they always hoped a human presence meant the possibility of a treat didn't make them any less welcome to Shiloh at that moment. They seemed to make things complete.

She and Zoe stood with Jericho where the ocean lapped at the rocks. He turned to Shiloh, pushed the urn at her. "You know *you're* the one supposed to do this. You *know* that."

She looked to Zoe who was tearing again. Her sister smiled, gave an acceding little nod. Shiloh took the urn, unscrewed the top. She knelt low, so the onshore breezes wouldn't just blow the ashes back, then shook them loose from the urn into the water frothing around the rocks.

"Go find her, Dad!" Jericho called out over the water, loud enough to even spook the gulls. He turned to Shiloh, brushed at something on her shoulder. "You got some ah Dad on you. Figures. You were always his favorite."

But it was said without bite, and the three did something Shiloh hadn't remembered them doing even as kids: they laughed together.

They turned back toward the house. On the porch, Shiloh lingered behind them, hugging the empty urn close and looking back out toward the blue, blue ocean. She remembered what Daniel Foy had said about pouring Evangeline's ashes into the ocean:

"We used to say the currents would take her all the places she wanted to see. You say that kind of stuff to make you feel better about what you lost."

"Does it work?"

"Not really. But it's all you got."

She thought of her father's ashes being carried out into the ocean, around the world, inevitably swirling into those of Evangeline. Like Daniel Foy, she knew it was just something to make her feel better, but if that's all it was... *Well, hell, then, so be it.*

EPILOGUE

Zoe was waiting at the bottom of the staircase for Shiloh as she jumped her suitcase from one step down to the next. She stopped at the bottom to catch her breath.

"Do you want some breakfast?" Zoe asked.

Shiloh shook her head. "I want to make the next ferry."

Zoe nodded, understanding.

Shiloh glanced at the front room, but it turned into more. She let go of her luggage and stepped into the front room. Zoe had remounted the two paintings back to where they had always rested on either side of the fireplace.

"Do you want to take one with you?" Zoe asked quietly.

Shiloh considered for a moment, then turned to Zoe, smiled. "If anything happens to the house. But for now, this was her home."

Zoe smiled, too.

Shiloh reached for her luggage, but Zoe stepped in front, extended the handle and rolled the suitcase out onto the porch.

Jay was waiting at the bottom of the porch stairs. He made a point of not looking at either of his sisters, his eyes locked on the horizon line. When Zoe reached the bottom of the stairs, he roughly grabbed the suitcase handle away from her and began rolling the bag down the walk without looking back.

Shiloh and Zoe exchanged a grin. This was what passed as gallantry from their brother, and it was probably as good as it was going to get.

They followed Jay out to the road, its potholes still brimming with rainwater from the recent storm. Before Shiloh followed her brother down the road toward the ferry slip, she took a step toward the rocks to take in a last view.

It was one of those brilliant fall days New England is famous for, one of the few things Shiloh missed about her home ground during the comparatively bland end-of-year months back in D.C. The autumnal angle of the sun gave all colors a vibrancy which tickled the eye, from the cornflower sky to the rich deeper blue dotted with sparkling white caps of the Atlantic, to the charcoal black rocks of Cape Elizabeth, and the white tower of Portland Head Light practically glowing. Tangy breezes skipped over the quiet seas, and she could hear the cries of gulls and terns hovering over the ferry, always hoping for a satisfying scavenge. She took one long draw of the salt air, then turned, saw a smiling Zoe waiting for her, and they trailed after their brother.

As they neared the ferry slip, Teddy Granier was waiting there holding a take-out cup and a small paper bag.

"Fuckin' Teddy, man," Jay said, it came off as something like a salute.

Teddy held up the cup and bag and Shiloh went over to him.

"I, uh, didn't know if you had breakfast," Teddy said. "Figgered even if you did, you could have somethin' for the road, ya know? I got a buttered roll in there. I didn't know how you took your coffee, so I got it black and threw some creamers 'n' sugar 'n' Splendas in the bag. I didn't know if you still ate 'em, but I threw in some Almond Joys 'n' Mounds; you know, munchies for the road. I 'membered you liked 'em, you know, back in 'em old days."

Fucking Teddy, and she smiled. She took the bag and cup, then took Teddy in her arms and gave him a kiss on the cheek. "Thank you, Teddy," hoping he realized she meant more than a thanks for a buttered roll and coffee.

Teddy stepped back, red-faced. "'S'ok, um, yeah." He pointed to the store. "I, uh, gotta, you know…," nodded an awkward goodbye, and headed back toward his store. Then he turned, still walking. "Don't wait so long to visit next time!" and more comfortable with the distance, smiled broadly, gave her a wave, and kept on to his store, now almost bouncing in his steps.

Shiloh handed the bag and cup to Zoe and turned to her brother.

"Don't think anything's changed," Jay said.

"I haven't," and she hugged him tightly. She felt him slowly – reluctantly, no doubt – put his arms around her.

"I still want Dad's guns," he mumbled into her ear.

"We'll talk."

"'N' I'm still gonna give you shit 'bout the will."

"I wouldn't expect anything less."   Then she pulled him even closer, kissed his cheek through his thick beard. "Thank you, Jay. Thank you for my life."

"Fuck you."

God bless this pain-in-the-ass sonofabitch, and she laughed.

The ferry whistle blew.

She turned to Zoe. Zoe had set the cup and bag down on Shiloh's suitcase, held out her arms. There was nothing to say other than Shiloh muttering her sister's name, Zoe whispering Shiloh's name. The only thing that had them part was a second whistle from the ferry.

"It ain't Uber," Jay said. "He's not gonna wait."

Shiloh grabbed up her bag of snacks and coffee and the handle of her suitcase.

"Thanksgiving," Zoe said. "You promised."

"I promise."

And yet Shiloh still couldn't turn away.

"Go!" Jay snapped.

Shiloh turned, saw the ferry deck crew waving frantically and impatiently at her to hurry.

Then she was at her usual place on the upper deck, looking down at Zoe and Jay standing side by side on the shore, watching as the ferry pulled away. Zoe reached out and Jay took her hand. As the ferry backed into the bay, Shiloh expected them to turn back to the house, but they didn't. They stood there on the shore, growing smaller as the ferry put more and more water behind it, and Shiloh thought they might've still been there even after they had disappeared from view.

When she closed her eyes, she could still see her brother and sister, hand in hand, waiting for Shiloh to come home, again.

Acknowledgements

Because I'm not a native Mainer, one of the locals I rely on to keep me on a path of authenticity is Amber Soha. If *Casco Bay*, like my other Maine novels, has any true sense of the place, a lot of that credit goes to Amber.

It's also been a long time since I've been an age where I had rock star posters on my bedroom walls. Many thanks to Rabia Ashraf, one of my former students and a fine writer in her own right, for helping me get those details right.

My thanks to my colleague, Bill Mesce, Jr., for connecting me with his lawyer, Robert Shanahan, who was a tremendous help on the legal aspects of this story, so thanks to you too, Bob.

To my publisher, Abby Macenka, my deepest gratitude for her ongoing support for my work. Also, a tip of the hat to her whole team who help turn out a finished product of which I am always proud.

And, of course, thanks to my family who always have to put up with a lot when I'm at the keyboard.

Although a writer sits alone at the keyboard, it takes a team to turn out a book, and I'm lucky enough to have a great one.

About the Author

Aja Holland lives on the coast of southern Maine where she teaches at a small university and loves to watch storms come in over the ocean. She shares her home with an adventurous shih-tzu and one judgmental cat.